T0167339

MASTERS OF FIRE

Derrick John Wiggins

authorHOUSE®

AuthorHouse™
1663 Liberty Drive
Bloomington, IN 47403
www.authorhouse.com
Phone: 1-800-839-8640

First published by AuthorHouse   06/06/2011

ISBN: 978-1-4567-5089-3 (hc)
ISBN: 978-1-4567-5090-9 (sc)
ISBN: 978-1-4567-5088-6 (e)

Library of Congress Control Number: 2011903855

Printed in the United States of America

Any people depicted in stock imagery provided by Thinkstock are models, and such images are being used for illustrative purposes only. Certain stock imagery © Thinkstock.

This book is printed on acid-free paper.

Special thanks to Sandra, La Shawn, and Kenneth Greene. My mother, sister, and friend. For all your help.

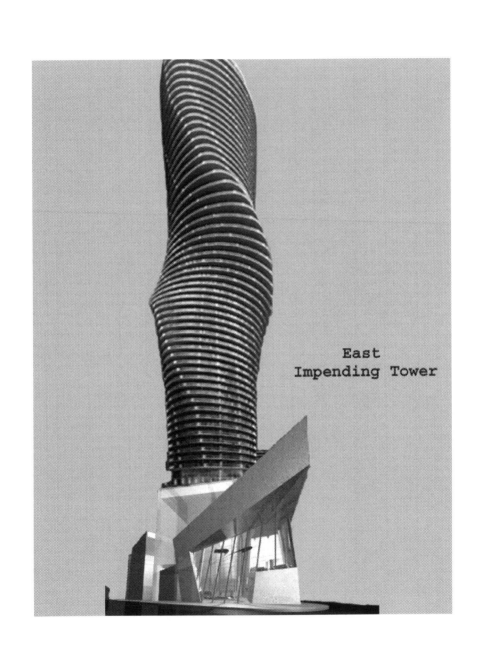

East
Impending Tower

INTRODUCTION

THE ANCIENTS WHISPERED, whoever controls the fire, controls the world.

Today, whoever controls technology controls the universe. Technology has won wars. Technology has shaped our very lives from the light bulb to the radio to the television. Now the venture into space and delivery of the computer has become the new god of innovation. Cyberspace is born.

Where are we going? What have we learned? Who will be the new, masters of fire?

PROLOGUE

THE NIGHT WAS INK BLACK. The Atlantic Ocean waters emulated a flat black still marble floor. No wind blew this calm night in the middle of nowhere. No clouds and no moon shone tonight. Only stars brightened the darkness like a million still white fireflies. The large three-floored luxury white boat cruised a thousand miles from the African continent shores and about a hundred miles from St. Helena Island. The yacht knifed the glossy oily water, its engines hardly making more than a soft humming sound.

Among the crew she knew a few important men made this entire trip possible. The crew of eight, mostly escorts, were well dressed in business type attire. She watched as they just finished eating in the dining room and now sat back in their comfortable chairs to chat in the salon. She observed the helmsman with his co-pilot on the helm guiding the yacht *Firestone* steadily through calm seas.

She surveyed her stepfather, Xavier, and his partner Morris sit below deck in the Aqua lounge. Both men, ties loosened, sat comfortable across from each other on brown leather couches. They couldn't see her but she heard them clearly.

"I don't trust our interest left alone with this new regime," the taller man, Morris, said. His blue Valentino suit was tidy as his short brownish frizzy hair.

"I have a good feeling about these guys," Xavier spoke. "Out of many Nigerians I know, they seem the most sincere in helping the country." Xavier was dressed in his black pinstripe Caraceni suit. His goatee refine didn't match his full-head of wild black hair. It reminded her of an untamed afro. She distinguished Xavier and Morris were clearly the controllers of the vessel, the money-makers.

"How many regimes like this have survived?" Morris asked her stepfather. "These countries are never stable. This is a big risk we're taking." She sensed worry in Morris's voice.

"It's going to work," Xavier responded. "I've things in play of surety that this government is strong. Trust me. Haven't I come through before?"

"I have to say, your methods are crude, but I admit you haven't failed us yet."

"Listen, my money is in this, too. I'm not going to let anything go wrong."

"You always did things behind our backs." Morris squinted, examining Xavier. "What are you up to this time? Is there more to this business deal than automobiles?"

Xavier chuckled.

"Come on man, I want to know the formalities," Morris said. "Stop putting me in the dark until the last minute."

"Do I have to? It's always much more fun this way." Xavier continued smiling.

"I'm putting a lot of money in this." Morris folded his arms.

"Okay, okay, you got me. General Snigiw is part of the Fulani people who make up most of the Region—" Xavier stopped in mid-sentence when the lights flickered and went out for two seconds.

When the lights came on, she sensed the boat had stopped, and they were slightly rocking back and forth. She watched them stare at each other puzzled. They then moved through the ship's many levels to the helm.

"Something must be wrong with the engines," Morris suggested.

The lights flickered again as they passed the crew in the salon. She saw that the bunch had looks of concern.

When Xavier, Morris, and she made it to the helm, the lights went out completely. The reflections of stars swimming in the ocean's tiny ripples were their only source of light. It made everyone look like defined shadows.

Upon entering the helm and her eyes adjusting to the dark, she could see the helmsman and his mate vigorously running their hands over the implements.

The helmsman, Ralph, had been sailing with her and her stepfather for a long time. They knew each other well.

Ralph was a mellow fellow she thought, as was his casual wear, and she knew he was doing all he could. She observed Ralph and his associate check the navigational indicators, magnetic compass, and computer modules. Ralph looked to his mate. "See if you can lower the anchor, then check the engine room." Turning on a portable flashlight, his aide left the room.

"What's the problem?" Xavier asked as the younger guy, the aide, brushed past him to leave the helm.

"Strange," Ralph responded without turning around. She knew Ralph was talking to her stepfather. "The computer is still up, but everything else . . ."

"Any idea?" Xavier pressed on curiously, but not meaning to be pushy.

"No idea," he replied, staring at the computer. There was dead silence for two minutes before some crackling interference came through a walkie-talkie on Ralph's hip.

"Ralph, you there?" The co-pilot's voice came through the receiver.

Grabbing the small transistor radio, Ralph answered, "Yeah. How's it going? See anything?"

"Nothing unusual. I'll call you back in a minute." The portable radio crackled off.

She perceived another two minutes of soundlessness.

"That's weird," Ralph spoke, cutting the silence. "The computer is showing all functions are on, yet we have no lights, and the engines just cut off. I don't understand it. The computer indicates all the ship's functions are normal."

She deemed this was the epitome of serenity. When she couldn't hear the tiny waves in the ocean lapping into each other was her assumption of silence. When she couldn't hear herself breathe. That was silence. For one full minute she thought her entire body was in molasses. It was like screaming in the middle of the ocean and expecting someone a mile away to hear her.

Then something supernatural happened. Xavier, Morris, and Ralph were suddenly lifted two feet off the floor of the ship. It was as if some kind of force stopped gravity and made them hover. They were in a form of zero gravity. Suspended in mid air, she could see the dumbfounded looks on their faces, even in the dark. They wanted to speak, but nothing came out, only their lips moving.

She then realized herself drifting on her back near a window. It was fun. She felt like five years old again. Morris floated forward. Ralph stayed suspended over the wooden wheel on the dashboard, and Xavier levitated on his back.

The events that took place next were unprecedented to her. A light shone over the ship as if someone turned on a million powerful helicopter spotlights, like a flashlight shining over a hairpin in the dark. She noticed the ship vibrating as pens and paper fell off the dashboard and shelves. Slowly she tried to glide herself more to the window by flapping her arms to see outside. To her surprise, after looking out the window, the entire ship was at least fifty feet suspended in mid air over the sea. She saw large drops of water tumble back into the ocean from the hull.

The next thing she noticed was that her stepfather was staring at the computer. They both watched the processor go crazy. Letters, numbers, and symbols streamed vertically. The computer didn't have the means to work symbols moving this way on its viewer, only across. That was weird she thought, but then why not? They were already in an unnatural position. It wasn't like this trip from this point was normal.

She then sensed the sensation of falling as the boat tumbled to meet the sea again. She felt it in the pit of her stomach, like an elevator going down.

The whole ordeal ended as gravity became a reality again. She fell on her rear end to the floor with a light thump. Morris fell on his stomach, Ralph fell on his butt, and Xavier fell on his back. Her notion was that a minute had passed and she heard Morris moan from getting the wind knocked out of him. The powerful spotlights from above went out, and they all managed to sit on the helm floor.

They squinted at each other in the dark, dumbfounded, waiting for the other to speak. The lights on the ship flickered on, and the engines roared back to life.

She had forgotten why they went to Africa. She stared at her stepfather and his friends. As puzzled as they were, she contemplated what just happened. She never believed in U.F.O.'s before. At the moment she still refused to believe it. It must've been some kind of test government craft intervention.

The story had been in her stepfather's company, Livenal for a long time and seemed to be in her head forever. The consequential story was said to start off the Livenal Company's science division many years ago before she was born. She had dreamed about it again. Why? Maybe because she, too, had ventured out into the sea. She liked the sea; it was comforting to her. Yes, that's why she fantasized this story so much.

Nzingha Chelsea, a mature woman now, had awakened in the master suite of her three-deck yacht somewhere on the Atlantic Ocean. It must've been 3AM Eastern Time as she lay still under satin brown sheets. She thought about the dream she just had. Why was she dreaming this same dream so many times this year? She couldn't remember exactly how many times, maybe six, maybe seven.

Usually she had nightmares that she never told people about. They made her uncomfortable and probably would scare anyone else. This dream, of Xavier's happening at sea, was puzzling to her. For some reason, she felt this dream was important; so important that it would soon unlock a great virtuous event or demons of her past.

CHAPTER 1

MARK DOUGLAS KISSED HIS DAUGHTER and wife before he left his summer house this early warm morning. In his Range Rover he picked up three of his life-long friends. They all had vacation homes about ten miles apart, give or take. They had done this for six years.

Mark felt pleasant today. He was going to fish at Chesapeake Bay with his friends half of the day, then spend time with his family the other half. He and his buddies Larry, Raymond, and Carl all picked the last week in August as they always did for the last six years. Larry had picked the spot, and Mark had suggested they all build homes in the area. Mark, bring chief executive of Clive Inspirations, felt he was an expert at building on land.

Larry was a fat guy who was always joking around. Typical, Mark thought; there was always some fat guy who went around the room telling comic stories. It was probably so no one could make fun of his size. All his friends were typical; middle aged, white, wealthy, with egos.

Raymond had light brown hair, blue eyes, five feet and eleven inches, he loved his job as an executive at Mate's, a banking firm. Then there was Carl, who was a banker at Adams & Abraham. He had the most problems of all, Mark believed. Probably was paid the least, too. So what? Mark laughed to himself. They all owned houses, many cars, and loved to go on vacations every summer.

"Hey, can we talk about anything else but work?" Mark requested, cutting off Larry and Raymond from verbalizing about labor. "We're going to have a good time this week, okay?"

"Don't get angry because you don't deal with real live clients," Larry spoke.

"I don't care what type of jobs we have," Mark said. Then demanded more than asked, "let's talk about something else." He changed lanes on a highway almost void of automobiles this early morning.

"Okay," Carl voiced from the back seat with Larry. "My wife had another miscarriage."

"You sure she's alright?" Larry asked. "That's her fourth one this year."

"I don't know," Carl said to himself more than answering Larry.

"I saw on TV once . . ." Mark spoke reminiscing. "I'm not saying your wife, Carl, but this lady on TV was making babies and purposely killing them. They say it's some kind of disease where a person wants you to feel sorry for them all the time. I forgot the name of a person like that."

"You've told us about problems of depression your wife had," Larry spoke to Carl directly, then to Mark. "I think it's called an over excessive co-dependency disease."

"Yeah, I think she might have that?" Carl said to himself again more than anyone else.

"First, we didn't want to talk about work," Larry spoke to everyone. "Now do we want to talk about Carl's co-dependent wife?"

The guys laughed and said, "No," simultaneously. Carl then gave a smirk and folded his arms.

There goes Larry again Mark smiled, always trying to make jokes out of a predicament.

Chesapeake Bay took in a light breeze from the Atlantic Ocean. Mark's Sabreline 47 white motor-yacht took off toward deeper water, moving past the estuary. This now late morning was lightly cloudy, and yachts littered the ocean as far as Mark could see. He steered the boat, *King*, for ten minutes before coming to a halt.

Some hours had passed as four fishing lines disappeared into the green-blue salt water. They soon filled white buckets with small Cod and White fish as they sat in small wooden chairs on the stern.

Mark moved to the galley to get his mates more beer and homemade sandwiches. His wife made ten sandwiches of ham, turkey, and bologna as she always did. She was a traditional wife, Mark thought, and loyal. He wouldn't give her up for Carl's attractive co-dependent wife for the world.

He couldn't stop his friends from talking of work again. Money seems to make the world go around. Mark sighed. So they spoke of investments and banking, for that's what they did all their lives.

SOMEONE HAD BEEN WATCHING THEM CLOSELY since they left the bay. She was fifty feet from them in a dark gray and navy blue jet boat. She scrutinized them carefully with powerful ultra-bright pocket size marine binoculars. She squinted her slanted gray-blue eyes as she peered through the lenses.

In her skin-tight diving suit that matched her boat precisely, she started the engine. It was time. She waited for most of the boats in the area to drift away from the King. It was so crowded today, she thought. It took two hours for most of the vessels to float enough away out of view. Her whole persona was about time, and she lived by it. Precisely two hours of waiting, she said to herself, as she eyed her two waterproof watches on her wrist. She was on a tight schedule, yet patient. Her mission estimated to now be thirty minutes. She then eased on black gloves and directed her boat toward the King.

CARL NOTICED HER FIRST. He felt he would have never recognized her except for the fact that she cruised her small jet boat straight toward them. She looked ten years younger than he and maybe Philippine or Korean. Her long straight black hair would have flown all over the place except it was neatly in a firm bun. Carl also recognized her attractive tan round face and likely healthy curved-shaped rump in a skintight full swimming suit. Nice body, Carl thought, not chubby and not skinny either. He waved at her, smiling.

She moved closer now, six feet from the King. Carl noticed Larry also waved, observing her. Smiling, she waved back, steering the boat with her right hand to come abreast to their boat.

"Ahoy there, how are you?" Carl asked, standing. It was something he'd wished he'd never done, because he was the first to be caught off guard.

SHE RESPONDED WITH A WIDER SMILE, now three feet from the King, and shut off her engines. Time was of the essence, a principle she lived by. She understood her target, and it was time to take it out before more boats drifted back this way. She didn't know the other three men and considered them collateral damage. They were just in the wrong place at the wrong time. There's that word time again, she said to herself as she smiled.

Finding her brown air-pistol that was hidden in a dashboard under the steering wheel, she grabbed it in a tight grip. She took-out the guys who waved at her first. Before the guy standing, waving, could do anything, she shot him in the neck. She was inhumanly fast and fired again at a fat guy sitting, hitting him in the calf.

She saw that they realized the pinky-finger size dart she shot them with didn't kill them right away. They moved about, aggravated at the tiny thing in their neck and leg and knocked it out for it to bounce about on the deck. They also moved about just enough for her to get a clear shot at another man sitting next to the fat fellow. She fired again hitting that man in the shoulder, and he cursed. Then she spotted her objective in the galley—Mark Douglas.

He looked just like the photo she was given of him and she studied his features, salmon complexion, light brown eyes, and straight neat short cut hair. He wore a white short sleeve Lacoste sports shirt and shorts. Precision was another trait she owned as time and speed.

She saw that Mark was confused about the circumstances, and she capitalized on it. They locked eyes for what seemed like the longest split second. She fired again, and he ducked. *Got him!* She yelled in her head. Although there was a window between them, the dart still made it through. It chipped a round hole in the glass and hit him square in the earlobe. Then he ducked, dropping sandwiches and a open beer that was in his hands.

She worked expeditiously as she dropped the pistol in the water and grabbed an air tank she brought with her and scuba diving gear. Now floating two feet from the King she tossed the equipment aboard. Being extremely athletic, another hobby of hers, she leaped for the side of the boat. Catching the steel rail, she flipped aboard, landing next to her supplies.

She looked around, still no other boats had drifted near. She glanced at her watches—time gone by so far, three minutes. The strong anti-anxiety drug she shot the three with worked quickly, as did she. The three she hit first lay out on the stern of the boat, moaning. Taking out a hypodermic syringe from a pouch at her side, she hastily stabbed the three men in the same location where the first darts entered. From the syringe she squeezed detoxification drugs into the fat guy's leg, the other guy in the neck, and the last man in the shoulder.

When she walked toward Mark in the galley, he was still stumbling about on his knees mumbling.

"What are you trying to . . ." He then for some reason tried to reach out toward her and fainted.

When he dropped to the floor, she grabbed a cone cylinder from her pouch. She fit the cylinder in his mouth and picked up the spilled Budweiser he dropped. She poured the rest of the beverage down his throat. Next to a counter she calmly opened a large blue cooler full of ice and all types of beverages. Finding a six-pack of Budweiser, she ripped out four cans. Opening them, she continued to pour the contents into Mark's belly. She crushed some of the empty cans with her hand and threw them across the floor. There, she thought, now it looks like a real man drank those beers. She then neatly put the cylinder back in her pouch. She retrieved the four darts she shot at her victims and also put them in her sack.

Moving upstairs to the open helm, she started the engine and directed the King deeper into the Atlantic. Time now, fifteen minutes into her assignment. After estimating she was about forty yards from her jet boat and more away from the yachts in the area, she stopped the King. Moving back downstairs in the galley, she lifted Mark onto her shoulders and carried him to the helm. Laying him on his back on the floor, she dressed in her scuba diving gear.

Starting the ships engine again, she drove it at top speed. She then made a sudden left turn against the current of the waves; a left turn that she knew the yacht couldn't handle at fifty knots. The bow lifted straight in the air in an acute angle. With a loud moan of wood and metal, the King top-sided. Humans and supplies dispersed everywhere into the sea. For now she was sure no other vessels saw the King's huge white belly bobble in the middle of the blue ocean.

Underwater now with regulator and tank, she watched more supplies empty below the waves. Waving her arms and peddling her feet about six feet under the sea, she watched chairs, buckets, and cans float slowly past her. The sun shone bright, making the water around her reflect beams of light with flickers of grays and dark blues. She also observed two dark silhouettes of bodies in a dead-man's float above her; their bodies breaking the beams of sunlight.

Her diving gear matching the sea made her virtually vanish below the waves. With powerful kicks and waving arm movements, she swam the forty yards back to her boat. Climbing into her boat, she stripped out of her gear and swimming-suit down to a dark-green and blue bikini, showing her body had black tribal tattoos on her left shoulder, lower back, and left side of her buttocks. Her light caramel complexion made the tattoos define.

Time now, thirty-five minutes, she thought, five minutes over schedule. She quickly let her hair out to fall down her back, then started the engine.

She drove back to the docks in the bay, still avoiding most of the yachts in the area.

She was annoyed with herself. She spent too much time gloating at the beauty of the ocean under water. Or was she merely taking pride in her work by staring at it? Or was it both? It was neither, she thought. Her mission was strictly business. She didn't care about the ocean and didn't care about the humans she just dumped into the sea. Next time she was going to be faster; a promise she made with herself. Time was her everything as were her missions.

CHAPTER 2

THE IMPENDING TOWERS, also known as the Chelsea Towers, went up a towering sixty stories in the daytime downtown skyline of Columbus, OH. The blue and light brown twin buildings replicated cylinders connected at the bottom by a ten-story triangular building. To Maddox, it reflected an architectural construction for show. Obviously, it was, he thought. Look at the building's lobby.

The entire entryway was a rapture of Egyptian fashion. There were statues of sphinxes and obelisks with walls and floor that mimicked limestone. Palm trees and huge water fountains decorated the five hundred-foot triangular lobby. The entrance hall housed golden elevators, four to the left going into the west tower and four on the right for the east tower. Four colorful Egyptian palm-style columns held up the four-story ceiling, giving the atmosphere a true historic feel Maddox thought.

Maddox Mathews sat quietly on a black leather couch in a large waiting room outside Chelsea's main office. On the twenty-first floor in the east tower he stared out a large window looking down at the city of Columbus. He saw North Bank Park and the Scioto River, but still didn't get the full effect the building had to offer. The higher floors had a grander view of the full city landscape of the Leveque Tower, William Green Building, and One Nationwide Plaza.

For four years Impending Towers towered over the Rhodes State Office Tower, making these building the tallest in all of Ohio state. Yes, Impending Towers was even taller than the Key Towers in Cleveland, Maddox believed. He wasn't even going to witness the beauty of it all here on the twenty-first floor. He wasn't here for that.

He was here for pure business, like the black guy in the dark blue suit who sat on another identical couch across from him. The guy held a brown briefcase and looked nervous as he switched positions in his seat for the eighth time.

Then there was the secretary. She was calm, Maddox thought—too calm. Aggravatingly calm, like he hadn't been sitting here for almost fifteen minutes. She was a black woman wearing a gray skirt suit. Attractive face and figure, shoulder brown highlighted straight hair, French manicure, and he could smell her saccharine perfume from where he sat.

The reception brown desk sat near two large brown marble doors. The desk with computer was large enough that Maddox couldn't see supplies or what the secretary was doing behind it. All Maddox saw was her phone headset attached to her head. She could have been hard at work or playing around for all Maddox knew as he eyed his silver Omega watch. Twenty minutes waiting now.

Two Oriental men, one in a navy blue suit and the other in brown, emerged from the marble doors. They mumbled cheerfully in their foreign language passing Maddox. Happy from some deal, he supposed.

"Mr. Mathews, you may go in, sir," the secretary said, peeking her head over her desk at Maddox. Maddox finally got up, nodded at the secretary, and pushed through the brown marble doors.

He walked slowly down a long dark-brown hall with paintings on both sides. Lights above and below illuminated three oil paintings on the left, a flower in a vase, a shipwreck at sea, and woods in front of a snow-topped mountain. On the right were paintings of a lagoon, a sky over a pond, and a bridge over a bayou with an eighteen-hundred style house in the distance. The portraits were huge, Maddox thought, in his opinion five by five feet. Was Nzingha trying to throw him off on why he really came here by blessing him with these magnificent portraits, so when he approached her, he'd make a comment about them.

He walked to the end of the hall, the heart of the office. The office was the size of a huge studio apartment, and its' windows followed the round of the building. Lime-green walls mixed with brown paneling ran into a lime-green ceiling and black marble floor. Surrounding the room were many dozens of Weeping Figs, Bamboo, and Reed Palm plants that stretched toward the ceiling. The plants seemed in competition, trying to reach a huge round light almost as large as the ceiling itself.

A large man in black suit and tie sat to the far left of the room with a woman in a dark-blue skirt suit. They sat in cushioned lime-green chairs mumbling over charts in brown folders.

Then there was Nzingha's desk that sat somewhat in the middle of the room close to the right wall where a sixty-five inch plasma television was a part of. The television on mute showed images of CNN Live.

Nzingha stood behind her brown and ivory desk on her cell phone as Maddox slowly approached. She politely put her hand out for him to sit in one of the two black chairs in front of her desk. He, for some reason, chose the one on the left. Her desk was sparkling clean, with a lamp, black office phone, and fifteen-inch flat screen for a computer. Three spider plants were also spread out on her desk in glass canisters.

Then finally there was Nzingha Chelsea. She was pretty, Maddox thought, staring at her on the phone. She resembled a Rio de Janeiro woman with short straight brown hair and gray-asparagus eyes. This all sat flawlessly on her oval head. She wore a special designer's black pants suit. He couldn't smell her perfume at all. He smiled. She sure was beautiful, though.

"Yes, please sell it," Nzingha spoke on her cell phone. "Sell it all. Stock like that is of no use to us in the near future. I'll call you back in forty-five minutes. Okay, bye." She then put the phone in her pocket.

As Nzingha sat in her large black leather office chair, he detected her looking at his gray Yves Saint Laurent suit. He also hoped she was looking at his well-cut wavy Caesar hair-style.

She smirked, then eyeballed him directly before speaking. "Alright, Mr. Mathews, I have twenty minutes." She crossed her hands on her lap.

His company, Alona had been negotiating with Chelsea for about eight months, and this was the first time they met in person. Wow, Maddox thought, no handshake, just straight to the point.

"You could call me Maddox," Maddox said sarcastically, as if to say, *I'm doing fine, how are you*? "Alona is aware that you'll attend our first face to face board meeting presentation. We want to be well prepared to where and how it'll go."

"I apologize, Maddox." Nzingha quickly stood and extended her hand.

He also stood, and they firmly shook hands. Man, Maddox said to himself, she shook it so fast and firm he couldn't even get the feel of her possibly soft hands.

"I've had so many meetings today and phone calls," she said. "I also spoke to you so many times on the phone, I feel I almost know you. Sorry, I seem to forget sometimes how to be formal."

"It's alright I understand. Have you ever envisioned how I looked on the other end of the phone from my voice?" Maddox smiled as they both sat. She stared at him strangely by tilting her head a little to the left. Yeah, Maddox said to himself that wasn't professional, more personal.

"I don't know. How does one sound how they look? I would place how your personality sounds over the phone to your looks, but I've been wrong before—then again I haven't given it much thought."

"Just curious. We've been communicating on the phone for so long. So how will this first meeting go?"

"We'll have the presentation in this tower on the forty-third floor conference room, our advertising department. I'll have three of my administrators in that department along with my personal assistant attending the meeting."

"Are you still attending the meeting?"

"Yes." Nzingha gave an expression as if to say, *why did he ask?*

Well, it seemed like that expression to Maddox and his smile widened. In his heart, of course, he wanted her to show up, but he had to keep it professional. "Um, the time and date will stay the same, right?"

"Yes, four o'clock—two weeks from now, Monday." Nzingha looked puzzled. "We could have spoken about this on the phone."

"Well, I personally wanted to meet you before we got deep into the politics of this merger. Even if it's for twenty minutes. You see, this merger is a big thing to my company. Our board of directors feel we're going to make a lot of money. They feel it's going to be a future climbing, um roller-coaster. They feel you're growing rapidly."

"What do you feel?"

"I agree with the council. I always admired your company, distinctively your computer department. You've made remarkable discoveries with nanotechnology."

"Really," Nzingha responded, raising a brow.

"Yes, I had to meet the person behind all this. The phone calls weren't good enough. Conducting business face to face is always good in my opinion."

"Very good, Maddox." Nzingha leered. "Yes, you do look as you sound on the phone. Handsome in stature, I suppose, for a chief executive of your designing department." Nzingha stood again and extended her hand. "Nice meeting face to face, Maddox."

This time when Maddox shook Nzingha's hand he remembered to feel it. It was soft and warm. For some reason he could now smell her perfume. It had a clean soppy vanilla fragrance to it, like if he just walked into a Bath and Body Works store. He smiled. Mmm she smelled so good.

CHAPTER 3

SPECIAL AGENT JOSEPH JOHN CLAY stood on a wooden pier with his hands in his pockets staring into the sea as the sun set behind him. The wind in Chesapeake Bay had picked up since the afternoon, whipping his gray tie about. He looked into the darkening blue sky full of silver-purple clouds sprawled everywhere. Stars started to twinkle to life, and he wanted to count them. It took his mind off this case that puzzled him like others. He even started counting seagulls as a flock flew past him over his head out to sea. Seventeen, he said to himself, as he watched the white and gray birds dissipate over the water.

Familiarity in cases had brought him here to Virginia. It all started in Columbus, OH and he had the strangest feeling it was going to end there. Jeffrey Wells and his wife died in a skiing accident in Canada. Now Mark Douglas and his buddies also died by mishap, so one would say, *what's the connection?* Well, a company in Ohio has profited from these misfortunes. Simply said, but hard to prove in a court of law.

Mr. Wells, president and owner of WCBH-TV, didn't particularly want to sell his company to the Chelsea Corporation. He wanted to sell it to Media Widespread, based in Richmond, VA. Chelsea, already fixed in Columbus, OH had great interest in the TV station for many years. As soon as Mr. Wells had a fatal accident, WCBH-TV, with its three sister TV stations, sold to Chelsea. Now the TV network was the major news for Ohio.

Also for some years Mr. Douglas, Chief Executive of Clive Inspirations, a real estate firm, didn't want to sell land out of Harlem in New York to the Chelsea Company. Mr. Douglas then buys an unfortunate casualty and

13

the Chelsea Corporation buys up land from Clive Inspirations. Hmm, Joe said to himself, that raises a red flag.

Then one would ask the question, *what brought him to realize all this in the first place so soon?* Columbus, OH Homicide Detective Peter Greenhill pointed this out, and he was a good friend. He met Peter eight years ago on a case they did in San Juan, Puerto Rico.

Eight years ago Peter worked for Florida Homicide and dealt with a Puerto Rican drug cartel that reached all the way to the island's own PRPD, La Uniformada. The case took two years to solve before arrests were made. He and Pete had kept in touch since Pete moved to Ohio five years ago.

Pete had talked to him in March, six months earlier, about this case in Columbus that stretched to Canada. Local Canadian authorities ruled the case as an accident. Pete always for some strange reason had his suspicions about the Chelsea Company. The Company had grown rapidly five years ago through takeover after takeover. It was eating up companies left and right in Ohio and Chicago. Growing to the billion dollar conglomerate it is today. So it wasn't a surprise to Pete that when Mr. Wells passed away, his TV enterprise went to Chelsea.

Then Joe got a call earlier today that a week ago Mr. Douglas had an unfortunate accident. The Chelsea Company was now making preparations to buy up land in Harlem New York. It was this day Joe took the case seriously.

Joe's partner, Special Agent Allen Valentino, was younger than him by ten years and new to the Federal Bureau of Investigation. They both wore a white shirt and black pants, but everything else was different. Allen wore a light pink tie and expensive Oxford light brown shoes. His light brown hair was wet and slicked back, and he wore Versace sunglasses almost all the time on his heart shaped-head.

Joe was against him wearing the pink tie, but if he argued with Allen, Allen would have only said he was old. Joe didn't like to be reminded that he was fifty years old and had been a lead field agent for twelve years. He didn't like to be advised his hair was graying rapidly, so he left Allen's tie alone today.

"Check all the flights from Ohio to Virginia from a week ago and prior to that about three weeks," Joe spoke to Allen, who had just walked up from behind him.

"Sure thing." Allen held a black E-Keeper pad holder and fumbled a little as he opened it to write down what Joe said.

"Also check all the boats rented at the bay at those same weeks," Joe said, "and see if we could get video surveillance at the piers and rental stores."

"Got it." Allen jotted all this down with his define pen. "I also have the police and coroner reports of the incident."

"Good, so let's go look at our boat." Joe and Allen spontaneously walked off the pier. "What's your take on this matter so far?" Joe knew everything there was to know about the case. Though fresh eyes was always good to consider, the possibilities were endless he thought.

"Well, as we speak, it's obvious Chelsea has bought land disputed by Mr. Douglas, but not so much by some people in his own company," Allen spoke as they walked down the boardwalk. "All this could be a coincidence, but my gut feeling is that coincidences usually only happen once. Therefore, that brings a lot of suspicion to Chelsea. My guess, we're going to have to interview people in Clive Inspirations and find extensive history on Chelsea, particularly Chelsea's pattern of takeovers."

"I couldn't have said it better, sport." Joe smiled. They stopped in front of a lot that held boat trailers and cars. Ten boats sat on the back of trailers, and sixteen cars of all types sat in this yard. Joe counted them all.

Two Virginia State Police officers in blue shirts, gray pants, and champaign straw hats approached the large aluminum fence from within. Joe took his badge from his pocket and showed the officers.

"Hi, I'm Agent Clay, and this is my partner, Valentino. We called earlier."

"Yeah, we were waiting for you guys," the older of the two officers spoke as he unlocked a chain and opened the fence. "Officer Austin, and this is my partner Blangard." The pairs shook hands quickly. "The boat is back here. So how was your trip to Virginia?"

"Long, but you got to do what you got to do," Joe responded with a smirk as they walked to the back.

They arrived at the back of the yard and stared up at a two story white motor yacht mounted on a trailer. Joe inhaled deeply, expecting to take in the strong aroma of the salty sea air. Instead, he smelled death. At first look, the boat seemed intact. He examined chipped black letters on the side of the vessel. The letters read, *King*.

CHAPTER 4

RAIN POURED FROM THE HEAVENS over downtown Columbus. It rained so hard it blurred the city streetlamps and building lights. It rained so hard, when raindrops hit puddles, it exploded on impact, splashing water in every direction. Lightning flashed and thunder roared. Huge dark cumulonimbus clouds darkened the night more.

The devil is really whipping his wife's ass, the man in black thought, as he stared at the Impending Towers. He stood over a manhole two blocks from the towers. His face was saturated with rain, but he didn't care. He was no ordinary citizen, he thought. He was on a mission most people seldom traveled.

He was dressed in a black custom-made full scuba diving wetsuit with beanie and boots. Black gloved hands, utility-belt with pouch on his left hip and night vision goggles on his head made his wardrobe complete.

With a crowbar in hand, he lifted the manhole and went down a ladder into the darkness. Closing the manhole cover over him, he hung the crowbar on the steel ladder and descended. Flipping his night vision goggles over his eyes, he reached the bottom of the ladder. He moved through waist-high sewer water rushing against him, emptying out somewhere far behind.

His world was now the vision of a green sewer, wet and full with crud. It kind of reminded him of what he called, *The Wizard of Gunk*. To take his mind off the musty shit smell, he thought about his purpose.

He drove a brown Dodge Plateau van two blocks from the towers because of his diagramed information. He attained the map of the towers and the streets around them. Based on the layout, he plotted his mission to take one hour. It didn't take long for the streets to vacate one o'clock in the morning. He made sure no one saw him take the crowbar from his van and slip into the hell he was in now. He analyzed the building windows. Maybe somebody was peeking at him. Not likely. No one will be watching him one o'clock in the morning in the midst of a thunderstorm.

The mission was simple. He had much harder assignments in the past. All he had to do today was download data from a computer in Impending Towers.

They were of death, to describe his missions of the past. He didn't know how many people he killed, but it was for the better of the United States Government. He hoped he didn't have to kill today. All he was doing was collecting information, he kept saying to himself.

Rushing black sewer water now only covered his boots as he made his way crouched through a narrow cylinder tunnel. Strings of rust mixed with muck hung over his head as he briskly moved through the loathsome funnel. All the while he just remembered he'd been through worse.

He'd been to the worst jungles of Brazil and through the deserts of the Sahara. All his missions were life threatening, nerve-racking, and at the highest of confidentiality. He lived by a principle—if I have to tell you my story, I have to kill you. He hoped he didn't have to kill anybody today.

Grabbing his Meizu M8 cellular from his belt, he studied the tiny screen. He clicked to the GPS to show a map of the sewer system connected to the bottom of Chelsea Towers. He checked his bearings, then picked up his pace through the gutter.

In the burrow, he made it to a rusted locked gate on his right. Picking the lock with an electronic master key from his belt, he pushed the gate open. Walking out of the sewer stream, he moved to a concrete wall. The wall was dirty, but clearly newer than the surrounding sewer. About a foot above his almost six-foot stature was the vent he was looking for. This was the vent to the Chelsea East Tower waste facilities.

Reaching up at a grid covering the vent, he tugged at it. Cemented shut, like he thought. Taking out a Tomahawk Eagle knife from his belt, he dug into the wall beside the grid. Chipping away at the cement, he exposed the ends of the iron frame, then did the same to the other side. Removing the grid, he placed it on the ground and pulled himself up into the crawl size shaft. He was pleased to escape the sewer to squeeze in this tight duct. Shimmying he followed a faint light about ten feet ahead. He passed fans embedded in the left and right walls of the passage. They were off now, but when turned on, they obverted the smell of the trash in the buildings compactor room toward the sewer.

He made it to a second grid, and beyond it was a small room full with huge black bags. Even though the dimly lit room had one overhead light, he saw it as clear as day. It was the size of a living room with two green trash compactors full with black bags. One compactor sat over a hole in the ceiling, his destination.

He looked around the room. There appeared to be no cameras. This grid was screwed into the wall, so he took out his electric screwdriver from his belt and went to work. Placing the four screws in the vent, he detached the grid from the wall and placed it sideways there, too. He then lowered himself out of the vent to touch the waste facility floor.

Like a ninja in the night, he moved through the shadows of the room to a door. Checking the door, he could tell it was locked from the outside. He opened it, and with all his might with his boot, broke the steel handle on the outside. The loud snapping sound of the handle echoed in the vacant underground parking lot beyond. He then quickly closed the door, shutting himself back in the waste room, and peered out the small door window.

He waited two minutes to see if any parking lot security heard anything. All the cameras on the top part of the parking lot wall faced away from this door. Nobody cared for the waste room. Bad for them, good for me, he thought. He was ten minutes into his mission. He'd best get moving.

He moved back to the shaft in the ceiling over the compactor full with bags and climbed in. From his pouch he took out four magnetic suction-cup shoes and strapped one on each knee and one for each of his hands.

He climbed into the silver shaft and moved now vertically with tremendous speed. He pushed his back against one part of the duct and attached his suction-cup knees and hands on the opposite side. In a fetus-like position he crawled quickly upward, sliding up the tunnel like a black human beetle.

Fighting gravity, using the leverage of his back and his special suction-cups, he took twenty minutes to make it to the thirtieth floor.

The thirtieth floor, his destination, was presumably going to be the hardest part of the mission. It was better than climbing this smelly garbage chute he thought. He couldn't wait to crawl out of the incinerator. Sewers and trash compactors wasn't his line of work, but hey, he'd been in worse places.

Climbing out of the thirtieth floor trash compactor, he was in a new room. It was small, but it smelled a lot better than where he came from. He took off his suction-cups and put them back in his pouch. He then took one end of a rope from his sack and tied it tightly to the door handle of the trash compactor door. Uncoiling it he threw the rest of the three-hundred foot rope back down into the shaft. His quick insurance route out of here, he said to himself.

The room he was in now, no bigger than a large closet, was going to be his surveillance post. Peeking out the glass window of the door, he observed the sea of glass offices across the white hallway from him. He was searching for cameras. Found them. One was in the upper corner left wall aimed at the entire collection of offices. The second he couldn't see, but knew for sure would be there, in another office at the opposite end. That was the CEO's private media office, Nzingha Chelsea's, and the end of his mission.

Emerging from the unlocked door of the incinerator room, he moved into the dull lit white hallway to a locked glass door. Taking out his electronic master key, he picked the lock and opened the door in about two minutes. This door was much harder to open than the one in the sewer.

Opening the door just enough to squeeze his body inside, he moved to the left of the room. Of the fifty large ceiling fluorescent lamps, only eight were on, scattered about the room. Good, he thought, because now he moved like a phantom along the wall of the twenty glass offices he counted. Lightning flashed and thunder rolled like bowling balls as he could see the rain washing the outside windows.

Moving past exposed desks, he never bothered to notice insignificant things like computers, pens, papers, desk name plates, and soda cans. He was going for the camera on the left side of the room.

Unplugging the wire under the camera, he knew he had seven minutes before the guards noticed and eventually would come. He had put the situation to a test last week. He had paid an eighteen-year-old mail-carrier two hundred dollars to drop some magazines off to this floor and find these offices. He told the boy if he did it in ten minutes, he'd get another hundred. He came back in six. "Here you go, kid, you just saved me another trip back upstairs." He remembered lying. "My friends really needed those."

He came up with a theory of how fast it would take to get to this floor and find these rooms. If it took the boy six minutes to go up, then come back down, then he figured it would take the guards about three minutes to just go up. He added four more minute for the watchman to figure something was wrong. Seven minutes was all the time in the world he needed for this part of the task.

He dashed across the room to the right and fiddled with the private office door using his master key. It clicked unlocked, and he emerged into the core of his sortie. The room was dark, but he needed no lights. His green seeing world showed him where everything was just fine. Right away he unplugged the camera in the ceiling above the door he just came in. Then he sat behind a glass desk with name plate that read *Chief Executive Nzingha Chelsea.*

A minute went by already, he said to himself, looking at his watch. Turning on the PC he took out a USB size hard drive from his belt and connected it to the back of the computer. It was a special portable hard drive not out to the public yet, built to specifically adsorb data and programs like a sponge.

The computer's flat screen asked for a password as it finished booting up. He typed in *download*, and the screen went blank again, then powered back up. Though that wasn't the catchphrase and he knew it not, it was his drive's shibboleth, and it was all he needed. Now the screen flashed white a couple of times, indicating the portable hard drive was bypassing the computer's catchphrase.

He was in. The screen wallpaper showed a huge colorful outside garden. Icons and folders of things saved on the computer hard drive showed up on the left. In the center of the screen a white bar showed the data the portable hard drive was adsorbing. Ten percent, twenty percent, forty, the bar was rising every half a second.

The whole tribulation lasted five minutes. Meanwhile, he glanced at pens, scribbled writings on note pads, folders, and papers neatly placed on the desk. Nzingha must be an orderly person, for things like *Nerocom three dollars a share* and *the Dow Jones dropping* was scrawled neatly on a small pad.

A hundred percent, the bar read, and he turned off the computer. He took his hard drive from behind the PC and slipped it back into his belt. Six minutes, he said to himself as he eyed his watch and re-plugged the camera. When he left the office the door automatically locked behind him. He also reactivated the other camera across the room of desks and left as he came, like a shadow.

The mission was almost flawless. His watch read one forty-six. He had enough time to get to the van to make his whole time spent, an hour.

"Hey, you there, get down on the floor!" a guard shouted. He was in a black suit and tie. The guard routinely had been walking the floor, the man in black custom-made wetsuit figured. He couldn't have made it here from downstairs that quickly. Hum, the man in goggles sighed. Just my luck. Soon, though, the downstairs guards were going to get fishy about the surveillance on this floor and be here in a minute.

He had to act fast. He flipped up his goggles so his adversary saw his eyes. He saw his opponent clearly, escaping his green seeing world. The watchman using his black laser sighting mini taser, fired it quickly.

As the watchman fired, the twin wire prongs flung threw the air toward the man in black wetsuit. He effortlessly dodged the flying twine by flinging his body against the hallway wall. The man in black wetsuit was much faster than his adversary. Maybe two moves ahead of him, no three.

The man in black wetsuit used his fist to punch the guard in the face, square in the nose. He followed by a swift kick in the groin, then another punch in the face again. The guard never met the speed of the man in all black.

The watchman, the man in the wetsuit thought, was probably surprised there was going to be a fight at all, slumped forward, nose bleeding. Then, just the man in the wetsuit's luck, the elevator door opened. Another watchman now stepping out the elevator moved toward the commotion.

The man in the wetsuit elbowed the first guard in the back of the head, knocking him out. As the first guard collided with the hard polished floor, the man in black, like a flash of lightning that lit the place momentarily, shifted toward the elevator.

The second guard, who was much taller than the first, also wasn't expecting a fight. His bad luck, the man in black thought. The second guard fumbled with his taser as he tried to reach for it at his side. *I just couldn't get that damn gun out quickly enough,* the man in black knew the watchman had to be thinking. The second guard never made it two steps from the elevator.

He punched the second watchman four times in the face from four different angles before the guard joined his partner on the floor. Nose bleeding, busted lip, swollen jaw, and soon to be black eye, the man in black understood the second guard was going to wake up with.

He then fled to his surveillance room, the incinerator. Shutting the door behind him, he climbed into the tight two and a half foot trash compactor quadrangle hole. He closed the hatch his rope was tied to and climbed down hastily. He was sweating as he climbed down from the thirtieth floor. Though he couldn't hear them, silent alarms must be going off all over the building, he thought.

It took eight minutes to make it to the basement compactor room. After a couple of times sliding down the rope, it still took about eight minutes, he contemplated. Soon letting the rope go, he plunged about ten feet into the bin full with black bags. As he slammed into the bags, cushioning his fall, he stood quickly and drew his black .45 with silencer from his shoulder holster. A black net covered the back of the gun so he could catch his shells. He aimed at the door in the room. Nothing. Nobody was there, *yet.*

Holstering his pistol, he hopped out of the compactor and jumped into the vent in the wall. He did it in two motions. He was fast, like a cat. Finding the grid in the shaft where he placed it last, he put it back in its place. Taking out his screwdriver, he neatly screwed the screws back into the four corners of the vent cover. Then he wriggled backwards down the shaft to the vile-smelling street sewer waiting beyond.

He back-tracked all his moves in the sewer, closing grids and gates behind him. He flipped his night goggles over his eyes again as he jogged in the gutter channels going with the flow of water.

It was five minutes after two o'clock as he glimpsed at his watch. He was five minutes over schedule, which he blamed on his encounter with the guards. Authorities will see his rope in the incinerator and will trace his steps to the basement compactor room. They won't know that he used the sewer system, but they'll see the broken compactor door in the underground parking lot. That will lead to the obvious conclusion.

The assignment could have gone smoother, but, hey, mission accomplished, he thought. His contact will be pleased. Furthermore, he was pleased with himself. He hurt individuals, but didn't have to kill anyone today.

CHAPTER 5

"SCRATCHES AND A NEAT SMALL ROUND HOLE in the galley window, but no real damage to the boat," Joe said to his partner as he examined twenty small photos of the King again. He laid them out in no specific order on his bed in an east end downtown Richmond hotel called Makso's.

"I have some interesting information for you and possibly some foul play which might draw more clause to this case," Allen said as he sat on the bed next to the photos. They both wore white shirts and black pants, but this time Allen wore a light purple tie and Joe wore an off-shade gray tie. I hate Allen's ties, Joe said in his head. He was going to tell Allen later, after Allen spilled the information.

"I have to show you something you're going to like," Allen spoke as Joe sat on the opposite bed parallel to the other. Allen opened his E-Keeper pad and scrambled with four small hand size photos and his notes. He handed the Kodak photos to Joe.

The pictures showed four different individuals. A diminutive puncture wound was on the neck of one person called Carl Matheson. His name was in black marker on the back of the photo. The second showed a puncture wound on the right calf of a man called Larry Tombling and a third photo showed a tiny pierce on the right shoulder of Raymond Davidson. The last photograph was of Mark Douglas. There was a prick lesion in his earlobe. Joe studied the snapshots, making a mental note of the similarity of abrasions.

"The Virginia Coast Guard recovered the four bodies in Chesapeake Bay two weeks ago," Allen spoke as he looked through some notes he had jotted down. "This tack-like hole obviously shows some kind of foul play. I also checked people's ID's on flights from Ohio to Virginia and matched them with flights from Ohio to Canada. Nothing unusual. No phony ID's, no usual occurring faces, nothing. Nothing unusual on the rented boats at the bay area stores. No matching faces with anybody coming in from Ohio to Virginia with rented boats for at least a month."

Joe sighed and tapped the photos on his leg.

"We're going to have to go to Ohio and see about that Canadian accident and check the bodies," Joe said, then sighed again.

"I suppose we're going to have to interview the TV companies here and the people who used to work for the old Ohio TV station," Allen inquired, staring at his notes.

"Yes," Joe answered, then paused for a while, thinking. This was turning into a major case, and it began today. He had to report this to his director. Welcome to our third case together, champ. "I also want to interview Mr. Douglas' company in New York. What's his company again?"

"The . . . it's right here." Allen rummaged through his notes to find the right one. He found it upside-down, then turned it right-side-up. "Clive Inspirations."

"What exactly did the accident report say how Mr. Douglas and his friends died? Was there anything in their blood unusual?" Joe stared again at each of the pictures.

"No." Allen went through his notes again, finding the right one. "The coroner's report said that they all drowned, but Mr. Douglas was the only one with a blood alcohol content of 0.11. He was well drunk driving his boat, so authorities figured he flipped it."

"I wonder did the authorities ever stop to wonder could any of these guys swim, or did they just figure they were all drunk and drowned?"

"There were no abrasions on the bodies except for those pin marks." Allen gave a quick smirk. "I guess they all got knocked out at the same time when the boat flipped."

"I hear your sarcasm, but they could have got knocked out when they hit the water. I've heard stranger things."

"A James Blatty of the Virginia Marine Police said it was crowded the day of the accident, but nobody saw anything, no witnesses," Allen continued reading his notes.

"So-called accident," Joe mumbled to himself.

"Oh, and there's about five boat rental stores big and small at the bay.

Four have cameras. It's going to take some time to look at all the video footage from those stores."

"First I want to go to our forensic lab right here in Virginia and have them check the bodies of these guys again. Then I need to see the coroner's photos of Mr. Wells and his wife in Ohio. I just hope we don't have to exhume bodies. There's a lot of legal work and family feelings in that. We could also have our analyst at this branch look at the video of those boat stores around the time of this incident. Maybe store some faces. So what do you think?"

"I agree with everything you said. You want me to make the call to the boss?"

"No, I'll call him. I'll sweet talk him again." Joe stared at his partner's tie. "I see we have one disagreement, though. Why don't you work on better ties?"

Allen smiled. "What do you mean, what's wrong with this tie?"

"It's too bright. Feds never wear ties like you."

"There you go hating again. I think you tenured guys know I look better than y'all, so y'all stay criticizing."

"You need to dress as the Romans dress."

"The Romans need to get with the program and see something new. Their ancient ways are—well, just ancient."

Joe shook his head in disagreement, but smiled. Yeah, Allen won the tie argument for now. He didn't want to quarrel to long. He'll talk that old stuff again.

Joe was going to talk to his Assistant Director Jacob Kordey in Washington D.C. and tell him it's a go on the case. Kordey will probably say it's not in your jurisdiction. Why do you want to take the case? He'll explain, well, my old friend Greenhill had told me about a suspicious company in Ohio profiting off unfortunate deaths. A Mr. Wells, owner of a television station and an executive of a real estate firm, died in unfortunate accidents. Sequentially, the Chelsea Company profited big from.

Kordey will tell him it's his call and the case will be a go. He didn't know what he wanted to call the case because Kordey sure was going to ask. Bad profits, illegal business; he just didn't know yet, Joe thought. He handed the four pictures back to his partner.

Joe checked his watch. It was 11:50, time for lunch. It was still early in September, it couldn't have been a better time to start this case. This could be something big; he just had a feeling about his assignments. He solved all his twenty-one cases as a field agent. Knock on wood, he was going to unravel this one. This was the kid's third case, and he felt it was going to be a big one. Could possibly take some years to resolve.

"So, kid, where do you want to eat?"

While Allen thought, Joe collected the pictures of the King and put them in his old and torn black E-Keeper. He counted the photos again, twenty. Counting, for some dumb reason, made him at ease.

Chapter 6

MADDOX FINALLY HAD THE OPPORTUNITY to see it all.

The Leveque Tower, William Green Building, and One Nationwide Plaza constructions glistened in the afternoon skyline of downtown Columbus, OH. It was what he saw through the window on the forty-third floor of the East Impending Tower.

More important was this meeting. It was his first company sit-down meeting with the Chelsea Corporation. He was excited about the seminar, but more thrilled about meeting Nzingha again.

The conference room was as large as two usual size living rooms with a light brown rectangular bamboo table in the center that stretched long enough to seat eight gray-cushioned chairs on both sides. Half of the room was surrounded by glass windows and doors, the other half by an oak wall. The windows showing the exterior showed the curvature of the building. One part outside displayed the identical reflecting windows of the west tower. The brown oak wall housed a fifty-inch plasma television. Another part of the wall on a ledge, in some kind of shrine, sat a large Yucca Elephantipes plant in a green abstract vase.

On the table at both ends in glass vases filled with water and flat stones were Bonsai plants. In the center was a black remote control conference room phone that also controlled global video conferencing. Apart from the main lights, four tiny silver lights hung from the ceiling, each having its own long finger-size silver tube so that they hung five feet over the table. Sixteen wine glasses filled with mineral water were placed in front of the sixteen chairs.

Maddox and his two assistants, Bernard and Charles, sat on one side of the table with the Chief Executive Assistant of Alona, Jason Culver, and his assistant Kathryn. Nzingha, her assistant, and three administrators of her advertising department as promised, occupied the opposite five chairs across the table.

Nzingha stood and walked to the end of the table. She wore a black long sleeve business suit, blue shirt, and black aerosols shoes. Her assistants were all male, in business attire.

"I'm glad everyone made it today. I want to introduce my design team executives. First, there's Ryan Peck. He's our art director." Nzingha began pointing each one out. Ryan nodded in the dark purple suit. "Then there's Assistant Executive Gregg Reid." Gregg put his hand up in the dark blue suit. "Then we have my Chief Executive Aaron Lerman." A man in a black suit signaled with his head. "And last, my personal assistant, Christopher Shaw." The last man of Nzingha's group nodded also in black suit. "Even though I know we all spoke on the phone many times and have seen each other through video conferencing, I'm glad we could all meet like this. Maddox, please introduce your team."

Maddox stood in his gray Brioni suit and spoke, looking at Nzingha's executives.

"I'm Maddox Mathews, Chief Executive of Alona's Designing Department." He then pointed to his group. "These guys are my assistants, Charles Quinn and Bernard Young." Charles was in a dark blue suit and Bernard was in black. "And the one and only Chief Assistant Executive of Alona, Jason Culver, with his assistant Kathryn Miller." Jason wore a brown suit, and his assistant wore a pants suit of the same color.

"It's an honor to finally meet you all face to face," Jason said as he stood and looked to Nzingha first, before everybody else.

"Please, have a seat." Nzingha gave an indication with her hand for the two to sit, and Maddox and Jason sat. "Today I'm not going to talk much because this is your first presentation on why our companies should merge." Nzingha held a straight face. "I have to start by saying that I like the idea and want to make it legitimate. I've already gone over what Alona has done in the past twelve years, and I'm pleased to say I'm impressed. And my assistants know it's hard to impress me."

There were giggles among Nzingha's team and smiles on the other. "I know we're about to hear more on what you offer, but I want you to know what type of business I offer. It might even be off the subject of business a little, but you have to hear this.

"I run a clean and respectable business and believe in purities. It's sort of like religion, a way of life. Like the water in front of you. I put it in wine glasses because I want to show people water is finer, richer, than wine. The point is, simple life is the most powerful thing in the world. We don't need fancy cars and jewelry. All we need is a roof over our heads and clothes. I want to show the world that doing the right thing gives you a positive charge on the mind and, with that, you could physically and creatively do anything.

"So basically my company is about purities. I believe being real and positively imaginative is the key to the mysteries of the universe. So, enough about the religion of my company. Maddox, please, begin your presentation."

Maddox didn't quite understand her, but he could have listened to her all day. Not only was she physically attractive, she had something to say. She was intelligent. He guessed she had to be, to possess this huge corporation.

He liked thinking women. Hell, he liked positive thinking people. He understood she was right about one thing. A positive thinking world would be a better place, though he was sad to say, that's not the way the world worked. The world was full of snakes, back stabbers, and cut throats, and you have to wiggle your way through that. That was the ultimate certainty, he thought.

Maddox stood again and walked to the front of the table as Nzingha sat.

"Alona, which has been in existence for twelve years has served huge companies like Fay's, Ralph n' Peggy's, and more than twenty small businesses," Maddox spoke, looking at each individual for a few seconds, picking them randomly as if he was talking directly to them. "I must say we've made great profits in this destabilized economy and hope to continue with even bigger earnings to come. I think I could speak for Alona, which we hope the merger will be a smooth transition, for we have much to offer each other. Today we'll show the Chelsea Corporation in more detail what we do and how we do it. So guys, you're on." Maddox pointed to his two assistants, then sat.

Bernard stood in front of the table while Charles went around handing everyone small color brochures from his briefcase. Charles then went to the television, turned it on, and fiddled with the remote.

"While Charles sets up the video presentation, I'm going to discuss a better view of what we do," Bernard spoke. "First, we're thankful that

Emmanuel Wade, our Account Executive, put this all together, or all this wouldn't have been possible.

"We're a full service and interactive agency. We're the eighth largest in the U.S. and tenth in the world and growing. With this merger it'll bring us higher on the scale. That's why we believe it's so important that this happen.

"As you know some things already, on what we do, I'm just going to go over it again, getting more into the essentials. We do e-business, mobile devices, digital platforms, radio, and television with many contacts with various media. We also deal in marketing, graphic design, and sales promotions. Along with the top executive thinkers of our company, we've specially picked individuals who are our art and creative directors. They do the ground work to make this all happen."

Maddox felt the first presentation went well. After Charles demonstrated and explained his video of the clothing commercials he did for Ralph n' Peggy's and other new advertisements, it was over in an hour. Everyone clapped, shook hands, and smiled.

It was like going to a first interview for a job. Did I say everything right? Was my tie straight? Did I say everything I wanted to say? Is my hair in place? Did the employer like me or was he just smiling, hiding the fact that I was never going to get the job? Half of him felt that way. The other half, he was confident he got a positive vibe and that things flowed well. It must have gone well, because the assistants of both teams set up meetings to see each other again.

Maddox took his mind off the meeting for a moment and focused on Nzingha. He wanted to know more about this mogul. At first glance she was calm and in control of everything around her. She had no rings on her fingers and wore a lot of black or blue expensive pants suits. She rarely smiled, was never alone, and always seemed busy.

Maddox saw something else in Nzingha that she didn't portray outwardly. She was quiet, because she was hiding something. She wasn't married because something in her relationships must have gone dramatically wrong. She wasn't as young as he thought; she looked in her mid-twenties, but she had to be at least thirty. A woman of her stature and money had to be married by now. Though she surrounded herself with a lot of people, she must be lonely, a workaholic perhaps. All this, of course, was speculation.

He liked something about Nzingha, but he just couldn't put his finger on it yet. Something else about her was soothing and innocent, like if she was kept out the loop about the evils of life. If that was so, then how did she get rich so quickly? Not by being naïve, Maddox thought. She talked about the purities of her company, Maddox figured: Well, we're going to have to see about that.

MADDOX STAYED AT THE HYATT REGENCY HOTEL in downtown Columbus with the other executives of Alona in separate rooms. The hotel had its entertainment, but he needed to get away from his associates for a while. He'd been with his acquaintances for a week, and tomorrow they were going back to New York. He didn't want to hang around his boss, Mr. Chief Assistant Executive. He and his colleagues will talk about business all day, trying to impress the manager on how well they worked. The little time he had left in Columbus he wanted to share with himself and his thoughts.

He rented a four-door silver Cadillac Escalade. The car for now was his sanctuary. It was five o'clock in the afternoon as he rode down Main Street heading toward the Main Street Bridge. He didn't have any particular destination. He was just driving.

Downtown Columbus was nothing like downtown Manhattan, Maddox thought. Not as many stores, people, and businesses. Maybe that's why some companies here started so quickly. Not much competition, where in California, Chicago, and New York there was an overwhelming amount of competitors. Then, the down-side of places like Columbus, because it wasn't a top major city, there was a lot of poverty, and that wasn't good for business.

Then, there was the Chelsea Company, which was doing well. For what he knew, it grew out of Columbus. Maybe the Chelsea Company was the start of Columbus becoming a part of the top major cities. Perhaps it was all a fraud and the Chelsea Company wasn't as pure as Nzingha said it was. Many fast growing companies in the past went down because of swindles and the Crash of 2008.

Speak of the devil! Maddox said to himself. As he drove down the street in what some New Yorkers would say *light traffic*, he spotted Nzingha. He watched her get out of a black Rolls-Royce Phantom SUV, escorted by a chauffeur also in black. Through the sea of people, probably just getting off from work, he watched Nzingha disappear into an art gallery called, Nouveau of Art.

For a second, Maddox viewed clouds that seem to want to produce rain. They shrouded the soon to be setting sun, yet it didn't rain. The clouds only covered the sun momentarily, then showed it again. The clouds did this about a hundred times as if playing peek-a-boo. He glanced at the wall of skyscrapers as he drove down the blocks of downtown Columbus and glimpsed at the shopping stores trying to mimic larger cities of the country. Trying to collect his thoughts away from work, the last thing he theorized was that he was going to see Nzingha in the middle of Columbus, OH rush hour.

Excited, he felt this was the perfect opportunity to maybe get to know her, if she allowed him to. He just had to approach her the right way and see. If she gave him the cold shoulder, hey, he was going back to New York tomorrow anyway.

It took five minutes to find a parking space two blocks from the art gallery. It wasn't like Manhattan, where parking was unbearable.

As he walked down the street through the groups of pedestrians, he smelled his breath with his hand. It was okay, but he still popped a Certs mint in his mouth. He glanced at his white shirt, dark gray slacks, and gray Ralph Lauren blazers' reflection in the gallery front window. He looked fine, not one wrinkle.

Before stepping into the gallery, Maddox noticed behind Nzingha's chauffeur who waited outside he wasn't alone. A black tinted window four-door Hummer sat bumper to bumper behind the Rolls-Royce, both double parked.

In the front seat of the Hummer with the window rolled down was a woman he couldn't forget easily. She wore a black shirt and blazer. With black gloved hands she tilted her shades just enough to get a look at him, then covered her eyes again.

It was her eyes Maddox thought, that made her eerie. First glance, she looked extremely attractive. She might have been Korean, maybe, he didn't get a good look. He couldn't, though, forget those eyes. Her eyes, sky-bluish gray, glared at him for that split second with intent. It reminded him of a Clint Eastwood movie, how Eastwood frowns at his adversaries before doing something sadistic. There were more people in the car, but he couldn't make them out. Obviously they were all Nzingha's security. That female protector sure gave him chills.

Inside, the gallery was a lot larger than he thought. The gallery owned the entire building, which was about a quarter of the block. After paying twenty dollars contribution admittance to the desk attendant, he stepped into long corridors of paintings. The building had seven stories of art. Nzingha could have been anywhere.

Despite the large area, he found her pretty quick. After walking past large and small iron sculptures of detailed animals, people, and things he couldn't make out, he located Nzingha in the back of the place on the first floor. The hallways of photographs and figurines were lit with orange spotlights, but where Nzingha stood was lit with ordinary bright lights.

She stood in a hall about as big as a public cafeteria, and the ceiling went up as high as an everyday cathedral. Two life-size in-depth bronze male statuettes of what resembled ancient warriors stood on rocks at both ends of this huge room.

One warrior with only camel skin covering his waist was stuck in a forever pose with one arm behind him, winding up a sling shot. The other man, also clothed in camel skin, was in an eternal posture of hurling a javelin stick. Both statues faced away from each other. The walls surrounding these two combatants were full, with abstract paintings as massive as an average size living room rug.

It didn't seem crowded today at this hour as Maddox counted about ten people in each hall or passageway.

Nzingha, wearing a long navy one-button tightly-fitted suit jacket, white shirt and slacks, just hung up her cell phone as Maddox slowly strolled up behind her.

"You're into the arts, too?" she asked, not turning around to face him.

"Yes, I am. I wouldn't have made it to where I am today if it wasn't for the love of the arts." She turned around, arms crossed, and viewed him. She was a little tall for a woman, maybe five feet, seven inches, judging the four-inch difference from his height over her. Her dark brown short hair appeared wet and very much in place in beautiful wave formations. Her myrtle eyes were piercing and innocent, he couldn't decide which at the moment.

"You saw me come in here, no doubt. You following me?" Nzingha raised her right eyebrow.

"Well, actually, um, yes," Maddox spit it out. "To tell the truth, I was just tired of hanging around my boss. So I decided to take a little stroll, and I happened to see you duck into this art gallery. So I figured, what opportunity was I ever going to get again if I didn't take the chance at meeting you like this? Well, and there you have it, the truth, and hey, no offense about the boss thing."

"None taken." Nzingha smirked. "Very brave of you." She looked away from him and back at the painting on the wall in front of her. "So, what do you see?"

The square painting she analyzed was twenty feet high and eighteen feet wide. It was a painting of what displayed a purple, red, silver, and black ceramic perfume bottle that exploded from the inside-out in slow motion. The top part detonated first as the bottom portion was still intact. It also had two long thin purple ribbons that also looks like it was blasted out of the top of the bud vase. Some purple, red, and black pieces of the jug trailed to the bottom of the canvas. The top left corner of the painting showed what mimicked blades of grass trying to extend out toward the explosion. The background was milky white, showing the shadow of the exploding vase, like a mirror.

"Hum." Maddox thought for a moment. "It looks like something beautiful and valuable, exploding from the inside by some unseen force."

Nzingha uncrossed her arms keeping her eyes on the painting.

"Sorry, that was the first thing that came to my head."

"I didn't say I disapproved of your comment," Nzingha spoke, still not looking at him. "I tend to agree, actually. It's my thoughts precisely. I'm not convinced, though, that we think alike. What about this painting?" She walked to the next painting and nudged her head at the wall.

This portrait, the same size as the other, showed what looks like a picture of a plant from the top looking down at it. It must have been at night, for he hardly saw the emerald green foliage coming at him in all directions. The background was pitch black except for the center of the image. The center glowed with white light as if someone turned on a flashlight at the bottom of the plant. The light was then distorted in what patterned smoke. Vapor and light seemed to entangle with each other as it came at him almost three dimensionally.

"Well." Maddox folded his arms, standing behind her. "It could be someone lost in a misty forest, and the searchers are shining a light in the person's face. The picture is from that lost person's point of view."

"Not a bad perception." Nzingha glanced at him seriously, then brought her full attention back to the picture. "But I knew we didn't think alike. I see something in a deep void creating some type of life. Out of chaos comes order, is what I would name this portrait. The ancients believed the same for thousands of years."

"Really?" Maddox moved closer to the picture to get a better look.

"So, how long are you here in Ohio?"

"Until tomorrow. Like I said, I was strolling around looking for something to do before I head back. I had to get away a little and take in the sites of Columbus."

"Hum."

"You know any nice restaurant around here where a guy like me could dine? A nice dinner before I go would give me a lasting impression about Ohio."

It took Nzingha, still staring at the painting, a full minute before she responded.

"I'm about to get something to eat," Nzingha finally replied.

Yes! Maddox shouted in his head, but he knew she was probably going to direct him to the nearest restaurant and that was going to be it. Give him the cold shoulder, so to speak. He didn't care if he had to eat with her and three executives. The chance to eat with this entrepreneur came once in a lifetime. He had a gut feeling not many people got to mingle with Nzingha on a personal level. The bodyguards themselves would keep the average Joe away from her.

"I don't have time to show you what Columbus has to offer, but I could take in a meal about now," she said, then asked in a demanding way, glimpsing at her silver Rolex watch. "Do you have anything to do, or shall we go now?"

She didn't have to ask twice. Actually he was expecting to eat with Nzingha and maybe some friends of hers, but to his surprise it was just the two of them. *How lucky was that?* Maddox asked himself.

They didn't go far from the gallery. River on the Edge Restaurant was about ten blocks away. It sat a mile from the Main Street Bridge near the edge of the Scioto River. It was built on a large hill, which out of massive windows gave a grand look at the downtown city skyline.

The Italian restaurant was impressive for Ohio, Maddox thought. Brown carpet floor, tan cushion chairs, and neatly dressed tables with a green glass vase which held a red rose in the center decorated the main area. A strange slanting ceiling that went up thirty feet held huge glass icicles going in every direction. There were VIP sections off to the side in glass booths. A bar sat in front of the huge glass window that went as high as the roof. Outside, it showed the downtown Columbus city skyline. The place was spacious, and jazz played from unseen speakers.

Maddox checked his watch. It was almost seven o'clock by the time they ordered their food and the sky outside dimmed to navy-blue. The lights of the city began to flicker on one by one as time slipped forever by. The dim lights inside the restaurant had a cozy feel, Maddox deemed, as were the guest. All the customers, napkins on laps mumbled under their breath, as if they were too good to speak loudly.

Though he wasn't particular about race, he did notice everyone in the dining hall was white. He and Nzingha were the only black couple. Well, plausibly they weren't a couple, but these people didn't know that. Hell, he didn't even know if Nzingha was black.

They sat in the middle of the dining area with cloths on their laps. Maddox had a view of the place from all angles. The place was nice, he thought, but not as pleasant as the person before him. Though she didn't smile much, she still looked attractive, particularly up close. Besides small freckles above her nose, her smooth bronze skin was unblemished, like an adolescent.

Today she smelled of strawberries. He knew this from sitting with her in the back seat of her car. On the drive here, and before their food was served, they conversed scarcely about da Vinci, Cappiello, Picasso, Van Gogh, and other artists. So Maddox felt it was time to open up and get more personal.

"I see you're a vegan. What else do you like?" he asked as he ate his veal parmigiana with rice. She had potatoes, small portions of broccoli, carrots, spinach, salad, and whole wheat bread. To drink, she had a glass of water, he had a Malibu and cranberry in a wine glass.

"I also like water," she responded, raising her glass, and drank a swallow. Detecting she was being sarcastic, he pressed on.

"What kind of activities do you like?"

"Philosophy and art, like most magnates." He still felt she was being derisive, toying with him, he sensed. It was true, though, that most industrialists studied arts and science. Okay, Maddox said to himself, enough of the small talk. It was time to get serious.

"Didn't know that was an activity," Maddox said knowingly more than asking.

She didn't retort. Using her fork, she ate some of her spinach.

"Well, I guess that's why you're into nanotech," Maddox spoke on. "We have that in common. I like the branch you have in your company of new materials of medicine, electronics, and energy. Your ambient intelligence department is outstanding. I read some articles where the government wants to regulate this technology. It's most interesting—"

Nzingha cut him off and glared at him with her army-green eyes. He seemed to strike a nerve in her, not meaning to. He just wanted her attention.

"You seem to be greatly interested in my company, for someone who was just hired at Alona eight months ago and now has just made it to chief executive since a month's time. You have a lot on your plate for a new guy."

Interesting, Maddox noticed, she didn't want to chat about work, so he guessed it was back to small talk.

"I suppose I do. I do like to do my homework, know everything about a company, before merging with it."

"Very good, Maddox."

He smiled, even though she didn't. As he took a couple of bites from his food, he observed they actually weren't the only black couple. Seated at the bar about fifteen feet from them were two large black males in black slacks, shirt, and blazer. They glanced his way every now and then. Nzingha's henchmen, Maddox figured, and probably the same people who were in the tinted Hummer who followed them here. He hadn't seen that Korean girl.

"You have some serious protection. Do they protect you when you sleep every night?"

"Why, you plan on doing something to me in the night?"

"No. Not unless you want me to," Maddox spoke under his breath, then giggled.

"What did you say?" Nzingha asked, but Maddox knew she heard him the first time and changed the subject.

"I've looked into your company since our executive accountants got together. I've read a lot about your company, and you're actually impressive, whether I thought you were or not. The world thinks you're impressive. *Forbes* puts you as one of the richest women in the world. So who is Chelsea? You must have been born with a silver spoon in your mouth." Yeah, Maddox felt, he had to stroke her ego and get her to open up and talk to him, but he had another suspicion he was failing miserably.

She ate a couple of bites of her food. She then wiped the sides of her mouth with a white handkerchief from her lap before she spoke.

"Some of it was inherited, but most of it I made on my own. What about you? Are your parents rich?"

"Hell no, they were poor," Maddox answered quickly. "I earned every penny of my currency fighting my way up in this corporate jungle. I notice you don't like to talk about yourself and your company. You're always evading questions."

"Not always."

"You should be proud of your accomplishments."

"I should give *you* some advice," Nzingha said, with that fire in her eyes again. Maddox knew it was coming; it was a matter of time. "It could be dangerous fraternizing with the owner of the company you're about to merge with. Things could go deadly wrong." She then smirked at him.

He was willing to take that chance. He was trying to figure out, was she sneering at him trying to be sarcastic again or was that a grin to say *are you up for the challenge of courting someone like me*? It could have been both. If she leaned more to the meaning of sarcasm, this personal meeting could have been all for nothing. Oh well, he was going back to New York tomorrow anyway.

CHAPTER 7

IT WAS EASIER THAN HE THOUGHT. Joe was finishing his conversation with his boss.

"It's your call, son," Kordey said in his Southern accent. "If you feel this is a major case, then I'm hundred percent behind you." Joe listened to him on the phone in an office at the Virginia, Clarksburg FBI Building.

Kordey, who was fifty-six years old, six years older then he, made him feel good to be called son. It almost made Joe feel young again. He was tired of calling his partner son. It was good to be the son, even if it was for ten minutes until the dialogue was over.

"Have you got a name for this case already?" Kordey asked.

"No, I'm probably going to make it up as I go along," Joe responded with a smile. "Don't worry, you'll be the first to know." He could tell Kordey felt his smile on the other end of the phone. Kordey gave a chuckle.

"Just be sure. I'll do what I can to get as much men as you need on this."

"Thanks, sir." Joe hung up. The conversation went just as predicted.

Joe then realized where he was, in someone's cubby that was no different than the other twelve cubicles centered in an auditorium-like area. Four glass offices were off to the right wall, probably for the lead special agents, like the office he had back in Washington.

Each field agent's cubicle had a computer, books, and files like any other detective desk. Some were messier than others. It depends on the agent, Joe supposed. There were organized people, then there were organized messy people, then there was that messy individual. He was organized, where his young partner was not. Well, not by his standards anyway.

Allen stood by him, waiting for him to get off the phone. Joe saw that he had a better tie on today. It was most likely because he knew he was coming to this branch. All the agents here, who were vigorously working at their desk or walking around toiling, wore black or blue suits and ties; even the young fellows. Allen also wore a navy blue suit and tie. Do like the Romans, my boy, like the Romans, Joe said in his head.

"I take it, that's a go?" Allen asked with confidence.

"Sure is, kid." Joe leaned back in a swivel chair, and Allen sat on the edge of the desk. Allen stared at a letter size picture hanging on a board above the desk that showed seven individuals in green camouflage uniforms. They were in a forest, all holding M-16 machine guns. Across the photo in black marker it read *Remember The Plot.*

Allen thumbed at the photo before inquiring, "What's that about?"

"In 1996 a group called Mountaineer Militia led by Floyd Looker, conspired to blow up this building; to no prevail."

"Really?"

Youngster, Joe said in his head.

"So, let's take this slow." Joe rubbed his eyes, then opened his pad and pen on the desk. "We examined the autopsy on the four boy's drowning and personally talked to the pathologist. Besides water in their lungs and beer in Mr. Douglas, there was nothing unusual in their blood."

"So for now we have to rule out they were drugged before they fell in the water." Allen took out his pad and pen and started to jot some things down.

"I know a good place to start this investigation before we start interviewing people. We're going to Ohio to have a chat with an old friend."

"Peter." Allen grinned. "Great choice. I also have some color pictures coming by e-mail that we're both going to like. I found some information about the Chelsea Company this morning online and on file at our Washington branch."

"Great," Joe said, astonished. Maybe this kid isn't wet behind the ears after all, Joe thought. "Here, have a seat. Get on the computer and see if those pictures came in." They switched places, and before Joe could settle down at the end of the desk, Allen was off typing in his e-mail address online. Youngster, he said, in his head again.

"Nothing, yet." Allen now leaned back in the chair.

"So what do we have on the Chelsea Company?"

"Oh yes, I have it all right here." Allen fumbled through his pad and found the right piece of paper. "I pieced it all together from the Internet and Carmela in our science and technology branch."

"Science and technology?" Joe asked, astounded. "How did you find out about this company there?"

"I was just snooping around this morning on the files we have on people and just decided to type in *Chelsea Company*. It guided me to the Science and Technology Division."

"Okay, go on."

"Well, after chatting a little with Carmela online, she forwarded some information on the company, but she said some information was blocked; classified or something."

"Interesting." Joe was becoming more amazed by the minute.

"It seems in 1999, when the Chelsea Company was just starting, the company gave millions of dollars to a company called Livenal. The Livenal Company was big into unregulated human reproductive cloning. There were many debates on whether it should be outlawed. To make a long story short, Livenal was evidently forbidden to practice the procedure. We monitored the Livenal Company's actions after the prohibitions, then the Chelsea Company, one of its biggest contributors, stopped contributing." Allen then paused, looking at his notes.

"Well, go on," Joe enticed, anxious for his partner to continue.

"Well, and that's it."

"That's it?"

"Yeah, that's all Carmela could find. She said the rest was confidential."

"Interesting. Did you find anything else online?"

"Yes, in *Forbes*, the CEO and owner Nzingha Chelsea of the Chelsea Corporation today is the richest woman in the world. She started out as an orphan in Ohio and became a success story. She's a self-made investor who owns a law firm, computer software, and telecommunication programs. She's the co-owner of a Major League Baseball team. She's also the shareholder of eight percent of her common stock. Her company has a trillion customers world-wide and sales assets of over two hundred billion. Her shares fluctuate, and get this, she personally practices frugality. She's individually worth twenty-five billion."

"Gosh, who the hell is this?" Joe asked himself more than Allen. "I never heard of Nzingha."

"Me neither." Allen put his pad down on the desk. "One thing is for sure, convicting her of anything isn't going to be easy."

"I'm not worried about that. The bigger they are, the harder they fall. It seems like the more money people have, the cockier they are. They think they're above the law. It only brings them down faster. Look what happen to Bernie Madoff, so I'm not worried about her wealth. It's just strange there's a woman of this day and age with so much currency and I never heard of her."

"She possesses one of the few corporations that weren't hit that bad during the Crash of 2008. While everyone was excepting the bailout from the government, her bailout came from, no other, you guessed it, Livenal. Get this, she's thirty-eight years old, never married, no children, and not bad looking."

"Yeah, let me see?" Joe nodded toward the computer.

Allen's fingers went to work on the keyboard. Before he went online to the *Forbes* site, the screen showed an e-mail that came in.

"What's that?" Joe asked, "you left your e-mail open?"

"Yeah, it's those color pictures from the Canadian coroner."

"Great, let's see that first."

Allen opened his e-mail and clicked on the message that read *Mr. and Mrs. Wells file*. When the message opened, it was from Dr. Lisa Stevens, and it had twenty attachments. Eight of the jpg files read police photos and the others read coroner photos.

As Allen opened each jpg file, it showed the bodies of Mr. and Mrs. Wells individually. First, the eight police files showed four pictures of Mr. Wells and four of his wife, fully clothed, sprawled out on the side of a snowy rocky mountain. They were both in white North Face coats, scarves, fleece pants, and boots. Mr. Wells was bleeding from a head wound, and Mrs. Wells was in an uncomfortable position in the snow. Their ski blades were both shattered.

The next bunch of attachments that read *coroner* had seven photos of Mr. Wells and five of his wife. They were both nude. Each of these photos were named Jeffrey Wells and Allison Wells. Jeffrey had more abrasions on his cerulean body of broken ribs, arms, legs, and a large gash on the left side of his temple. Allison had black and blue marks on her torso, and her right leg was clearly damaged.

In the writing part of the e-mail it read, *Expired at Sun Peaks Resort. Conceivably Jeffrey Wells drop from about twenty feet, died on impact from chronic injuries. Allison Wells feasibly after plunge, died slowly from leg wound. Initial death, by hypothermia. Sincerely, Dr. Lisa Stevens.*

Joe stood and leaned over Allen as they went through the coroner photos over and over again, looking for similar pin mark abrasions anywhere on the skin, like Mark Douglas and his crew.

"I don't see anything," Allen said as he opened his pad again and pulled out Mark Douglas and his friend's coroner pictures. They both looked up and down at all the snapshots for another three minutes. "You see anything?"

"No." Joe then inquired, "You know what? Print all the Wells photos. We'll take all of this with us wherever we go." Allen started clicking on all the jpg files one at a time, sending them to a color printer about three cubbies away from them on a table. "Be ready, five A.M. tomorrow, we're heading to Ohio."

"Five . . . morning . . . tomorrow?" Allen asked, as if to say he wasn't ready.

"Yes." Joe folded his arms behind Allen and sighed, staring at the screen of photos. Joe saw that Allen knew he was taking this case all the way, like all his assignments. When he folded his arms and groaned, it was time to get to work. "So, let's see this Nzingha."

"Sure thing." Allen pressed the mouse for the last coroner photo to print. Then, going to the *Forbes* magazine site, he typed in *Nzingha Chelsea* under the richest women in the world column. Her photo came up right away with a paragraph underneath.

The article read basically what Allen spoke of. What stood out to Joe was the article's first line. *America's first youngest self-made female billionaire.* Also what stood out was how she looked.

The photo was small, of just her head and shoulders in an office. She looked twenty-five years old, had short brown-black hair, and wore a blue business suit. She looked Latin, maybe Brazilian. She had a golden-brown complexion, full lips, and appealing eyes. She was stunningly exotic, Joe admitted to himself.

He had a gut feeling, behind her eye-catching looks, there were many secrets to her success. Joe had a hunch not all the secrets were going to be unsoiled. He felt, no matter how young, how famous, how much power, they all slip up and fall flat on their faces. He was just one of those agents who felt, like he presumed most, that nobody was above the law. That's why he did his homework, studying most of his investigations enthusiastically, and the result was that he solved them all.

This being his twenty-second assignment, he felt it was a lucky number, though on his last task, he said it was his lucky number. This was his third case with his new partner. Man, Joe said to himself. That had to be a lucky number.

CHAPTER 8

SOME PEOPLE IN THE UNITED STATES GOVERNMENT called him a hero. Some folks in the American military called him Superman. Most foreign countries called him a terrorist.

He thought of himself as not ethical, but more as a survivor of the fittest. He believed in collateral damage for the greater good. If a thousand and ten people had to die to save a million, where is the button to kill the thousand? He had to press it. The United States Government was the most influential society in history the world has ever known, and he was going to keep it that way. He was going to maintain it for the good or bad of other peoples' cost or agenda, foreign and domestic. If he was to sacrifice his life to save the inner workings of America, he would in a split second.

He wasn't as patriotic as some would think. To be patriotic, he would know, follow, and act out the traditions of America, like raising an American flag all over the country, reciting the national anthem, or celebrating Christmas. He didn't care who did what or what was to be celebrated. His primary mission was to preserve the American society intact the way it is.

If that meant killing American children, then so be it. If that meant slaughtering foreign children, then so be it. America was here to stay, by any means necessary. That was his religion.

To have the belief he had, had one flaw. Being Superman was lonely. Believing in the concept *survival of the fittest* produced him no true children of his own, no offspring to raise and teach the true nature of the world. Having a child was also like surviving, so his offspring could march into the decades of time. Nobody lives forever, that was an inevitable fact; quite possibly the strongest fact in the universe. Everything dies, even Superman. Nowadays, after twenty-six years of serving his beliefs, he had the thought of quitting. He wasn't that old, only forty-six.

Maybe this was his last mission, but he said that on the assignment before this. Stay focused for now, he said to himself as he drank some water in a coffee shop in Manhattan.

The shop was called Café Works. It resided on Spring Street in the Village. He waited there about fifteen minutes before he was to meet an individual, scoping the place, always looking for avenues of escape. He trusted no one.

On his trip here, he brought along a disguise and two guns. He wore latex cheeks to make his face fat and a couple of layers of clothes. Even though it was September, it was still hot in New York, and he perspired a little in the layers of clothes to make himself appear a little chubby.

Outwardly he resembled the average chubby black guy in black jeans and brown long sleeve collarless cotton shirt. He wore a short curly black wig and plain black baseball cap. With dark-brown contacts in his eyes, he felt he looked ridiculous, but the crowds of people around him didn't see that. They also didn't see the Desert Eagle he had in his front waist and Glock strapped to his ankle.

It was rush hour, and the store was packed, as were the streets. He sat on a stool in the front of the store peering out a huge glass window into the organized confusion of the afternoon pedestrian and automobile traffic. As he set his water on a ledge in front of the window, he saw Brian walk into the store. Five o'clock on the dot, as usual. He was never late.

Brian was the common well-built Caucasian guy in a yellow Lacoste Polo short sleeve shirt, blue jeans, and blue tinted shades. He moved his hands through his light brown hair showing off his black Omega watch. Brian looked in his late twenties, the man in disguise contemplated as he watched him for five minutes standing in line buying coffee.

Brian finally found his way through the crowd of people to sit next to him at the front window ledge. The swarm of people around them chatted away in a hundred conversations. The outside multitude of honking and screaming was music to the man in the concealing-outfits ears.

"I'm surprised you held this empty seat so long," Brian spoke, then sipped his hot coffee.

"You gotta scare people the right way, that's all. Besides, most people just want to go home after a hard day's work."

"Yeah, I suppose so." They both chuckled.

"So what did you find?" the disguised man asked.

"Practically nothing. Just a bunch of crap, like job salaries, takeovers, and company expenses."

"Practically nothing, huh? Well, what's in the practically part?"

"Matt, I always wondered why you needed to know so much for an army hero guy. You know, they say it's a go, and you just say where."

"No, I don't know, and *Brian Glyn*, first, don't call me by my name," the man in disguise Brian called Matt said, getting agitated. "Second, don't mess with me on the particulars."

"Okay, but the less people who know about this, the better, I always say."

"I'm not those people, and I think we've been through this dance already. I don't know why Taffy resigned in the first place. You new people, I don't know."

"Yeah, well, Taffy's old school. The world's different now."

"That's what I'm afraid of. Not keeping it how things used to be done, could be dangerous." Matt looked Brian straight in the eyes. "So what have you found?" he insisted, more than inquired.

"Okay, it seems like now the company has been receiving large donations from the Livenal Company. This, by the company records, has been going on for the past five years."

"That's about as long as we've been involved. Can't convict on accepting donations, I suppose."

"You're going to have to go in again, you know. This time you're going to hit the CPU. We need to know why so many donations and what they're doing."

"How much in donations?"

"Over the past five years, two hundred million. Going to something called the M.E.G. Foundation. It's a part of the company's NPO businesses. What they do exactly is a mystery."

"You mean to tell me, you young brainiacs haven't figured out this foundation yet? You know, like it might mean megabyte something or a million something. A megohm, high resistance testing."

"No, we don't know," Brian spoke sarcastically, with a smirk. "Could be a simple term, could be sophisticated. That's why we need you to determine that."

"Thank you, and that's why I need to be in the loop about all this, so I can stay abreast of what we're doing. You know what I mean?"

"Yeah, whatever." Brian shrugged him off, and took another sip of his coffee. Matt responded with a sardonic frown.

Does this kid know who I am? Matt thought. Taffy, before he retired, put this new team together, but for sure he could take them apart. What the five of them were doing now, back in the day, he was doing by himself.

Brian, himself, with three others, were a part of a special operations group, a part of the CIA only known to the President, Commander-in-Chief of Forscom, who sometimes was a four-star General, Director of the CIA, and Taffy. The name of the special unit was classified. Matt and this team's names were classified, as were their missions.

The new team was young, Matt thought. With youth came cockiness and ruthlessness. It was then turned into making mistakes. To Matt, this team was going to have to do better. There was a way to be ruthless, but this group had to use their heads. On the other hand, he was going to have to trust this group somehow, if he was to also retire like his old contact Taffy.

WEST COLUMBUS OH, just outside of the metropolis, sat a new fifteen story building, The Columbus Homicide Division. It looked nice, Joe thought. It was a peach color building with flowers lined in front of the entrance. The back of the half block-long almost windowless building was a park half the size of a football field filled with Maple trees and a path that went through the area. Some brown wooden benches were also placed along the path.

The three slowly walked on this trail leading to nowhere, Joe thought. He knew the park was made to relieve stress, and he welcomed it.

Today he wore a dark brown suit and, surprisingly, his partner Allen wore a black one. Peter Greenhill was in blue shirt, tie, and black pants.

Joe was ecstatic to see Pete. Though he was here to question him about a few things, it still felt like old times. Pete, with full mustache that he never cut, looks like a fifty-nine-year-old guy who didn't know when to retire. He kept working like he just started the job. He wore the same brown and gray mustache under his nose from eight years ago. Some things never change.

"This is my new partner, Allen," Joe said to Pete. "He's been with me for, what, four years now." Allen and Pete shook hands.

"It's an honor to finally meet you in person," Allen spoke. "I've heard a lot about you and your Death Squad case in San Juan."

"Yeah," Pete replied, "it was a hell of a case, but Joe saved me from embarrassment."

"Please, if it wasn't for our combined notes, we both wouldn't have accomplished anything," Joe responded, smiling.

"Well, anyway," Pete said and gave a smirk.

"How's the girls?" Joe asked.

"They're good. The wife is fine. Kids growing fast. My youngest Jackie thinks she's the head woman of the house now."

Joe hooted in response to Pete. Kids are something else, he thought.

He then watched Allen partially open a cellophane wrapping as he ate little by little a lamb gyro. He juggled between holding, drinking his red Gatorade, and eating his sandwich. Youngsters always hungry, Joe thought. He just has to eat at twelve o'clock, the time now. He figured, if that got his strength up to help solve this case, then eat away.

It was windy this afternoon in Ohio and as Pete fought to stabilize his aqua-blue tie, he spoke.

"This is the eighth most dangerous state in America and that's why you don't see anyone back here walking around. Everybody's busy picking up dead bodies off the streets, instead of trying to find a piece of mind. This place keeps me busy. That's why I called you early this year about a particular company that I knew I didn't have time for. The company is too big, too powerful. The little guy is dying every day out here, and this one case would have taken, I predict, a long time to solve. With my resources, could be some years. With your sources, maybe within a year."

"Thanks for putting me to work, big guy," Joe said.

"Don't mention it." Pete chuckled.

"So, how did you come about figuring the Chelsea Corporation is profiting off other company executives' deaths?"

"A high executive WCBH-TV board member came to me in the beginning of March about his boss, Mr. Wells. This executive who wanted to remain anonymous because he feared the board at the time will hate him for continuing Mr. Wells's dreams, felt the Chelsea Company got what they wanted underhandedly.

"Mr. Wells, who owns a lot of his stock, always wanted to move to Virginia; a childhood dream. He had the opportunity at the beginning of this year. He was going to merge with Media Widespread already based in Virginia and soon retire. The Chelsea Company here in Ohio offered more money, and I mean a lot more money, to keep WCBH-TV here. A lot of people on the board and employees liked the Chelsea Company idea better, plus more money, right? But Mr. Wells and his wife was set on a dream.

"As soon as Wells was ready to seal the deal and head to Virginia, he has an accident in Canada where he always skies twice a year. The board then votes unanimously that they stay in Ohio, and they got big bonuses from the Chelsea Company, who now owns WCBH-TV."

"Okay, but the accident could have been set up by the TV station's own board members."

"Right, that's the same thing the anonymous guy said, until he looked into the Chelsea Company and did some research. He found out the Chelsea Company was in the newspaper a lot in Chicago. And guess what? Owners in two different cases in Chicago have died in accidents, and their companies are now owned by Chelsea."

"Really?"

"And if that was it," Pete said sarcastically. "At one time the owner, Nzingha Chelsea, was a part of some black Muslim militant group out of Cleveland in the early nineties, called Crescent Enterprises. This could very well be some kind of new form of terrorism. So that's why I called you about this whole thing. With Mr. Wells death and all, I figured this to be a serious case."

"After all that said, Chelsea seems to be a busy lady. This is going to be a serious case. There has been more death, this time it was pretty sloppy. Could very well be a quadruple homicide, sparing the particulars."

Allen finished his sandwich and wiped his mouth with some tissue. They had walked the length of the park and now turned around to walk the length of the park again back to the precinct building.

"How does this anonymous board executive know the owner of Chelsea was part of a militant group some time ago?" Joe asked.

"The Columbus public library newspaper article archives."

"Now why didn't I think of that?" Joe posed the question to himself not trying to sound ironic. "What about this anonymous person? If he came to you anonymously, will he come to us the same? Of course, we'll keep him under wraps."

"Don't know." Pete scratched his head. "Don't know if the same number he gave me works. Or if he even wants to talk again. I'll tell you what. As soon as I can get a hold of him I'll try my best to set something up."

"That would be great, thanks."

"We have some work to do," Allen said, putting the empty cellophane and tissue into a brown paper bag, then crumpled it up. He tossed it into a nearby black garbage can and continued to drink his now half-full Gatorade.

"We certainly do," Joe responded, most seriously. "Pete, you've been a great help, and I hope to call on you again if anything else."

"Sure thing, buddy." Pete smiled. "Hey, try not to keep me too far out of the loop."

"Of course not. If I get anything, you'll be one of the first to know. Besides, a person of this status will be hard to keep out of the media. Thanks for the info. It feels like old times." Joe then smiled, and they shook hands.

"No, thank you. I have a feeling this case isn't just going to roll over. I hate to say this, but I knew this was going to be too big for me."

"We'll get on it right away, sir," Joe said, playing around, and they laughed.

Soon, after Pete, Allen, and Joe shook hands again and said their goodbyes, Joe and his partner sat in a gray two-door Lexus LS. The car was parked in a lot in front of the precinct with many other unmarked police cars like Dodge Chargers and Ford Expeditions. Joe, in the driver's seat of his car, opened his pad and jotted some things down on a fresh page.

He wrote, *Look into Chi-town companies Chelsea owns. Check into library. Check FBI science division again.* He then put his pad in the back seat of the car and started the engine.

"I want to go to the library and find the history of Ms. Chelsea," Joe said. "Then we might have to go to the Windy City."

"Sounds good to me," Allen responded then finished his drink. Joe drove out of the lot and onto the main street.

CHAPTER 9

FOR SOME REASON IT WAS HOT this late September in Ohio, and Matt felt it. He was sweating in his black custom-made full scuba diving wetsuit with beanie and boots. Though he had to crawl in this tight space again, he welcomed the strong breeze of the fans. This time they were turned on. Again squeezed into this crawl-size shaft, he took out of his pouch an electronic screwdriver and went to work on the screws that held the vent in front of him.

He was a little more equipped this time. Besides his utility-belt, .45, and night vision goggles, he brought two sleeping gas grenades, fog spray canister, and grappling hook attached to a three-hundred foot rope. The grappling hook was to speed up his getaway in the compactor shaft.

After placing the grid and screws in the vent, he dropped down to the compactor floor. Déjà vu, he said to himself, as he looked around again. The door he broke before was fixed, and the rope he left in the compactor shaft was gone. Peeking out the compactor's small door window, he noticed the parking lot where this trash facility shared space. Cameras were facing the door.

He moved his head back quickly and strolled to the shaft in the ceiling. The security of this building changed things, but they still didn't know his little secret. They didn't know that he hadn't come in through the garage, but through the sewers. He had to tap himself on the back—good decoy in breaking that door.

Putting suction-cups on his knees and hands, he crawled upward, sliding like a human bug in the tunnel, leaving below huge black garbage bags in giant green bins.

Tonight, he figured his operation should take him no more than an hour and a half. He parked a black four-door Chevrolet Express two blocks from the towers where he entered the sewer system. This time knowing where he was going, he took three minutes to get here.

He had a new destination. He had to go to the fifteenth floor in the west tower and download the company computer mainframe. Here was the trick. The west tower didn't have a compactor room connected to a sewer system. Actually, there was nothing outside connected to this tower except the front doors. That's why his team called him for this task, because he was known to accomplish the impossible.

Sara, Brian, and he mapped it out on the GPS system on his cellular phone. After attaining the blueprints of the building four years ago, they studied them extensively.

Simple, all he had to do was climb this garbage chute to the tenth floor. The tenth floor was the last floor of the triangular building where the two towers grew out from. Then he'd have to climb into one of the ceiling tiles and crawl between floors to the west tower elevator shaft, climb the elevator shaft five more flights, sneak past some guards, a laser sensor system, then find the computer, and download the mainframe, which took about five minutes. Then, while waiting those five minutes, dodge more guards who possibly might detect that something is wrong. Then go back the way he came. No sweat, Matt thought. I got this, he said to himself with a nervous giggle.

After making it to the tenth floor trash compactor, he was drenched in perspiration. It took about five minutes to reach the floor, it seemed like a harder climb than before. It was about seventy degrees outside this clear night in downtown Columbus, therefore it was about eighty in the shaft.

He glanced at his watch. It was eight past two o'clock in the morning. He wanted to do this later than before and try and beat the heat of the day. It didn't work. The humidity was still up well into the night, and the sewer stunk so bad he felt the stench was still with him as he went. And the rats, God, the rats were so huge in the gutters. Sweating like this didn't help either.

The compactor room, no bigger than a closet, didn't have a window on its door. He was going to have to take a chance and peek out and make sure there was no camera staring back at him. After putting his suction-cups in his pouch, this time, he didn't tie a rope to the trash handle door. He figured shimmying back down this shaft using his grappling hook, ten floors down, wasn't going to be a dilemma. Unlocking the door, he inched it open.

He saw a brown paneled hallway with many office doors. Looking at the ceiling, so far he saw no cameras. Inching the door more to look at the right side of the corridor, he saw more offices, a reception desk, and black dome camera. The camera hung over the desk.

That was a great place for the camera to be, Matt thought, as he inched himself out of the maintenance room. Placing himself flat against the wall, he moved swiftly to the far end of the hall, away from the main desk. At the hallway's end he jumped over an office door with gold plaque that read *Chery Scott* and hoisted himself through the white acoustical ceiling tile.

He knew the objective of most surveillance cameras, especially in this building. He knew the camera had a blind spot at the very end of the hall and so took the advantage.

He moved promptly and precisely, bending low through the workings between floors. He moved past a maze of installation, tin air ducts, and wires. He knew the joists that could support his weight from the beams that couldn't and he squirmed through cautiously. He moved like the technicians who built this network, for he calculated the path to his destination well. If someone was to stand under him and listen, someone might have thought there were rats in the ceiling, but certainly not a man, Matt thought.

He made it to the west elevator shaft to find it incased in cement. No problem, he said to himself. He took out his electronic master key and easily opened a lock on a silver hatch built in the wall. Opening the cover, he squeezed through the toilet bowl-size hole into the elevator shaft.

The passage appeared to go on in both directions, up and down forever. It was pitch black in this well that housed cables in the center and rails on its walls.

With his goggles he saw everything the roped style elevators had to offer. There was a ladder about three feet to his left. If he didn't have his night vision, he could have plunged ten floors down. The steps were built into a groove in the wall just enough for a average human to fit. He reached for the ladder and started his climb.

He could feel the wind pressure from the elevators moving in this four elevator shaft that shared this concrete casing. The cool air felt pleasant compared to the humidity of the day. Actually, it felt too good as he watched the counterweight behind him in his shaft's lane fly up passing him. It looks like ten machine weights were just lifted by a giant's muscular arm.

Matt thought for a second about the mechanics of elevators. Oh yeah, he remembered, that's right. That meant the elevator was coming! Matt pressed himself against the wall in the crease so that his entire body was inside. In exactly three seconds as he did so, he watched over his shoulder the elevator in his lane smoothly and quietly descend over him. Shit! he said to himself, another second and the elevator would have smacked him in the face, sending him tumbling to his doom.

The elevator at five miles per hour flew past him. He could feel its metal cage brush his back, then disappear into the darkness beneath. That was close, he thought, as he continued his climb.

Making it to the fifteenth floor in two minutes, he pulled a black dusty lever and cracked the elevator doors just enough for him to peer through. White light washed into the shaft, almost blinding his night vision. He then turned it off and positioned the goggles on his forehead.

He was about to open the doors more and slip through when he saw two security guards dressed in black come from a stairway somewhere from his right. Matt closed the doors fully and moved back to his ladder in the darkness that engulfed him.

Only two elevators stopped on this floor, and the guards moved directly toward them. Matt hid in the channel of the left elevator ladder as the right elevator came and picked up the watchmen. He heard them converse about their boring jobs. As soon as the right elevator doors closed, he opened the left doors just enough for his body to slither through.

Matt walked into his new world with buoyancy. First, he knew how the building's security worked. Second, he knew the design of the floor and moved around smoothly like he worked in the building every day.

The sky-blue floor was shaped like a capitol T. The elevators were at the top part of the T and the CPU door was at the end of the long part of the T. A ceiling dome camera was mounted on the top center part of the T floor so that it saw a three-hundred and sixty degree look of the entire place.

Matt casually walked up to the camera in the ceiling and took a small gray spray-can from his pouch and lightly sprayed the side of the globe facing the CPU door. He did this hoping the spots of the paint imitated dust, making it a blur to what he was about to do at the end of the corridor. Then, without hesitation, after passing a couple of black doors he found the door labeled in white, CPU Room.

The door, was electronically locked with a white keycard indicator box on the left side of the wall. He went to work quickly on the keyhole part of the door using his master key. Lucky this door still had a keyhole, Matt contemplated. It would have been a lot slower but he had ways of picking a lock on a door even if he had to go between the slot or bypass the keycard indicator. He had a bag of tricks in his utility belt and pouch.

He knew now, he didn't have much time. Those two guards will soon double back and whoever was watching the cameras will soon get suspicious. It's going to get real nasty in here in a few minutes, Matt spoke to himself, but about five minutes was all he needed.

He unlocked the door and watched a green light brighten on the keycard box. Opening the door, he walked into a white two living room-size area that was well lit. The white floor tiles and walls sparkled, making the centered black huge components of the IBM computer stand out more. To the left of the room was one huge window with no blinds, and to the right of the room were two watchmen seated at a desk. One guy was reading a paper as the other was watching a movie on his iPod.

Matt nonchalantly walked past the guards like he worked there himself. Not paying attention to them whatsoever, he dropped two sleeping gas grenades in their direction. The grenades exploded, sending light smoke every which way.

The right-side of the room was spray-bombed in a cloud of what seem like bug repellent. Emerging from the thin haze, the two guards stumbled over each other trying to reach the door. One of them yelled, the other cursed. The smoke was too thin to set off any fire alarms. The grenades were made just how he liked them, Matt thought, smirking.

As these guys staggered about, Matt simultaneously moved to the disk drive part of the computer and put on a small gasmask from his pouch. Before he sat at the terminal he sprayed more smoke in front of him with his fog spray container. Seeking a thin laser surrounding the computer perimeter, he found it. Stepping over the red laser beam of light a foot above the floor, he then sat in a black swivel-cushioned chair. He turned on the computer in front of him and took from his belt two of his specially made USB size hard drives and connected one to the back of the computer.

He noticed how the central processing unit operated as he sat back in his seat and let his device go to work. The disk drive part of the computer was the largest part, taking up most of the space in the room. Then he saw the CD drive, cartridge drive, front end processor, and CPU. The connecting terminals filled up a good portion of the room in the center, which was surrounded by alarm baring lasers. He could tell also that the make of the components were a mixture of IBM and Fujitsu.

Almost knocked out cold, the two guards made their last attempt to escape the room. Their crawl on the floor, almost making it to the door, was abated by sleep. Not bad, Matt spoke to himself. He was halfway through his first download and already had two sleeping guards and hadn't alerted the entire security. He had to get a pat on the back for that. By the time these suckers got up from a splitting headache, he'll be long gone.

He glanced at his watch. It was twenty past two o'clock; he felt he was making impeccable time. Yes, the security will know they were breached, but hey, they were violated by the best. Me, he said to himself and smiled as his first portable hard drive was almost done.

SURAKSHA KNEW ABOUT THE BREAK-IN on the thirtieth floor of the east tower. What were they looking for in Nzingha's media office computer? The rope in the garbage chute was cute, but why go through such lengths? She wondered about these things as she made her way to exit the building. Or was it perhaps some rival cooperation trying to put the squeeze on Chelsea? Chelsea had profit much in the recent years and it seemed another company wanted a piece.

The Chelsea Company paid her well as head of security, so Suraksha felt it was her duty to get this varmint. She felt she was the best in securing anything—hell, she was the best the world had to offer, and she was going to show it. She was going to show it one of these nights if the phantom came back. Almost every night she came to the towers around one o'clock in the morning and left about two AM since the incident occurred three weeks earlier. That was determination—and she was just getting warmed up, she thought.

Just as one of the front glass doors slammed behind her, a guard called her and waved her back. What now? Suraksha said to herself. All day she wore tight black slacks and black long sleeve shirt that she wanted to get out of. It was almost two-thirty in the morning; the bandit should have showed up already. She hoped these incompetent guards didn't call her back for something simple and stupid.

Opening the door again and entering the enormous lobby, she just stared at the gold and black marble information desk where a guard was located on the right.

"Woodbury wants to see you," the guard in black suit and tie shouted. "He says you'll want to see this." She knew that he knew that she wasn't walking across this atriums shiny tan marble floor again unless it was important.

The young guard smiled at her as she ignored him and went into a room behind the massive reception desk. She knew he was looking at her figure that went well with her five-foot six-inch height. Typical immature boy, she said to herself as she closed the door.

The dimly lit room was as big as a good size bed room. The wall to the left was crammed with eight-inch television screens, fifty in all. Two watchmen sat in front of a large terminal that took up the entire bottom part of that wall controlling the televisions. The muscular heavy-set older of the two, a fellow named Woodbury, turned his head acknowledging Suraksha.

"I'm glad I got you before you left," Woodbury spoke. "I was just going to routinely check it out, but I decided to show it to you first. If it's nothing, I'm sorry."

Suraksha yawned, folded her arms, and stood behind them, looking up at the screens.

"It's monitor number fifteen-sixteen," he continued. "The CPU floor. I've just noticed a smudge on the lens facing the door. It could be a bug or dust. I called the guys on that floor, but I haven't got a response. Do you want . . ."

Woodbury's voice seemed to fade away as her eyes dilated, keenly focusing on monitor fifteen-sixteen.

Incompetent, amateur, fools, she spat in her head! Glaring at monitor fifteen-sixteen, which was almost in the middle of all the other screens, she saw light smoke come from under the CPU door, though she could barely see it, for the screen was almost fully covered with a large gray splat, except for the top edge. The top edge of the screen showed a tiny portion of the bottom of the CPU door. What little she did see seemed like someone was smoking a cigar under the door.

The place would burn down and these idiots wouldn't know a thing until it's too late, she thought.

". . . Ralph and Barry just did their rounds on that floor and—"

Suraksha then realized Woodbury was still talking.

"Get on the radio!" Suraksha demandingly shouted. "Tell the men who survey that floor to meet me there. *Now!* Cover me. Take the safety off your guns."

"Yes, ma'am," Woodbury said, surprised of Suraksha's outburst. The younger thinner guy and Woodbury almost stumbled over themselves as they rose out of their seats.

Adrenaline flowed through her. She felt they had caught their rat. *No,* she didn't feel. She *knew.* This is what the Chelsea Company paid her for. She was trained to catch rats, especially human ones. She was also qualified in other things much more dangerous than this situation, things she dare not speak about in public. But this guy, who snuck around Chelsea Towers was going to get a rude awakening.

HE FELT HE WAS MAKING GREAT TIME. The bar on the computer in front of him read a hundred percent. Matt reached behind the computer disk drive section of the gigantic processor and took his second hard drive. He turned off the computer and slipped the hard drives in his belt. He then took out his fog spray.

The smoke in the room now dissipated. He used his smoke bottle again, spraying it low to the floor just enough to see the red laser and step over.

He took off his gasmask and put that and his container back in his pouch. He was out of here, mission accomplished, and not one alarm went off. Somebody had to respect him for being the—He spoke too soon.

Alarms blared, and white blinding light from the ceiling's four corners of the room flashed off and on. *What?* What happened? Matt thought. He didn't touch a laser—nothing.

As he was about to open the door to leave, the door opened all by itself. Not actually just opened, but swung open, with Matt standing face to face with his assailant. Surprised, but not taken off guard, Matt dodged the watchmen's first move.

The first guard extending his hand fired his taser. The taser's prongs flung through the air, hitting nothing. It was because Matt quickly moved to the side, then grabbed the man's right firing hand and twisted his wrist. As the watchman yipped in pain, hearing his own wrist snap, Matt then knife-hand struck him in the throat. Matt was so fast, it looked as if he hit him in the throat and simultaneously punched the guard in the face, all the while using the man's momentum as he walked into the room. The watchman was knocked out before he hit the floor.

The next watchman, about five feet eight inches, the same size and build as the first, was fully caught off guard. As he saw his companion fall to the floor, Matt wasted no time. He grabbed the surprised man's arm and lifting him over his shoulder flipped the man onto his back like a neat forward summersault. This security guard also lost his taser as it bounced across the floor to land next to the first bunch of knocked out guards. Matt then hastily, without thought, kicked the man square in the chin, knocking him out cold.

He noticed these were the same guards whom he saw enter the elevator when he first made it to the floor. They must have been doing their rounds, and for some reason doubled back sooner than expected. He remembered their conversation of boredom. Not so boring now, huh? Matt said to himself.

Then he thought about the camera. The camera trick he did was foiled. The central security room must have called the watchmen back to check it out.

The way was now clear, so it seemed. Holding the door open, looking down the hallway, he saw no more guards. This was the only way out. He knew more security was on the way. He had to make it back to the elevator and somehow muscle it open to attain his freedom from this floor's piercing alarm. He wondered, how did he set off the alarm anyway? His plan was so perfect until now.

As he stepped over one of the guard's legs to leave the room, to his astonishment he found himself back in the room on his back, on top of the guard he just knocked out. His chest was stinging. Apparently someone had kicked him in the torso incredibly fast. That someone was hiding against the right of the wall just outside of the door where Matt was blindsided. As fast as he fell, he was faster getting up. With a robust flip using his back and legs, he was on his feet again. Now he saw who his attacker was.

At first glance she could have been a black female. As he looked more closely, he noticed her slanted blue eyes, and features were Korean or Philippine. Also at first glance, she was exceedingly attractive, but he had to dismiss that for her now distorted face. It was a mean face, as if to say *I got you, you son-of-a-bitch.*

She didn't think. She didn't hesitate. She attacked. She flung a series of three perfect kicks that reached his head in a-half-a-split-second. And they weren't soft kicks either, Matt said to himself, as he blocked them. As he blocked the lashes, the sting went through his gloves, knocking dust off.

Matt came to the conclusion she wasn't playing. He had to back up into the room again to get some leverage to protect himself. Mastering the art of Aikido, he tried to grab her wrist or spin her using her momentum, but it didn't work. She wormed her way out of every hold, then flicked out a two-foot bamboo rapier somewhere from her right long shirt sleeve.

Matt noticed her style of fighting as she slashed at him left and right in succession. Kenjutsu at its finest—she was no beginner. He dodged out of the way of her strikes. He could feel the power of her thrust from the breeze as the hard wood just missed his chin, arm, and neck.

She backed him up more into the room. It was then he realized his way was forever blocked as he watched two more guards step into the room, guns drawn.

"Get down on the floor!" the larger of the two watchmen shouted.

"It's over, there's no way out!" the other smaller guard hollered.

Theoretically, they were right. Matt knew, though, he was the best at what he did. This little party didn't know about his plan B. He would have loved to grapple with this chick for her body's curves were so defined as well as her wallops.

His position was obviously compromised so there was no need to be skittish on what he was about to do next. All he needed now was a means to escape.

For a moment in time he and the girl were in perfect harmony. He then got through her defenses with a straight punch to her chest, which backed her up a little. That second was all he needed as he picked up a taser from the floor. He fired it at the girl, but to his surprise she was inhumanly fast. They both were. As she dove to the right he sprinted to the left. The prongs missed her, then burrowed themselves into the big guard's firing arm. He then fired his Glock into the space where the two warriors fought. The bullet slammed into the base of the huge black computer, giving off a ricochet sound. The big man then fell to the floor and shook.

Matt, as he ran, concurrently dropped the taser, took out his .45 and fired three shots at the huge window with no blinds. It all happened so fast. Matt holstered his gun as the window cracked into a million segments. He then whipped out his grappling gun, all the while still running, and slammed his right shoulder and back into the cracked window like a linebacker.

He was only going to get one chance at this. The window burst outward in an explosion, as he came crashing, plummeting backwards through it to converge with the warm outside air. It rained glass onto the tenth floor platform. Gravity took over his body quickly, so he didn't waste the seconds he had. He fired the grappling hook into the floor's windowsill. As he descended the hook latched into the ridge of the window. The rope, uncoiling out, tightened and swung him into a thirteenth floor window which he cracked.

He then pressed a button on the grappling mechanism handle. The rope uncoiled rapidly but smoothly continuing his descent three more floors down. His boots hit the mammoth tenth floor podium with a tap. Uncoiling the rope more, he then moved to the edge of the platform. Climbing over a small fence, he continued his journey down the building. He had ten more flights to go. I bet they didn't see that coming, he said to himself.

SURAKSHA GOT UP FROM THE FLOOR and watched the man in black slam through the window. That was close, she said to herself. She could have been electrocuted or shot. She looked around the room and saw the devastation of the other guards laid out. He was no amateur. She underestimated his fighting skills, too. By now the average guy would have been laid out from her assaults. Who was this guy? She concealed her weapon in her shirt and rushed to the shattered window.

The only watchmen left holstered his gun and knelt by Woodbury to see if he was alright.

Suraksha looked out the window into the night, gazing down at the figure she just fought. He was now past the tenth floor roof as she just lost sight of him as he maintained his descent. She had to think fast. Not many people got away from her—actually, nobody got away from her. She saw the hook imbedded in the windowsill below her. It would have been too late to pull it out; he surely made it to the ground. It would have been too late to take the elevator. He would have certainly been far gone.

So she reached into her back pocket for her black gloves and put them on. She then leaped out the bare window, leaving the only guard there with a dumfounded look. She also had one chance at this as she flung through the air and caught her assailant's rope. As she slid down the rope she saw the guard above look out the ruined window to see if she made it. She saw him shake his head and scrunch his face as if to say, she was crazy.

Glass crunched under her shoes as she made it to the tenth floor roof. Then at the edge of the platform she climbed over the fence and continued her descent holding onto the rope.

Suraksha vigorously wanted to know what this thief-of-data wanted. She couldn't get a true description of him, not with all that black paint on his face. She was willing to risk her life for the information. It wouldn't be the first time she put her life in jeopardy. Besides, today she brought along her best friend, her nine millimeter pistol.

AS MATT REACHED THE DESERTED STREETS on the right side of the building he felt a tug on the rope. Detaching the rope from his grappling hook, he looked up. Were they trying to separate his hook? he wondered. As he looked up, he found his answer. He saw the dark shadow of a woman smoothly climbing down ten flights using his very line. The very woman, he just fought. She doesn't know when to give up, a trait he found in himself.

He peeked at his watch. It was ten past three. Well, he did say the mission was going to take an hour and a half. He was still making great time, considering he was stopped. Going through the plate-glass window put him back on schedule. He sprinted in the opposite direction from where he parked his van.

When he made it to the end of the block he heard a bam. A bullet whizzed by his head. What the, he said to himself. Looking back over his shoulder, he saw the girl aiming her gun again. She hadn't even finished her fall to the pavement. The blast echoed through the buildings as she fired again from two stories up.

The second bullet hit the asphalt five inches from his boot. He flipped on his goggles and ran faster down the next block out of what he hoped was her firing range. Then, when he reached the cross street called Pearl, he turned, disappearing out of her sight indefinitely. He lost her, hiding behind the block's ten-story buildings.

He now watched her in his green vision world jog down Long Street, the block he just ran. She used the corner of the building to peek her head out and look down Pearl. He could see the gun in her hands clearly now. It was a silver 9mm Beretta. Nice, Matt said to himself as he took out his .45 and aimed it at her legs. He wasn't going to shoot her but, if she ever peeked under this car, he wanted to make sure it was her last. He then observed her curse, put away her gun, and walk back down Long Street occasionally looking over her shoulder.

When he disappeared down Pearl Street he doubled back and hid under the first parked car, this blue Audi. The street was littered with parked cars. It was also three o'clock in the morning, so nobody gave away his position. Now he watched her.

She was brave, Matt thought, and skilled. So the Chelsea Corporation has highly trained security. Interesting.

CHAPTER 10

TWO WEEKS INTO OCTOBER the wind picked up from day to day, and the temperature gradually dropped. Some days it was seventy degrees Fahrenheit, other days it was sixty-five. The leaves on most trees in New York were already yellow, orange, and brown.

It had that Halloween look, Nzingha thought, as she stood outside her rented silver BMW X8. She stared at a boarded lot as big as half the block. The surrounding boarded fence had posters on it of prominent movies and singers about to come out with their products. Also smeared on the wooden barrier were grime and spray paint of unknown artists. Inside this corroded wooden fence were dirt, bricks, and garbage of all types. She wouldn't have been surprised if a few derelicts were camped in there, too.

It was Saturday morning on 130th Street and Lenox Avenue. Most people hadn't come out yet and the cloudy gray sky didn't help much. Nzingha, wrapped in a button-less light brown hooded cashmere sweater, gazed at the huge vacant lot in thought.

She was going to build on this property that had been an eyesore for months on end. One thing puzzled her, and that was the way she attained this estate. Not many things mystified her, but this did.

She had put it all together for weeks now. First, it was strange how she got this land. The owner of Clive Inspirations, Mark Douglas, didn't want to sell the land to her because he didn't like her business ethics. She never met the man, but he reportedly had told one of her buyer agents that, "Nzingha is well read, a great orator if she was more public, but I just don't like her board of directors." She was never clear on what he disliked about her board of directors. As soon as Mr. Douglas had that accident, executives in his company seized the opportunity of the money she was giving, to get this real estate.

The same thing happened eight months ago with WCBH-TV. The owner Mr. Wells died in a skiing accident and the company's board members practically threw themselves at her to get the money she was offering for their corporation.

Then Chicago, years ago. She didn't detect anything suspicious then. Her company grew fast in Chicago. She never recognized two people died many years ago and that's how she got control of a law firm and co-own the Chicago White Sox baseball team. She thought she did this all on her own. She did grow that little law firm to becoming the largest in America. These untimely deaths where her company profited, was becoming far too occurring. Nobody was that lucky.

Then someone stole important files from her computer. She was told by her security, it was done by a professional. Someone was slowly setting her up for some years now.

She had supervised Chelsea Enterprises for fifteen years and had done it starting with five million dollars. This infuriated her. Was this someone's sick game to see how far she could take a company?

To capitalize on the blood of human beings to profit in billions of dollars was the American way, and she helped build this. She did it with pride and without thinking. But now, she thought.

She had taken over twenty huge companies through successful acquisitions in her years as CEO of Chelsea. Was that a set up, too? she questioned herself.

Then she thought of the things she'd done with her wealth. She had fixed schools in the urban cities of Chicago and Ohio. She had bought up land and made affordable housing, creating CGC, Chelsea's Gated Communities. She purchased land in African American districts where she helped business persons own blocks upon blocks of stores. Some said she was a bit of a philanthropist when she gave millions to start the first African American film directors guild.

Now she felt she was being set up. So all the things she was doing will be undone. Also someone hadn't forgot that she was a part of Crescent Enterprises. White America didn't like them too much. They spoke strong about black culture and sometimes even preached violence. The leader of that association was assassinated, moving her into that lead position. Did someone set her up for that, too? Nzingha deliberated long and hard as she climbed into the back seat of her car.

She was now building in New York, a museum, here at 130th and Lenox. It was going to have four floors. The first floor was going to have Egyptian artifacts, the next floor, Songhai Empire and Zimbabwe Kingdom models; the third, Mali Empire, Dogon, and Timbuktu society models, and the last floor, African and African American inventions and accomplishments ancient and modern.

Her chauffeur Thomas drove through Manhattan heading downtown toward her hotel. A black SUV followed close, her security. She felt she needed the protection now. Someone was after her, or in the least trying to make her look bad. With immense fortune came high-paid criminals trying to bring her down. She felt she was smarter than they, and she wasn't going down without a fight. She felt she was fighting them all through the years of her wealth; why stop now?

Laying her head on the door window, she closed her eyes and thought about her trip here to New York. It was of pure business, her visit, but for some reason she now reminisced on a dream she had on the airplane.

She saw a desert that had endless dunes of sand like the Sahara. These dunes weren't made of sand, but of white snow. The wind howled like a thousand wolves, and snow spewed out of a sky of fuming navy-gray clouds. No matter how many layers of clothes she wore, she was cold. She then for some reason saw Oriental-looking people migrating across this ice desert.

Their faces were the actual color indigo as were their eyes. The sky turned blue, then gray every two seconds, like pulsating light. A mist swirled around them, sapphire in color. Then night came upon them, and she grew colder.

Her face hurt so bad, it felt as if someone hit her with a bat. It was so bitter, her fingers and feet burned and turned black with frostbite. It all felt and appeared so real. She could smell the snow, smell the cold.

As far as she could see, dry ice-like snow surrounded her. Space must be this cold, she thought. She then awoke, but not shivering. She was sweating. Strange, she thought.

She wanted to share her thoughts with someone, but there was no one. She wanted to deeply converse with someone about her business phantom trying to bring her down. There were only executives and analysts to chat about the strategies of her paranoia. It was awful lonely being at the top. She wanted to cry and laugh at the same time.

She had three serious relationships in her lifetime. She first courted a man with a nine-to-five job. It didn't work, initially their status got in the way, then eventually he left her for a more down to earth ideological individual, so he said. The second guy made millions of dollars, but wanted to get married, and she wasn't ready yet, so that relationship didn't last long. Now she was ready, but she wasn't going to find that guy again, it being some ten years ago.

Her last attachment, about five years ago, didn't go so well either. The man was handsome, had millions, and they enjoyed each other's company, so she thought. He one day stopped calling and disappeared. It was funny the way he did it, but she knew why. Though they did have fun together, she knew he didn't like her ethics, her philosophy of exercising, eating healthy, and being proactive. She was strict in those things and he wanted someone, well, more adventurous, he would say.

All her monogamist relationships lasted about three years at a time, and all the while she felt lonely. No one was on her thinking level except, perhaps, her business partners. She had never thought about going out with any of them. Never mix business with pleasure, another strong principle she lived by. Then there was this guy Maddox. He was interesting.

Maddox was a handsome early middle aged man, defined square head, light brown eyes, tall, strong-build, and was well-off. He had a nice fragrance too. It had a distinguished light fresh citrus smell. Acqua di gio by Giorgio Armani, she believed. Interesting, she said to herself again. He was interested in her, she felt the vibe. She felt he was not only attracted to her appearance, but he seemed passionate about her endeavors. Well, she had to give him a plus for that. What about her code? Don't mix business with pleasure, she said in her head, louder. She had to be careful, people were trying to destroy her from all angles. She felt this was a bad time to court someone with all this death and computer thievery floating around.

Was she becoming so paranoid that she couldn't trust anyone? Yes, she was paranoid, and she was going to stay suspicious of everything until she had the feeling again that everything was alright. To stay suspicious, she felt, was healthy—it kept her alive, on her toes.

Maybe she'd give Maddox a chance at trust and see what his real aim was. He was no more an adversary than her closest executive.

She couldn't; her morality would be bent.

Maddox did, come from New York. She'd call him so he could return the favor by giving her some lasting impressions of the Big Apple. You know, she said to herself, prepping herself on what she was going to say to him, I was just looking around for something to do before I go back to Ohio. She then dialed a number on her cellular and put it to her ear.

AS LONG AS HE LIVED IN MANHATTAN, Maddox still liked what the night life of the city had to offer. Accessible bars, open all night. It was eleven o'clock on Madison Avenue and Fifty-Seventh Street. His night just started. It rained earlier, giving the street and air a clean smell. Early strong winds became a breeze and temperature now a steady sixty-eight degrees.

Though most of Manhattan was still crowded this evening, the spot he found was not. Sandles Saloon was most of the ground floor of a forty-floor story building.

The bar-lounge was about as large as a bodega. Most of the place was all bar, but in front were large white cushioned couches. There was easy access to the street with its wide open walk-in from sliding windows, where the sounds of the avenue flooded in. Soft music of jazz and rhythm & blues mixed with the outside, clattered perfectly. There were four other couples sipping their drinks spread around the small place being served by one male bartender and one waitress.

The place was expensive, snug, and private, Maddox thought, just how he liked it. Most important of all, he was with Nzingha in this flawless setting.

Nzingha sat with him at the bar on a tall cushioned white stool. She wore a black long sleeve tight Vera Wang blouse and black slacks. With legs crossed she sipped her orange juice with ice out of a large wine glass.

"Nice place," Nzingha said, then asked. "You come here often?"

"Sometimes. When there's a lot of pressure at the job. Sometimes I don't even come to drink. I just listen to a singer who plays the piano or guitar in that space over there." Maddox pointed over his shoulder.

In his burgundy Eton shirt and black slacks, he sipped a martini with lemon and olive. He wondered if she noticed the spot he pointed to in this dark cavern with no lights. The only thing that lit the place were candles set on low white long tables near the couches, and they would go out now and then. He then had to rely on the rim of the bar that glowed blue, casting an azure tan across their faces, until the waitress lit the candles again.

"I used to own a piano like that." She smirked peering over his shoulder at a large old brown piano hugging the left wall of the place.

"You have a nice smile," Maddox complimented, gazing at her. "I have some advice for you. You should smile more." Maddox couldn't tell if she continued smirking or if it was a blush; it was too dark.

"Thanks." She then took a long sip of her drink.

"Sorry for being strongly forthcoming the last time we met, but I'm truly intrigued about your company's new technology. It's just that I read a lot about it, you know."

"Where have you read this?" In a way he sensed she didn't accept his apology. She more demanded an answer.

"In *Newsweek*, from time to time."

"I have to look into that and cork that up. Someone's been leaking too much information."

Maddox was looking for Nzingha to smile again after that statement, but he perceived she was serious. "Why? The world needs to know about technology like that. You could help millions. And while you're helping millions, you could make millions."

"You know what I want people to know about my company? The reason why I'm here in New York is what I want people to know about my company."

Yeah, Maddox thought, why are you here in New York? It was not just to see me. When he got her call, he was purely ready to talk business, whatever it was. He made a gesture as if to say go on.

"I want them to know the unpretentious things in life. Like when I give money to better schools or improve housing. The media doesn't talk much about that. Instead, they gossip about the negative aspects of death and technology to inflict death." Nzingha took a breath as if she felt she spoke too much, then continued, "I'm building a museum in Harlem."

"Really?" Maddox said, surprised she cared for such things. "That's great." She came across to him as a stuck-up-tight-individual, personality and money alike, who just eats companies for dinner. "What kind of museum?"

"It's going to be called The Museum of African American Culture."

Maddox nodded in recognition and finished his drink. He waved the bartender for another martini and orange juice for Nzingha even though she was only half through her first.

"I bet *Newsweek* won't print that in their magazine," Nzingha said under her breath.

"They might," Maddox said, as the bartender placed another martini with napkin under his glass.

He then left and came back again, placing another glass of orange juice next to Nzingha's half full glass. "Anything else, sir?"

"No, thanks," Maddox answered.

The bartender left because someone else wanted another drink.

"They might, you never know," Maddox spoke, looking at Nzingha.

She then fell quiet for a second, sipped her unfinished juice, and stared at him. Looking back at her, he wondered why she really called him. Maybe for him to return the favor she gave in Ohio? Possibly to start a new introduction because she felt guilty she was kind of harsh on their first dinner meeting? Perhaps she just wanted to get off her chest and tell him about her museum and that she wasn't all about business? Maybe it was none of these things? Maybe she just liked his charm? Nah, he then laughed in his head, but if she did, she had a funny way of showing it.

Yeah, he figured it out. She was in New York for commercialism and just wanted to talk to somebody. She knew Alona was in New York, and he lived in New York, so why not have a little drink with a soon to be business partner. It wasn't a male-female thing; it was just business, and he had to treat her like any other *business associate*. What was that saying again? Never mix business with pleasure. He knew her type. They all think like that. "So how many times have you been to New York?" he asked and felt at ease asking her the question, for he had an understanding of her type now.

"About nine or ten times. Mainly for business purposes and to see sporting events."

"Yeah, what kind of sports?"

"Boxing, at Madison Square Garden."

"Who did you see?"

"That big fight with Panek and Klein."

"Get out, who did you think was going to win?"

"Klein, of course. He was too fast for Panek. Panek had the power, but he was never great with fighters who box well. I was actually surprised the fight lasted twelve rounds. Panek is strong, but Klein is the man."

"Oh, okay, so now I know who I'm going to bet with next time."

Nzingha smiled as they talked loud now, arguing over who was better, the New York Yankees or the Chicago White Sox baseball teams. Wow, Maddox thought, her smile was truly exquisite. Her dimples showed in the glow of the bar. They both hadn't realized they finished their drinks about an hour ago. He managed to make her smile that long—that was a miracle, Maddox laughed to himself.

"Well, it's kind of late," Nzingha said, glancing at her watch. "I don't want to keep you too late. Your wife or fiancé might be wondering where you're at."

"Well, if you must know, I'm not married or have a lady friend. To answer your next would be question, I probably don't have a sweetheart because I believe a lot of women like the bad boy and that I'm not. I'm the gentleman type."

Nzingha blushed, and he could see that even in the dark. She was about to sip her drink, but only found ice and water. "Every woman likes a little resistance from their significant other," Nzingha spoke. "You know, a little adventure. I don't know, maybe it's in our genetic makeup. The yes-man was always boring."

"Some time ago I hated the sea," Maddox said, reminiscing, changing the subject. "I went sailing one day and lost a friend, misjudging rough seas. It took almost three years to get used to the ocean again. Nowadays I try to get out on the water when I can to overcome that fear. To me, that's adventure. The sea is adventurous. Not many females I know like the sea."

"Sorry you lost your friend," Nzingha said, as Maddox nodded in acceptance. "What are you doing next weekend?"

"I'm pretty free on weekends. Why? What's up?"

"I go sailing every other week from Friday to Sunday with some friends who have similar stories like yours. Next week we're only going out for two days, and it'll be the last time we go before winter. How'd you like to come?"

"I'd love to. Where?"

"The Port of Boston."

Port of Boston, Massachusetts, now why hadn't he guessed that? It was a major seaport on the eastern coast, right down Nzingha's alley. He didn't know what to think of Nzingha's invitation. Was it a date? Was she trying to help him overcome his fears? Was she simply trying to be a friend? Maddox picked that she was just trying to be a friend.

The chance to go out to sea overnight with this beautiful entrepreneur was just—well, overwhelming. He never thought in a million years he'd get that opportunity.

He also wondered, would her bodyguards be going out to sea, too? There was a black SUV double parked outside the bar that just got a citation from a traffic cop. Maddox chuckled in his head. That traffic cop could give them a hundred tickets, that car wasn't moving until Nzingha was good and ready to leave.

CHAPTER 11

THE ARCHIVIST AT THE COLUMBUS, OH LIBRARY must have thought his job was easy when he flashed his badge at her the other day. She introduced herself as Julie and said she was going to get right on the task he asked of her. She said it, gesturing sarcastically, "Yes, Mr. Policeman, I'll get to it because your work is sooo important."

Joe felt his job was freaking arduous, and a lot of people couldn't see that. They just think he was here to harass them or abuse his power. Also people get defensive right away as if he was investigating them with every command or question he asked. They don't understand he needed information promptly to solve things in a timely fashion.

A lot of people needed to know he had a personal life with problems, too. He had divorced his wife of six years two years ago. She said she was tired of him coming home late almost every night and sometimes not coming home for days at a time. Sometimes he saw that she became a nervous wreck, thinking any one of those days he'd never come home because he'd get shot dead.

He tried to comfort her and assure her that everything was going to be alright. He told her all of his cases were tedious, and he mostly just took out his gun as a precaution. In truth, out of all his cases, he did draw his gun and fire it in two incidents, but he never told her about it. That wasn't so bad, he thought. It wasn't like he worked for the city police, who draw their guns almost every day. Well, she divorced him anyway, and they had no kids.

He was never crazy about having kids in a world like this. That was another issue adding to their separation. Now, though, he was sad to see it. Allen was going through the same thing with his girlfriend, only it was at its early stages. Joe held back from giving his partner advice. He giggled to himself. He couldn't even get him to wear a decent tie. Allen's girlfriend complained about him missing some nights, but she seemed understanding—for now.

Joe and Allen sat in the back of the Columbus Metropolitan Library. This was their second visit. Yesterday when they came, they didn't know the archives of Columbus in the nineteen-nineties were so extensive. They had Julie look up magazines and newspaper articles from nineteen-ninety to nineteen-ninety six. They gave her all day yesterday to search for those years.

Today at ten in the morning, Joe and Allen rummaged through eight full brown crate-looking boxes of magazines and newspapers. Two boxes labeled in black markers read the 90's, two more boxes read 94, then there was a box each for the years 92, 93, 95, and 96.

Julie, the archivist had an attitude saying, "Please, guys. Please, put the magazines back in the proper spots. It took many hours to sort that stuff out."

"Not a problem," Allen replied with a smile. The lady didn't smile back; she just walked away with a blank face.

Joe and Allen went out and bought Chinese food. They ate then spent five hours sorting through magazines and newspapers. At three o'clock in the afternoon they found what they wanted, narrowing it down to seven books—one *Fortune* magazine, one *Ebony* magazine, and five *Columbus Dispatch* newspapers. It took another hour and a half to read some of the articles, making sure they talked about the Chelsea Company, a group called Crescent Enterprises, or Nzingha herself.

Allen copied those articles from the magazines and newspapers on the library's twenty cent copy machine. Joe then neatly put the books back in it's places in the boxes and informed Julie. Julie came, they thanked her, and she slowly took away the crates. Picking the editorials they wanted to read, they sat another hour in the quiet building. They circled and underlined some of the paragraphs and phrases on the journal copies.

They then left the library and decided not to talk about what they read until they found a place to sit and eat. It was a quarter to six o'clock when Joe and Allen ordered dinner at Votano's Diner in the business district of Columbus. It was busy in the diner as waiters and waitresses scrambled about serving tables in their white uniforms. The sun was setting sooner now. It was fall, so people flooded the place earlier.

Allen got that call again from his girlfriend. Though he talked under his breath, Joe could tell he quarreled with her about when he was coming home. The many hours and sometimes days spent on this job comes with the territory, Joe wanted to say to Allen.

Allen spoke until their food was served. Allen had a steak, mashed potatoes, green peas, and a large soda. Joe was served a hamburger with cheese, fries, and a glass of lemonade.

Joe waited until Allen hung-up the cell phone and put it back on the holder on his belt before Joe asked, "Everything good, sport?"

"You know, same old story. When am I coming home? Our three-year anniversary is coming up next week. Am I going to be there, because she set up something big this year? You know, yada-yada-yada."

"It's hard sometimes, son." Joe put ketchup on his fries. "Comes with any job. Who knows? When that day comes, maybe we'll just say you came down with the twenty-four hour flu." Allen smiled as he poured some A-1 sauce on his well broiled steak.

"So, you go first, because I think I already put this whole thing together on what I think about the Chelsea Corporation," Allen said. Joe sensed Allen spoke in a way as to say he could focus on the mission at hand and not mix it with personal things.

"Well." Joe got his thoughts together, surprised he changed the subject. "What I read and gathered about Nzingha is, she seems to be a studious businesswoman. Orphaned, then graduated at MIT at seventeen. Fluent in seven different languages. She was the head of an organization of about fifty-thousand members at the age of eighteen. Then becomes head of her own company at twenty-three. That must say something about her. A child prodigy I suppose. She must be either snobbish or modest because she turned down every interview the journalists offered. So to really know what she's thinking is off the table."

Joe took a bite of his burger and realized he didn't have ketchup. He put it back on his plate, opened the bun, and poured some of the red stuff from the Heinz bottle on the meat, then covered it again.

"What do you think about the Crescent Enterprises organization?" Allen asked, cutting his steak with a knife and fork in almost perfect squares.

"Started by someone called Akeem Muhammad with a group of American Muslims, Crescent was for black pride and controversial on how black people are treated in America. The papers claim the association was militant—preceding Nzingha at the time it was led by a popular

Muslim orator named Hadrat Fatimah. But when Nzingha was moved up to lead this movement, she seemed to turn it from militant to conventional, from religious to skeptical." He then took another bite of his burger and swallowed some fries. Mmm, better, Joe said to himself.

"The thing that's disturbing and occurring . . ." Joe went on, and he noticed Allen nodded in agreement like Allen knew exactly what he was about to say. "Yeah, death seems to conveniently surround her at the right time."

"In her favor, to where she advances," Allen said, then ate a couple of pieces of his steak.

"Yes. The article in the *Dispatch* back in nineteen-ninety said there was some suspicion that Nzingha had something to do with the leader Ms. Hadrat's death in the Crescent organization. Then when Nzingha moves to Cleveland she becomes the head of the organization for five years. Crescent then flourishes in a more business aspect, and the black pride theme becomes almost depleted—or does it?" Joe drank some of his juice. "So, what's your analysis?"

Allen took a couple more bites of his steak and sips of his drink. "I have to agree on the timely deaths. I see things like this; I think that the Livenal Company and Chelsea have great common interest. I'm willing to bet, the Livenal Company that started in America, that's now in Nigeria, is pulling the strings."

"Why do you think that?"

"Because a man named Xavier, who heads Livenal, helped Akeem finance the beginnings of Crescent giving the organization its start. He then gave Nzingha personally five million dollars in ninety-five to start her business back here in Columbus. Whoever has the money has the power. Furthermore, if you remember, in our files, we were monitoring the Livenal Company in nineteen-ninety-nine where the Chelsea Company was giving millions of dollars to Livenal. To figure out any mystery, *follow the money.* It's all interrelated."

"That's right, the classified files of human cloning." Joe ate more fries.

"I'm willing to bet Chelsea *and* Livenal know something about all these mystery deaths." Allen then spoke sarcastically, "Oh, excuse me, accidental deaths." He then mixed his mashed potatoes and green peas and ate some more.

"So you think these companies have another aim besides making money from deaths?"

"Very well could." Allen took another fork full of steak. "I mean, we have a lot of technology flowing through these two companies."

Joe was about to respond when his cell phone went off, playing the song "Up on the Cripple Creek" by The Band. Recognizing the number on his phone, he smiled at Allen and answered it. "Hey, hi, Pete, what's going on?" Joe fell quiet for a minute, finishing his burger. "Really? Really? Okay. Tomorrow. I think we could do that." Allen's eyebrows went up as if to say *what's the great news?* Joe nodded as if Pete was in front of him, agreeing with him. "That's great, I'll be there by ten—oh and Pete, thanks."

He hung up, and his grin widened at Allen across from him. "Pete's lead is going to talk to us tomorrow."

"No way?" Allen joined Joe's, smile.

Joe nodded. It was a sure thing.

"This case could go quicker than first perceived," Allen said.

Joe felt good about this lead. He wished he felt the same about his health. He had to stop eating hamburgers and fries. He wasn't young anymore. He loved it so much, though. Oh, well, he did leave exactly twenty fries still on his plate. He wasn't going to eat those.

IT WAS FIVE AFTER TEN in the morning and still no sign of the anonymous lead. Joe and Allen scanned the parking lot full of cars near the Conrail and North Third Street.

"You think he's going to bail?" Allen asked from the passenger side of Joe's Lexus.

"Give him time. He'll show." Joe looked in the rearview mirror in the driver's seat. They were parked in a grassy field at the side of a parking lot, clearly visible for anybody who was picking up their car in the lot to see them.

Peter said the lead was going to find them at this excluded place, where a train on their left roared by every half hour or so. Another five minutes had gone by, and now Joe was wondering was this guy going to show. "That's him!" Joe said, astonished he spotted him.

Joe felt he was an agent long enough to recognize people's body language. A skinny man in gray business suit walked through the lot fast and nervously. He moved as if he was lost, like trying to get out of an alleyway full of thugs. He held a black briefcase tightly in his hand. Clearly he was out of place in this section of the city.

Allen noticed him now, and they both stared at the man long enough for him to turn and walk in their direction. The man walked up to the car, leaned in the passenger window, and asked, "Can you guys show some ID?"

After Joe and Allen flashed their badges, Joe pointed to the back of the car.

"Hop in, sir. We have a lot to talk about."

The man quickly climbed in the back seat and sat his briefcase on his lap.

"I walked about five blocks to see you guys. That's why I was late," the man said. "My name's Larry."

Allen and Joe, in the front seats, turned around, distorting themselves the best they could to talk to Larry face to face. They shook Larry's hand. Joe introduced himself and his partner. "I'm Special Agent Clay, and this is Special Agent Valentino."

Joe felt they looked proficient enough today in black suit vest, slacks, tie, and white shirt. Well, Allen had to wear a gray tie and Versace shades, but it didn't change the fact that they resembled typical FBI agents.

"Do you need me to drive you anywhere?" Joe asked.

"No, here is fine."

"Thanks for coming out like this. It's citizens you know, who solve most cases. You're braver than most."

"I wouldn't consider me brave," Larry said, and clearly he was sweating. His face was pale and perspiration showed on his brow. "I walked over here, knowing no one would follow."

"If the information you give is valuable, and you run into trouble, like the company threatening you, we have programs of witness protection?"

"Don't know if I want to go through with all that. I don't know if anything I'm about to say is even going to help."

"Every little bit counts," Allen said. "So what do you have for us?"

"Mr. Wells, who was head of WCBH-TV, was a dear friend of mine," Larry began. "I guess that's why I'm curious about his accident in Canada. I was suspicious because he knew those slopes like the back of his hand. I even went up there a few times with them. It was strange that they found the bodies way off the main trail of the resort slopes. It just didn't sound right.

"At first I had suspicion of my own board members because the Chelsea Corporation offered them a sweet deal. Then, bam, just like that, I remembered a friend of mine in Bernie and Ash's law firm. Years ago my lawyer friend said that Chelsea offered them a sweet deal to buy her firm, and they turned Chelsea down, saying they didn't want to sell their organization to anyone associated with malevolent associates. I never understood what that meant until I looked up the history of the Chelsea Company."

"And you found out that the head of the Chelsea Company was also the head of a militant black power movement called Crescent Enterprises," Joe said, finishing Larry's statement.

"So you guys know about that, huh?" Larry questioned himself more than asked them. "I figured so. You're the FBI. You monitor all those militia groups and stuff."

"We try," Allen said.

"Anyway, my lawyer friend at Bernie and Ash told me the head of the company had an accident, then her company was immediately bought by Chelsea," Larry spoke as Allen started writing in his E-Keeper pad. "When she heard that Chelsea was interested in my company, followed by the accident of my proprietor, we put two and two together. Then I presented this to Officer Greenhill."

They all paused from talking as a train with nine freight cars passed slowly by, bellowing, shrieking, and shaking the vehicle they were in for two minutes.

"Where's Bernie and Ash located?" Joe asked.

"It's now called the CBA International Law Firm based in Chicago."

"I heard of it," Allen said. "It's the largest law firm in America. I've seen the commercials. I knew Chelsea owned a law firm but I didn't know she owned that one."

"Do you feel your life might be in danger from word getting out that you're telling us this information?" Joe asked.

"It might be," Larry said. "My friend in Chicago might be in more danger. If these people are killing off top executives, then I know me and my friend's lives ain't worth spit."

"Who's your friend in Chicago?" Allen asked.

"Her name's Rachel," Larry answered. "Some days ago she told me she heard an inside scoop on what the Chelsea Company is planning to do in the near future. She said she was going to have to see me face to face on this one. It was something big."

"Do you think Rachel will want to talk to us?" Joe asked.

"I don't know what's going on, but for you guys to want to see me, it must be big."

The start of something big, Joe said, in his head. Joe of course, had a rule—all agents did—never tell any criminal or witness you're interviewing, especially the first time, what you know about the situation at hand. You have to make them think you know everything. It made some people by nature open up.

"I think she'll cooperate," Larry said. "I mean, we can't solve all this on our own. I just hope I'm not endangering her life. I want her to make that decision."

"Can you give her a call now?" Joe asked. "Maybe we could set up an appointment?"

Larry thought for a few seconds, hesitating. Then he pulled out his cell phone. "You know, I should get this over with." He then dialed a number on his phone. After a few more seconds Larry spoke again, but into his phone. "Hello? How you doing?" There was a pause. "I know you're at work, but I have the authorities here about that thing we talked about. Yes, I'm serious. I think they want to set up a meeting with you. Hold on." He passed his phone to Joe.

"Hello, Rachel," Joe talked into the phone. "I'm Agent Clay of the FBI, and I'd love to meet with you anytime you have free. Is next Saturday good for you?" The lady on the other end of the phone sounded young and nervous.

"That Saturday is-is fine," she responded stuttering her words. "It-It's going to have to be in the morning."

"Not a problem. Could I reach you again on where we'll meet with this number?"

"Sure, yes."

"Okay then. Thanks. Our meeting would mean a lot to me. Here's Larry." Joe passed the phone back to Larry. Joe told Allen the number he saw on Larry's phone. Allen then wrote it down on his pad and scribbled Rachel's name next to it.

Larry talked low on the phone as he continued his conversation with Rachel. With his low voice mixed with another train roaring by, Joe couldn't make out much. When the train finished passing, he heard Larry say, ". . . when you all talk? Yeah. Okay. Okay. Then I'll hear from you soon. Okay, bye."

Joe found his note pad in the glove department. He opened the pad to find another small yellow pad. He took out a pen and wrote his number and name.

"I'll be in Chicago ahead of you on business," Larry spoke. "You guys wouldn't mind if I tag along when you interview Rachel?"

"Not a problem," Joe answered. "Actually I was counting on it. Do you want a ride anywhere, Larry?"

"No, I'll walk back from here."

"If you feel your life is in any way in danger, call this number," Joe said, ripping out the page he just wrote on and handed it to Larry. "That's my personal cell number. Use it wisely."

"We'll be able to contact you with your 614-386 . . . number?" Allen asked.

"Yes," Larry, confirmed.

They all shook hands, and Joe thanked Larry again.

A lot was going on at Chelsea, Joe thought. He had a feeling this wasn't just going to stay in the States. This case could take them to Nigeria. Damn, he said in his head, he hated dealing with other countries. There was so much red tape. Other countries were so uncooperative because they feel they don't need American help. They felt they could solve their own cases.

Something was unquestionably wrong with the Chelsea Company. How many times were there going to be incidents where other company executives died conveniently, then the Chelsea Company made more money. How about the deaths of whom they didn't know about? Joe had the strangest feeling this company wasn't going to stop either. No, not at all. Because that was his job.

CHAPTER 12

IF HE WAS CALLED HERE, then something was dreadfully wrong. Somebody was in trouble and stumbled onto something that shouldn't be. He sure wasn't coming here for them to congratulate him and his team, but yet they were all called. This was no trip to say, *thank you for serving your country. You all are doing just fine.* There was something on those files he stole that must be valuable to the United States Government, because they never called a meeting like this since September 11th.

Matt had to use his full name to walk down this white hallway. Commander of 1st Special Forces Group Matthew R. Hellems, he had to voice into a computer on the wall to get past the door to this passageway. His whole team voiced their names as he met everyone in the situation room.

This situation room was about a half mile below the Department of Defense Building in Arlington, VA. This section of the building was called the "H Offices," and it didn't exist to most of the staff in the building and the world. This sector of the building had its own full staff. They worked there twenty-four hours every day. Of course, they were specially picked from the highest security in the country.

He hated coming to the Pentagon where cameras everywhere watched his every move. Today his disguise was a full head of curly hair and beard that covered the sides of his cheeks and above his lips. He replicated an old marine captain in his white suit and tie with gray shirt.

The situation room was a large office with three walls decorated in antique mahogany. The remaining wall in which Matt came in was made of sound-proof glass. Beyond this glass wall showed a command center where most of the staff of this department worked at terminals. Many flat screen televisions decorated the walls above those consoles showing different news channels around the world. Particularly CNN and BBC.

In the actual enclosed conference room it was equipped with secure advanced communication equipment and a huge mahogany table had fourteen black leather chairs surrounding it. One side of the room had three curved computer terminals, and another side had six flat panel television videoconferencing screens. On another wall hung huge lit framed black and white headshot pictures of a colonel named Leslie Groves, a major named Clarence Renshaw, and President Roosevelt. An American flag was also framed in the middle of those photos.

Everyone wore blue or black business suits except Matt and the most important person in the room who called the meeting. The person who called the meeting everyone knew as General Anthony J. Powell. He wore a green military uniform with many awards and insignias on the left side of his suit. The most important insignias he wore on his shoulders, which showed four stars.

Then there was Matt's team; Brian, Sara, Joseph, and John. They were all in their mid-thirties and the youngest in the room.

There were two more guys in the room who looked in their fifties who sat across from the rest of them at the table. Matt didn't know them. The General sat at the front of the table where usually the President of the United States would sit.

Brian had a folder in front of him and a cup of hot coffee like everybody else except Matt. He had a glass of water. The General also had a folder with papers sticking out and the two guys Matt didn't know had many folders spread out in front of them on the table.

"We're calling this part of the operation, Project Masters of Fire," Powell said in his deep over-powering voice. He seemed not to talk to anyone in particular as if he was talking to himself and was making a mental note, like if anyone was going to question him. He took out an expensive black fountain pen, clicked it so the point showed, and scribbled something down on papers he had in his open folder.

Anthony Powell who needed no introduction was about sixty years old, but looked in his mid-fifties. He was six feet four inches of pure muscle. His features were square and stern, and not one string of his slick white hair was out of place.

"I called you all here to get some definite answers and conclusions to a possible imminent threat to this country," Powell spoke loud and clear to where no one so much as coughed. "This appointment is on a black budget and won't be taped. The information negotiated here today won't leave this room. I haven't told the President yet about these proceedings for I don't know if I should. I need to know from you if the President and the world should go on a panic attack.

"Before I get into what precisely I'm talking about, I want to introduce the two teams here. Team SDA. This fellow here is Professor Scott Ying, who formally worked for the NSF for twenty years." Powell pointed to the Chinese man in blue business suit across the table with his would-be partner. "And this is Robert Summers, who used to work for NASA, also about twenty something years." Ying's partner, also in blue suit, nodded, then sipped some of his coffee. "Then we have team SOF-101, Brian Glyn, Sara Sanders, Joseph Healey, and John Goldman."

They all nodded as the General read their names from his notes. "They're a special team that works out of the CIA. I believe you all have been in Central Intelligence for about seven years now." Some nodded.

Powell then looked to Matt with a grin. "I always save the best for last. With us is a dear friend who should be wearing my uniform, Matt Hellems. He and another good friend, Taffy, go way back being a part of SOF."

Matt waved the glass of water in his hand to show the two guys from the SDA team who he was.

Matt recognized the General had many projects of compartmentalization. He didn't know all of them but he knew about the General's team names of the people present. The SDA, Science Division Alpha, always had a new face heading that branch. They always came from the National Science Foundation or National Aeronautics and Space Administration.

Then there was his team, Special Ops Force 101. The number was for how many times the special ops team was put together since it was formed in 1942. It was dismantled and reassembled a hundred and one times so no one person over the years knew everything the government was planning. It also made it hard for moles to penetrate the organization as it recreated itself without warning or supposed reason. Very few stayed on board.

Matt was part of thirty of them, outlasting many presidents since Ronald Reagan. So he wasn't surprised when he got stunned looks from his team's faces when the General said he personally knew him.

"I want to understand the dynamics of the M.E.G. foundation of this company," Powell spoke, folding his hands in front of him. He looked the SOF team up and down for any of them to speak.

Brian cleared his throat and stood before he spoke. "Hi everyone. Um, to start, we've finally found out what M.E.G. stands for, and we only attained this through Matt's enthusiastic abilities." He smirked at Matt and went on. "It stands for Matter, Energy, and Gravity component. Now, before I get into that, as you know the Chelsea Company has been monitored by us for the past five years.

"What we know for those years is that this corporation has invented nanomedicine. They cut a mouse in half, applied some kind of solution to the half of the mouse with the head, then the entire bottom part grew back—stomach, tail, and legs—everything. It grew back within a half hour, and the mouse survived. We checked the math of how this was done from the stolen data we attained. Not believing the technology was real, some scientists from your SDA team still tried to duplicate it. They actually succeeded in doing the same experiment with the mouse. A week later the SDA mouse died from complications of its lower body functions.

"A year after this, the Chelsea Company comes out with a new cell phone and computer system using nanotech components. These phones work ten feet underground, and computers have batteries that are presumed to last about twenty years. You could also talk into this computer, and it could write letters or stories as you speak. This could deplete the use of paper. The media goes crazy to interview anybody in the company who knows how they did this. Nobody comes forward.

"We purchased these phones and computers and gave it to the SDA team. To no prevail, they couldn't back-engineer the mechanics of dealing in nanometers. It was too difficult for our scientists.

"There were talks of regulating such technology from the CRN, Center for Responsible Nanotechnology. The CRN said, if Chelsea's nanotech is real, it could very well harbor untraceable weapons of mass destruction. This company has direct dealings with an overseas company called Livenal, based in Nigeria.

"Now it seems Chelsea has abandoned its nanomedicine capabilities and has embraced a more mechanical nanotechnology. It seems to work and sell high on the world market. The world is using these computers and phones on a daily basis. I own one of the phones myself as the rest of the team. We, sir . . ." Brian said, looking directly at Powell. "We're monitoring this company's every move to the point that we've come across something new. The new thing is called M.E.G., and most of the files in this part of the company are encrypted. So we handed them over to your science team."

"What do you know for a fact that's substantial in this company?" Powell asked.

"Well, we believe the company has achieved nanotechnology in medicine and mechanics," Brian responded apprehensively. "How well it works is an abiding debate, sir."

Matt never saw Brian this nervous.

"Have a seat," Powell said, and Brian sat immediately and looked through his notes nervously as if he forgot to say something. Powell looked around the room at his guests, sighed, then spoke. "Guys, ladies." Powell made a gesture at Sara that he recognized her. "What you're about to see in this room, try to keep in this room for now. I don't want the could-be adversary to know what we know. My new friend Ying here has decoded those M.E.G. encryptions. What we found is far more serious than nanotech." He then pressed a couple of buttons on a panel on the table in front of him. The sound-proof glass wall tinted black so the office personnel in the adjacent room couldn't see inside the situation room. "Ying, if you please."

Ying stood. "Hello, everyone," Ying said. "The M.E.G. encryptions have revealed a visual recording of something extraordinary." He walked to the front of the table where the General sat and moved behind him where there was a computer terminal. Everyone's eyes in the room followed him to the computer. He leaned over the console and typed a couple of commands into the processor. A flat screen television came to life over his head in the wall. "This is what I call example A."

Ying sat at the terminal. The television first showed a blue screen, then a white lab with a bunch of people dressed in white lab coats. On the left of the screen was a timer that read 9:03 PM Eastern with seconds counting. Under that were military hours that read 2103 and the date August 6 2010.

The camera didn't show any of the six lab-coated people's faces, only the equipment around the room. Then the camera focused on a blue and white electronic looking rectangular box about the size of a desktop computer. It resembled a large computer except it had twelve green marble-looking balls in a circle on the top of it.

Someone with white-gloved hands placed a brown mouse in what look like a Glad bag, sealed it, then opened a round panel on the top of the box in the center of the marble ring and put the bag inside. More gloved hands sealed the panel, then walked away from the box.

When the camera panned back showing the full public lunchroom-size area, it focused on a table. The empty desk was approximately forty feet away from the table with the container. The camera was positioned where now Matt saw both tables.

Then the right-side of the screen showed a countdown that read in nanoseconds. The camera time read 9:05. Someone off screen shouted, "Ignition!"

Then, when Matt blinked, the box on the screen before him disappeared entirely and reappeared on the table forty feet away. The camera then moved to the table, followed by the others in white. Someone opened the panel on top of the computer-looking box and took out the Glad bag. They took the mouse out of the plastic bag and started petting it as it sniffed about alive.

"Let me see that again?" John asked as he sat in attention. They all were now staring at a blue screen.

"Soon, we have more to show," Ying replied, smiling.

"What is this?" Sara requested. "Some magic trick?"

"You know, we said the same thing," Robert said and stood. "We first thought this company discovered a transporter machine until we studied some of the paperwork that went along with this project. We discovered all sorts of new bio-engineering methods. After painstakingly decrypting more files, we notice equations like E equals mc square, light in vacuums, and electromagnetic radiation methods. M.E.G. is also the name of this module."

"The ability to travel at the speed of light," Matt blurted out. "What the hell are we dealing with here? Is this real?" Matt kind of asked anyone, but was more directed at Robert.

"Actually you're wrong," Robert answered, focusing on Matt. "We might be dealing with something faster than the speed of light." Robert then walked to the front of the room where Ying sat and nodded at him. Ying then started the footage over again, but this time paused it when the nanoseconds appeared.

"Now nanoseconds in light travel in feet," Robert continued. "That table has to be at least forty feet away from the other. After the countdown, when this vessel is shot across this room the nanoseconds read twenty point six nanoseconds. They should read at least forty-five to fifty nanoseconds. Go ahead, show it again," Robert said, to Ying.

Ying let the recording play, and this time Matt didn't blink. Someone off screen shouted, "Ignition!" Everyone around Matt, including Powell, leaned toward the screen, eyes glued to it. The time on the screen ran smoothly, then the box that was on the table disappeared and reappeared across the room before anybody breathed in or out fully. To Matt, it mimicked something out of a movie.

"Could this be camera trickery?" Matt asked Robert or Ying.

"Yes, but we're not taking this lightly," Ying answered. "We're working on some equations as we speak. So far the information of this technology we attained from this company is equitable."

"Shall we show the next example?" Robert asked Ying, then sat.

"Yes of course," Ying said, as he typed into the computer again. "I call this example B."

The television now showed a split screen. On the bottom left screen it read *Quebec, Canada* and the right, *Adamawa, Nigeria*. On the left of both screens showed the time in both countries and on the right the nanoseconds. The time in Canada read 7:08 A.M. and the time in Nigeria read 1:10 P.M..

The people in white lab coats were outside. The individuals in Canada were in a mountain area in a spacious grassy field. The people in Nigeria were also in a similar setting, except Matt could clearly see the Nigerian grassy field seemed larger.

On the Canadian side people prepared camera surveillance equipment. This time using a much larger bag, some gloved hands put a Labrador Retriever puppy into a clear plastic bag, then sealed it. The screen then showed the container the plastic bag was now put in. The size of two milk crates, sitting in the grass, it appeared like a blue and white oversized desktop computer with green marbles on top. They all stepped away from the computer-looking carton. In Nigeria, the occupants there stepped away from a white cement platform in the middle of the field.

On the Canadian side of the screen Matt could still hear the dog yipping inside the box as a countdown was started. "Five, four, three, two, one, ignition!" someone said off camera.

As the dog yipped again, the capsule disappeared from the Canadian screen and reappeared in the Nigerian screen on the platform. The sound of the yelp was unbroken as the dog continued to bark. Matt didn't notice the difference in speed. Pretty much if you blinked, you missed it disappear and reappear.

Matt could hear the people in Nigeria clapping as someone took the dog from the capsule and plastic bag. Then after a minute or two the people in Canada started to clap. The monitor then went blue.

"Even though our eyes can't detect the difference in speed, it did take longer in nanoseconds," Robert clarified.

Ying walked to his seat at the table and sat.

"This time the nanoseconds ran out, and it started counting in microseconds," Robert continued. "That dog apparently made it to Nigeria in zero point six seconds. That's still faster than the speed of light. It takes light zero point thirteen seconds to move across the equator."

"I want to show you guys something," Ying said, holding a remote control. "I want to see this again because it amazes me every time. We slowed the footage down to where you could actually see it launched." Ying pressed some buttons on the remote, and the screen showed the capsule in the grass in Canada again. "We slowed this down in hyper slow motion. You won't hear any sound because of the severity of the frames per microsecond. Right here is where someone yells, ignition."

Everyone in the room watched as the box jumped out of the grass. The entire box turned blood red and lunched into the sky in an acute angle and disappeared into the clouds. Reappearing in the Nigerian side of the screen, it flashed in the sky like a star. Then it moved like a magnet toward the concrete platform. As it descended, it was all white, but right before it landed, it turned back to its original color.

Ying turned the television off from his remote.

"That gets me on the edge of my seat all the time," Ying said enthusiastically. "Scientists throughout our history on earth couldn't figure this out. I believe this technology is real, and we have to get it!"

"Easy, Ying," Powell said and smirked at him, then looked at Matt. "So, Matt, do you think this is still camera trickery?"

Matt gulped before responding, "It might be."

"I like that, you son-of-a-bitch. Nothing amazes you," Powell said, then sipped some of his coffee. He put his hands through his slick hair, sighed, and leaned back in his chair. "Let's suppose this is real, ladies. What are your opinions on this? What do you think this government should do? What sort of action would you take toward this Chelsea Company? Brian, you're up again."

"Sir, I definitely believe this company must have close continued surveillance, to say the least," Brian said. "Being that the technology is real, they could transport weapons of mass destruction in a blink of an eye to any country in the world. This could become a national threat."

"Can I say . . ." Sara said, putting her hand up.

The General nodded at her.

"Before we go too far putting up our defenses, we haven't even talked with this company. We don't know yet what their intentions are. This nanotech could be a cure to all diseases. Though I do believe we should play this cautiously."

"Robert, what do you think?" Powell asked, peeking at him, then sipped more coffee.

"I personally think this technology is groundbreaking, mind-boggling," Robert said, "but putting my personal feelings aside, I have to lean toward Brian. Power like this in one person's hands could be catastrophic to others, especially if the others are us."

"Matt," Powell said invitingly, then folded his hands in front of himself on the table as if to say he'd been waiting to hear from him all day.

"Okay, supposing this is real," Matt said, "I agree with Brian and Sara. Basically we must monitor this closely. I'm willing to do whatever it takes if it's true or not."

"Spoken how I figured you'd speak," Powell said, smiling at Matt. "Well, ladies, thank you for your comments, but this is what me and Director Grass strategized. We need the SOF team to go into Nigeria. There's a secret government unit there called the SMB who'll be your contact. The lead director there, a Mr. Bolaji, will be assisting you on your mission." Powell glanced at some of his notes in front of him as he spoke. "Your derivative mission will be to look into the Livenal Company's activities with unregulated human cloning or their connection with Chelsea. Mr. Bolaji will be fed the notion that we have suspicion that cloning technology is being illegally imported into our country by the Livenal Company.

"In reality, the primary mission is to gather information on what exactly the Livenal Company is all about. What's Livenal's goal? What the hell kind of corporation is it in the first place? And who's the head of this company?"

"Sir," John Goldman said as he raised his hand, and the General nodded. "We already know that Livenal is a financing, insurance, and oil company, run by a American born aristocrat, Xavier Kcired."

"Good. So that should give you a head start on the week you'll have in Nigeria to complete this mission. The Nigerian government is giving us a week to investigate our speculations about the company."

"Our relationship in that region should be pretty good," Joseph Healey spoke. "Our current relationship with that country is that it wants to establish a bigger arm toward its western allies, namely the United States.

I'm just curious, sir. How did they feel when you told them about our mistrust in Livenal?"

"They were a little apprehensive at first, like most third world countries. After about a week, they got back to me and said we could conduct an investigation for about a week. Mr. Bolaji did want to know what sparked our suspicion and assured us we won't find anything. He said Livenal happens to be the most protégés corporation he ever knew. I didn't tell that son-of-a-bitch how I really wanted to respond. I wanted to say, that's because Livenal has poured billions into your government." Powell chuckled to himself, then ogled the SOF team. "But I wonder what we'll find."

"Livenal has also given Chelsea millions towards NPO organizations over the past years," Brian spoke.

"This would give us a credible reason to snoop around Nigeria with real intent to disclose what Livenal is actually about," Matt said, then leaned back in his chair.

"I'm going to leave it up to you experts to figure out how you're going to execute this diagram," Powell voiced.

So just like that, they were off to Nigeria, Matt thought. Another exercise of excitement and intrigue. This time science fiction technology was on the line, and it seemed like it was going to be a race of wills to attain it. He was up for the challenge. It made his heart race. Maybe death was around every corner on this trip. Maybe some kind of enlightenment of future things to come. Maybe plain old hell was around this corner. He felt young again, but knew his body was aging. We all are. It's the natural order of things. This might be his last mission. God, he never thought he'd ever say crap like that.

He had a lot of brushing up to do in Nigerian subdivisions, environment, culture, and cuisine, and he didn't have a lot of time to do it. He had missions in the Middle East, South America, and Korea. He visited many parts of Africa and had contacts here and there over the years, but he couldn't remember any special assignments tangibly in Nigeria. This was going to be his first. He inhaled, exhaled, and said to himself, well then, here-we-go.

CHAPTER 13

DUSK HAD COME. The jungle was huge. Though this was the edge of the tropical forest, she would have never known. The world was green, full with vines, grass, and every kind of plant and tree she could think of. Vapor snaked between entangled trees, steam rose from the forest floor, and low clouds encircled tree tops. It mimicked the South American and Congo jungles wet season put together. Something was deadly wrong with this rainforest. It looked and smelled like a forest, but it didn't sound like one.

There were no sounds of leopards, tigers, birds, or monkeys. It wasn't just quiet; it was deadly silent. It wasn't because the sun was setting. It was silent because of what occupied its surroundings. The coming sounds of crushing bushes, branches, and wood didn't fully scare the animals. It was the bullets, lasers, and machines.

Twenty men wrapped in bulky metal armor fired into the trees at a yet unseen foe. Shiny green camouflaged body armor was part of the fifteen foot human robots with extended huge guns. The camouflaged armored men's metal skin was cloaked. When they emerged from the world of thick bush the metal turned back to its original color of gray and blue.

Retreating from something still yet seen, they fired a trillion bullets per second with laser fire. The sound of the guns gave off an eerie high powered fan sound with the swish of a plane taking off. The ammunition tore and ripped into tree barks and limbs, sounding like rain from a monsoon. The shells also ripped into something else, more mechanical, more with the capacity of returning fire, the unseen opponent.

The twenty sought refuge in a building at the edge of this jungle world.

Beyond this tropical place was a muddy empty field. The murky brown and black domain went on for thousands of miles in all directions. They all turned to the construction. They had no choice.

The building looked ancient, but still held strong by massive colorful stones. The structure's architecture she observed was a mixture of thirteenth century Muslim, French, and Indonesian styles.

Entering the mouth of the structure, they fired more into the forest. Now, she saw why they withdrew. Materializing from the jungle came forth a forty foot robot that had tank-like feet and a metal human-shaped torso with blaster machine gun arms. In the cockpit of this android, four humans sat at controls, like a brain, telling each part what to do. This one enormous robot fired back at the retreating men, blowing softball-size holes into the ground, building, and smaller android armor.

One of the twenty men were immediately torn to pieces. Hot metal, flesh, and wire were an entangled mess at the doorstep of this ancient hundred-story church-looking building. Another of the now nineteen men screamed as his arm was blown off from enemy laser-fire.

Sounds of distant explosions could be heard. Screams of a man who missed an arm echoed throughout the building with more screeches of bullets slamming into its frame. Bricks and plaster detonated from lasers touching the building, raining pounds of dust and pebbles upon the nineteen survivors.

Two men held the man with the lost arm on this once beautiful red tiled floor as ten more fired their guns from the inside confines of the building doorway.

She could now see where metal and wire differentiated from flesh and bone. One of the android battle-men took a bottle from the side of his waist. He opened the bottle carefully with his bulky robotic fingers. He poured an indigo-colored solution from this container on the bloody mess that was a shoulder with no arm.

From the man's shoulder, flesh started to return almost instantly. The man shrieked and squealed in unimaginable agony. After some time the building shook. Bricks and dust fell everywhere. Meanwhile, his arm, as if by magic, grew back.

His android comrade put a machine gun in his new well-made human hand and nodded. Through tears, the healed man nodded and stood to continue the fight.

ONLY A QUARTER OF THE PLANET showed through her view-port in her vehicle. Though she was a hundred thousand miles from the world, she still saw cloud, land, and ocean formations. She couldn't concentrate on that, she had freight to protect.

The cargo ship was about the size of a city, about as long as thirty miles. It was rusty green in color with a shark-shaped head and box-like body. Massive fins stuck out from both sides of the rear, and one on the top of the shark head. From a distance it matched a well fashioned man-made cigar asteroid. There were words on both sides of the neck of the ship that were unreadable to her. It was a jumble mixture of Chinese and ancient cruciform. One word did stand out to her. It read *Ylil*. She remembered the word from somewhere in the past.

Her ship was like a fly as it buzzed around the payload, zipping horizontally and vertically in quick bursts. Her ship, which was the shape of an angelfish, was accompanied by thirty other identical crafts, all green and orange in color.

They were escorting this freight, full with raw materials, from a planet called Anit, back to her home-world.

Then an enemy with only seven alike ships out of nowhere attacked them. The thing different about the ships were the color. It was black in color, blending in with the darkness of endless space. And if that wasn't enough to disguise this vessel, it also didn't show up on the radar of her ship.

Two of her fellow ships exploded around her, blowing metal in every direction. Though it didn't look like it, they were traveling at speeds of twenty thousand miles per hour, zipping and dodging each other. She yelled commands into her headset at her other companions to pick the enemy off by watching the flares of the sun on their wings. She was aware that the enemy knew they only needed seven ships that were practically invisible to overrun the freight ship. She felt she could outwit them as she shouted more commands into her wire headset.

She saw a bright white flare of metal in front of her. She fired her brilliant orange lasers in that direction without thinking. Black smoke exploded in a puff cloud followed by metal spit in every direction.

She was then hit by some of the metal from the rival craft. It thumped into her ship which vibrated it terribly.

"I'm hit! I'm hit!" she kept screaming into her headphones. Her ship then exploded in a mass of black smoke, wires, metal, and consoles. Like a bullet in air, her bare body was ejected into the void of space.

Everything around her was cold and silent in this endless epitome of night. She grew colder as her face and body began to hurt so bad it was as if someone hit her with a bat repeatedly. She, for some reason, felt a burning sensation in her mouth—the taste of a bad cigar. She began to gag as air rushed and squeezed from her lungs. Her body felt as if she was bathing in a bath of dry ice.

A minute had passed as she began to lose consciousness. Her body liquids and blood started to vaporize. She was so cold she couldn't even shake. She was turning into a shooting human freeze-dried popsicle. So this is what space feels like.

Nzingha awoke in the master suite of her three deck yacht as she lay under satin brown sheets. More strange dreams. She hated them. They were always about war or the cold. War or the cold. She wondered why it was always about one or the other. Was that going to be her inevitable fate? It seemed like she'd been dreaming about the cold and futuristic war as far back as twelve years old. She shook the sleep from her head. She had to get up, she had to get ready.

ARRIVING IN DOWNTOWN BOSTON, MA on this Friday afternoon, he felt a bit cold. The wind whipped around him and the massive pier, making sixty degrees feel like fifty.

Maddox had no problem finding Nzingha's yacht. It gave the impression of a futuristic miniature Titanic, minus the smokestacks, moored in front of the Rowes Wharf. He couldn't miss the Boston Harbor Hotel's multi-story arch over the public plaza on Atlantic Avenue. She had described the vessel to him and told him to avoid the many hotels and restaurants in the area because he'll be eating and sleeping on her boat, the Firestone II.

The Firestone II was a white luxury monster yacht, four stories high with three decks and huge blue tinted windows. The yacht's two hundred foot long frame didn't hide it easy in the dock where other mega-yacht's smaller than itself were also docked.

Maddox spotted Nzingha on the back of the boat high on the sundeck. She was in a black sweat-suit in some kind of yoga exercise position. She stood on one leg with the other leg in the air and arms stretched out. Her body was also leaned over to where she made a perfect capital letter T. A Oriental man who looked seventy years old stood in front of her in a brown judogi. He also could have sworn he saw a couple of swords at their feet, but he was interrupted by a big man in black suit and tie.

"Sir, this way please," the big guy said in a deep voice. "Miss Chelsea will be with you shortly. May I take your luggage?"

"Sure, thanks," Maddox responded as he handed the guy his small black suitcase and duffel bag on his shoulder. He then followed the man up the docking ramp into the vessel. Another man in black three-piece suit guided him throughout the ship as the other guy left with his baggage. The man he followed gave him a tour, showing him the formal dining room and bathrooms.

Maddox was shown the vivid grand salon, fully equipped kitchen, bar, and grand spiral staircase that went from the lower deck to the sky lounge above the main deck. He was then led through foyers of granite and marble to the master sitting room with custom furniture.

"Have a seat," the guide said. "Miss Chelsea will be with you in a minute Mr. Mathews." He then left down the hall from where they came.

Not bad, Maddox said to himself as he sat and stretched both his arms on the back of the peach crescent couch with tan pillows. The setting went perfect with his leather looking lambskin double collar brown jacket. He then crossed his legs as he got more comfortable and looked around.

The room was round with tan walls and tan carpet. A small gold and glass table sat in front of him with magazines and another crescent couch across from him. A huge white dome light illuminated over a black marble table in the center of the room. The windows on the left side of the room were covered by wood blinds that let in little sunlight.

The thing he noticed about Nzingha's style was that she was bland when it came to designing things, yet she had an artistic feel to it. Like, for instance, this room was simple except she had an interesting detailed African-style black marble statue on the center table of a nude woman on her knees praying. Also there was a painting on the wall that looked simple, yet interesting.

The oil painting showed a globe of the earth showing mostly Africa. It showed the longitude and latitude lines of an ancient tan color fifteenth century-looking map. On top of this globe-map was a meticulously drawn Egyptian clothed lady of justice. If he didn't have the eye for it, the picture almost blended with the surroundings of the room.

Then Nzingha strolled into the room, breaking his concentration. She wore a black tightly fitted blouse, slacks, and slipper-looking shoes. Her hair was in perfect slick wave formations. She was slimmer than he previously thought, like a female hourglass-shaped mannequin.

"My other friends couldn't make it," she said. "So it's just you and me. Do you have a problem with that?"

Maddox almost lost his breath. Was she serious? Just them out to sea together was a dream come true. Nah, she had to be kidding. He straightened up from leaning back on the couch and uncrossed his legs. He grew a face as if to say he didn't understand. "Fine with me. I don't have a . . ."

"I have a confession to make. When I said friends, I meant my escorts." She stretched her right arm in a gesture to say follow me. "I could explain better over a hot meal. Hungry?"

"Starved."

Maddox liked to call the dining room the square room. It was a perfect square with a round, polished mahogany table in the middle. The table was set up with eight Egyptian-style chairs ideally coordinated with brown mats, silverware, napkins, and wine glasses. Flowers of all type were on the center of the table where a chandelier hung over them connected to a pure copper ceiling. A genuine maroon rug coated the floor, and authentic tan and yellow drapes covered the rectangular windows. Brown panel walls held two oil paintings of Pablo Picasso's "Weeping Woman" and "Studio with Plaster Head." The chairs didn't look comfortable, but when he sat, they actually felt soothing.

Nzingha had him remove his shoes before he entered. They sat across from each other and placed the napkins on their laps as they were served food from a male waiter in all black. The waiter also took his jacket, exposing his white Eton shirt.

They both were given a plate of steamed vegetables, white rice, beans, and spinach.

"Sorry, this is all that's aboard today," Nzingha said, seriously.

"I suppose I'll survive being a vegan for a few days," Maddox lifted a fork full of hot beans and rice, sniffing them. "Mmm, smells pretty good."

"Wine or water?"

"Wine, of course."

"Of course," she said, and grinned. "What type?"

"Merlot."

"I have plenty, straight from France."

When the waiter came back, Nzingha ordered water and a bottle of Merlot.

"We're heading on the North Atlantic current toward Greenland," Nzingha spoke, with a straight face. "We'll actually travel through that thermohaline circulation which will soon shutdown and cause some serious global warming." She then ate a mouth full of carrots.

"Interesting to know where we're headed." Maddox blew a little on his hot beans and rice, then ate some.

"Which one? The world or us?"

"Both."

The waiter came back with a bottle of 1972 French Merlot and pitcher of water. The waiter poured water into Nzingha's glass, then popped the cork on the wine bottle and poured a glass for Maddox.

"That'll be all, James," Nzingha said, nodding at the waiter. The waiter placed the bottle on the table and left.

Maddox felt a slight shift as the room vibrated a little before turning into a smooth agile sway. Soon he noticed nothing as if they were stationary. Maddox knew they weren't immobile as somehow he could sense they were picking up speed.

"You're not scared or anything?" She asked. "You're not going to get seasick and throw-up are you?"

"Not at all," Maddox retorted, "I'm fine."

Nzingha smiled. "So how was your trip here?"

"Long—about four hours. I suppose if I could survive a four-hour trip by myself, I could survive this."

"This isn't going to be like any trip you've ever been on."

"What do you mean by that?" Maddox asked in a kidding way, as if he was frightened, but still serious to the question.

"It'll be unique. Maybe we'll get through some questions you've been asking, about nanotechnology."

That's what I'm talking about, and now was the perfect time, Maddox said to himself. After they finished dinner, she showed him more of the ship and introduced him to some of the security in the crew's quarters. He couldn't tell how much security personnel was aboard, but he wondered why she required so much. Was she trying to say, behave yourself on this trip because help isn't far away?

When she showed him the outside saloon on the upper deck, he understood the boat's surroundings and the time of day. It was about five o'clock because the sun was all red and seemed to forever sink into the western horizon every time he looked away for a minute, then looked back. It was that time when it was easier to stare at the bright red ball.

He also stared at miles upon miles of blue-gray water. The ocean went in every direction endlessly, and Nzingha's boat didn't look so big anymore.

He could still see water taxis far in the distance as they moved farther from them. He guessed in that direction was land—Boston, to be exact.

A gust of wind whipped around the boat, and the air felt like forty degrees. He was freezing to the point he was shaking and couldn't wait to go inside. He did notice Nzingha wasn't. She moved around outside as if it was a bright sunny day with a demeanor to say let's take in all this sunshine. Strange, he thought. When he really contemplated it, he felt the whole ship inside seemed a bit cold. Even as they ate, he felt a chill. He didn't say anything about it, figuring, hey, out here in the ocean, it's cold and she's used to this.

They soon settled in the lower deck private master sitting room, bigger than the other sitting room he waited in earlier. It was designed like a living room, with complete entertainment center, wall to wall white New Zealand wool carpet, and expensive maroon rugs. This part of the ship Maddox could tell was the bow. Wooden blinds covered the windows that went with the V front of the vessel.

In this room the walls were made of redwood, and on one side there was a library. A large polished round tan-wood table sat in the center with a five foot tan spherical woven termite mound on top. Two smaller tables sat near the entryway, and on top of those were woven round basketball-size spheres. Two tan couches with brown leopard-style patterns sat on both sides of the round table.

Maddox sat with Nzingha on the left sofa.

"Interesting," Maddox said, as he stared at the large anthill in the center of the room.

Maddox noticed her solemn eyes when she spoke.

"Nigeria; a long time ago, a Fulani priest taught me the secret magic of the termite hill. A non-human species that could build a complex mega-subterranean metropolis is equivalent to the wonders of the world. Their underground artistry is a marvel."

"You're becoming more intriguing by the minute," Maddox said. "I couldn't help but notice you exercising earlier. What kind of workout do you do?"

"That was Master Sun Lu-t'ang. He teaches old-style Tai Chi Chuan."

"So you know martial arts?"

"A little. It's a style of many cures, like for negative chronic conditions, stress, and positive for mental health. I've witnessed ADHD diagnosed persons become cured through its practices."

"I've asked you before, but I think now I understand. Martial arts, artistry, philosophy, and technology seem to be your forte."

"Just like I told you before." Nzingha sneered in a way to say obviously we know that.

"You did." Maddox paused, getting his thoughts together to ask a significant question. "What I believe *we* have in common is your technical interest. Why don't you advertise your AmI more, or is it real?"

Nzingha smiled. It was a wide, pretty smile. "That's where you and your company come in, Mr. Mathews. I've studied Alona for some time, and I fancy how you advertise and commercialize. I love what you've done with Ralph n' Peggy's. This merger is important to me. Soon *we'll* advertise AmI."

"So AmI is real and ready to go?" Maddox had excitement in his eyes.

Nzingha's smile never faltered. "Of course."

"How? How have you done this? Is this technology stable enough that there will be mass production?"

"It's securely established. Soon, in every home, an ambient computer system will control your lights and temperature. It'll lock and unlock doors just from your presence alone. It'll map the exact location of your loved ones, particularly children. It'll automatically tell you what utilities you need to have more in your home, like groceries and such. It'll automatically remind you when your favorite programs are about to come on. Not only in the home, but you'll be able to carry this information in the palm of your hand. This system is already up and running."

"You haven't told Alona these things. Alona believes and is ready to advertise your computer systems that you have running now."

"Alona believes they're making the right move because they feel my company is growing into a worldwide conglomerate. Many companies have tried to join me on this same conception. Most don't do their homework and are either rejected or in a takeover. You, Maddox, have dug deep. I know the 2004 *Newsweek* article you spoke of. It's a small article about half a page. The article only talks about how they believe it's impossible for the Chelsea Corporation to obtain such knowledge.

"I believe you lied when you said you've read from time to time in *Newsweek* about my technology. They only have one article that rejected the notion how far Chelsea has come in AmI and nanotech. I think Alona adores the idea that it *could be real* and sought my company."

"I have to admit, I did exaggerate, but I had to, to get your attention that I'm seriously interested about the technology and want to believe and prove it's authentic." Maddox had the sense she wasn't playing when she said she had this technology ready and up and running. But when? To him, this was like the beginnings of discovering how to control atomic energy. "Are you afraid or concerned the government or sanction groups might stop you from distributing this technology?"

"That's where Alona comes in," Nzingha said, smiling, showing her perfect white teeth. "You'll promote that this technology is good for human contact. This will better communities and cultures all over the world. It'll build knowledge and skills for better work quality. It'll make it easer to live and control your own life."

"All over the world?" For a second Maddox thought, what did he get himself into? "Did you consider the loss of privacy? You consider other organizations misusing the technology? And the government having a crisis on their hands with empowerment of increasing individualization. Have you told Alona about these things?"

Nzingha chuckled and made a face, as if she didn't understand. "Maddox. I thought you're with me in all this. Was it not the other day you said you liked the branch in my company of this technology? You said, and I quote, the world needs to know about technology like this. You said I could help millions. I figure I'm giving you a front row seat at this chance."

Maddox felt he put his foot in his mouth. He felt perhaps her beauty overwhelmed him. For some reason he felt she was using him. She was serious, and he had the strangest feeling this technology was real. He was in the middle of the biggest merger in his company. Don't screw it up, he kept saying in his head. He was sweating now.

Nzingha was attractive, no doubt a high empowered businesswoman. He found out today she was like no other woman he ever engaged. She was well informed and had a strategy. No, she had many plans. She was using him and didn't hide it. She innocently did this as if to say, *what? What did I do wrong? What? You thought you were going to come in here on this trip out to sea, make love to me, and the merger goes through. Ha, the laugh is on you, Maddox.*

"Well . . . Yes, I did say that, and I'm still saying that. But aren't you afraid other countries might use this technology improperly? I mean, did you have board meetings about this? This all seems sudden that a company just drops technology like this without many meetings and media coverage, uh, stuff like that."

"When is a better time to advertise this?" Nzingha continued giving a warm smile, but didn't wait for an answer. "Maddox, I see you're afraid, excited, and overwhelmed at the phenomenon of this technology."

"No. I'm not . . ."

She cut him off by putting her finger on his lips. "Shh, don't be afraid. My board members had many meetings. Other meetings with other interest groups—well, I say, don't let your left hand know what your right hand is doing. I say to the media, even a fool is wise if he keeps silent.

"I made this arrangement with Alona because of you. Your zeal on the technology. I hope you understand the gravity of this situation and will remain tacit until after the merger."

She stared at him with her hunter-green eyes. It wasn't a seductive gaze; it was innocent, drawing him in like a vampire to its victims. It was a gracious glare before an attack. "We do have an understanding, right?" she inquired, lifting his chin with the same finger.

"Yes," he said, then she attacked. She closed her eyes and kissed him on the lips. Her lips were full, warm, and soft as pillows. He could now see clearly the brown freckles on and around the bridge of her nose. He could feel the warmth of her body and smell her sweet cherry blossom scent. He could taste her tongue and lips. It was the flavor of strawberries. After one seemingly long minute of tongue-kissing, she pulled away and, with her teeth, almost pulled his bottom lip off.

"People and governments will fear AmI and nanotechnology," she said. Her dreamy, chinky eyes now open peered through him. "Not everything that's faced can be changed, but nothing can be changed until it's faced. Change is the law of life, and those who look only in the past and present are certain to miss the future."

Maddox thought, now where did I hear that before? One of the Presidents of the United States once said something like that.

"After I show you the authenticity of this project, I'll count on you to publicize it," Nzingha said, with a charming smile.

"When?"

"I'll call you."

The rest of the trip was odd as Nzingha excused herself to retire. Maddox had a lot to think about. Was that impulsive kiss to say I like you? Was that kiss to complicate things? Or was that a kiss to assure a deal gone well? It was a passionate kiss. Quick, but he liked it. Maybe the more he helped, the more he'd get some kind of genuine affection from her, even if it was true she was using him. To look at the bigger picture, he'd win her over, get the merger, and make lots of money. Who wouldn't jump at that chance—a fool, I suppose.

He slept in a lower deck guest cabin about the size of an average room under blue satin sheets. It was cold on the ship, and he meant to ask Nzingha about it, but he didn't see her for the rest of the night. He spoke to a crew member about it that showed him his room. The crew member walked away nonchalantly and said, "I'll see what I can do." Funny, Maddox said to himself, he hadn't felt a difference throughout the night.

He now had two things to dream about, Nzingha and her technology. Nzingha was attractive, equal to her science. Somehow he was going to try and juggle both. He laughed to himself, or perhaps die trying.

The Firestone II never made it to Greenland, but went as far as Newfoundland Island and the Labrador Sea before turning back around. Now, going against the gulf stream, it took the whole second day to get back to Boston. In the morning Maddox got a glimpse of an iceberg in the far distance. It appeared like a white island the size of an eighteen wheel truck. Appealing, he thought. I need to come out here more and experience nature. He missed going continually out to sea.

Nzingha and Maddox talked of sports and artistry most of the day. She also explained why she loved the sea. "I love the mysteries of the sea," she would say as they ate another vegetarian meal. "I can think out here, even in a storm. I just become overcome by a state of equations and ideas. To stop the progression of knowledge is like seeing the horizon as the end of the ocean."

CHAPTER 14

THE LAGOS NIGHT LIFE WAS IMPECCABLE, and the city was even more incredible. Lagos was nothing like it was fifteen years ago Matt thought.

The metropolis extended across the Lekki Peninsula as far as Mayfair Garden Estate. Skyscrapers ranging from forty to a hundred stories littered all of Lagos's islands, Ikoyi, Victoria, and Iddo. The skyline resembled Tokyo and Manhattan combined. Brightly lit highways and bridges like a spider's legs seemed to connect these islands to the mainland and end on Lagos Island as the hub. A sign over one of the highways read in a Fulani script, *All Roads Lead to Lagos*.

The Livenal main building sat in the heart of Lagos Island surrounded by about fifty sixty-story buildings. The Livenal structure towered over all of them, reaching a hundred flights. The tan-colored building was shaped like an obelisk with pure gold top.

Matt positioned himself on the roof of a fifty-five story building. He was dressed in his black custom-made suit. This time, not only did he have his night-vision goggles and utility belt, he had a knapsack on his back.

He had to be well prepared for this mission. There could be no screw-ups. It had to be flawless. He wasn't in his own country where authorities there could say, it was just a thief. Here in Nigeria if he was caught they'll say he was a spy. He was—that's exactly what he was doing. If he was captured, not only would his team be in jeopardy but the whole United States. Of course, he had ways around that. This part of the mission didn't exist. He didn't exist, and the United States Government saw it that way, too. That understanding came with the job.

He glanced at his watch, synchronized now to Nigerian time. It was three o'clock in the morning—mission estimated, one hour.

He took out his grappling-hook. Aiming low, he fired it into the fifty-first floor windowsill of the Livenal structure simply called the Obelisk Building. Giving it some slack, he tied his end of the rope to a steel ventilation pipe sticking three feet out of the roof he was on. He attached a locking carabiner to the rope. Holding on with both hands to a rope loop attached to the carabiner, he swung himself smoothly through the air heading straight for the Obelisk Building at twenty miles an hour.

Hanging and sliding along this rope, he moved through the dry night air like a silent Blackhawk with no wings. All the while, the few people below were totally oblivious to his presence. The city was like New York, a city that never sleeps. He could still see some cars and people below rushing about. It wasn't as active as the day, but he could imagine.

Lagos to date was the largest city in Africa and most populated. It's the financial capital of Nigeria and fastest growing economic center of all Africa. Nigeria alone accomplished this in fifteen years after many civil wars and internal conflicts.

Ezequiel, a good friend of his who lived in Nigeria after defecting Cuba following the Cuban Revolution, had told him of many rumors surrounding the Livenal Corporation.

After they got acquainted again, Matt asked about the Livenal Company. Ezequiel told him stories about how Livenal deals in many political issues in Nigeria. "Livenal is like the Rockefellers in America," he would say. The biggest rumor was that Livenal, Energ, and Xur Corporations controlled Nigeria's aristocracy like a secret society. It was said these American businesses have strong trade and financial connections in Japan and throughout Europe. Nigerian politicians and journalists called them, The Three Gods of Nigeria.

This was all new, Matt thought, and he had a lot of work to do. The first night he flew into Nigeria he saw Ezequiel and thanked him for the information. He then took him out into the musical night life attractions of Lagos.

Matt tightened his grip on the rope and carabiner as he slowed his tumble into the fiftieth floor window. He shot his grappling hook into the fifty-first floor windowsill so he could now dangle in front of the fiftieth floor window, his main objective.

He took out a suction cup from his pouch and placed it on the window. Taking a diamond-cutter from his utility belt, with one hand he slowly and painstakingly started to cut a five by three foot rectangular vertical hole into the glass around the suction cup. Perspiring now from hanging by one arm for almost five minutes, he was cautious not to knock the glass away when he finished cutting.

Though he was sweating, he didn't quiver, and moved about as if he was a window technician. Matt was well qualified for this, and he perfectly calculated it. There can be no mistakes, he kept saying to himself. Now removing the glass from which he cut, with the suction handle he placed it carefully on a desk full with papers inside the window.

He then, still holding on by one hand, gently swung himself through the five by three hole to land on the desk inside an office. A light automatically turned on, and he got a good glimpse of the office before he stepped off the desk and turned the light out again. Average business office, nothing to see here, he said to himself as he cautiously peeked out a door into the brightly lit hallway of office doors.

Fifteen minutes into his mission now—destination, the office at the end of the hall, the CPU room.

The SOF team came to Nigeria two days earlier ahead of him. They had to establish a surveillance of the place to make his operation run smooth. The team met the head director of the SMB, Secret Military Brigade, Bolaji in Abuja. Bolaji briefed them on Nigerian customs and the Livenal business.

Bolaji explained to the team, and they fed the conversation to Matt, that Livenal was the heart of Nigeria and a lucrative business. He said, "Livenal deals much in reconstructing Nigeria's business and political world. I doubt they have time to waste on such things as trying to clone things. I don't know of such a technology existing here in Nigeria. This sounds like more of a European dilemma. Cloning goats and such."

"You're probably right, sir," Brian said. "But if you recall in your records as well as ours we did have a slight predicament with this company around 1999 to 2000 about unregulated human cloning. Some things have come up in the States recently, and we've found a money trail leading here. We're not accusing the company's board of anything. We're just checking to see if any individuals are using this company for their own purposes of possibly starting this cloning thing up again. They could have connected with contacts in the United States on such matters. Something we can't have in our country."

"Very well," Bolaji said. "You have my full cooperation for a week. You'll be given a secret service escort who goes by the name Bayode."

On that first day, Monday, Bayode flew the SOF team out to Lagos, showing them the Livenal building—the Obelisk Building.

Matt moved back to the desk and stood on it again, cautious not to step on the glass he just cut and papers. He reached up into the ceiling and removed the white acoustical tile. He climbed into the darkness in the hole he made and began crawling through the installation and joists between floors. Flipping on his night vision goggles he was like a roach between walls, knowing exactly where the crumbs were on the outside. He had tentacles that knew where to search.

When he was over the CPU room, he removed the ceiling tile just a little and peeked down. The room was all white as were the many huge refrigerator-size computers. The huge circular room housed all the components of the mainframe in the center of the room also in a circle.

There were no cameras, guards, and laser detectors. Instead, five people were stationed around the CPU at terminals, working, wide-awake. This would be about the time the average person might say, damn. Matt was no amateur. He assessed his situation, found his target, and executed quickly.

Matt remembered Brian, Sara, Joseph, and John telling him that they interviewed many executives that first day in the Obelisk Building. They conversed generally about when was the last time the company dealt in cloning technology and was there anything like that going on today. Have they heard of such things? If so, where? If not in this company, could there possibly be another dealing in theses things? Is the Nigerian government dealing in this technology or other unnamed interest groups?

While asking these questions, of course, the SOF team asked other simple inquiries. "Can we check the basement of the building? How high is this building? Does Livenal have other buildings like this where we could talk to other managers? Is this the main hub of the corporation? Wow, nice building! When did they put this up? If we need more information, like computer records, where must we go? Not that we need to take it that far, but I'm just asking."

Everyone on the team scrutinized the building itself, probing for name brands and manufacturers. Then, after the first day, the team took in the information and went to work.

At the end of the second day in Lagos in the confines of a hotel they picked randomly, they had the information needed for Matt to do his job.

Of course, all the executives had no idea what they where talking about when it came to the cloning questions. From the simple questioning, they attained an abundance of information.

They found out the building had a hundred and five floors, to be exact. Livenal also had business buildings in Abuja, but this was the main hub. The CPU room was on the fiftieth floor and the company that made the building was a French company called Noah Constructions and RWI Haruna steel company from Japan. One executive spoke about looking into a secret organization called the Yoruba society, saying they might be dealing in such things as cloning. The SOF team agreed that they could learn a lot by asking dumb questions.

The team told Matt that Bayode eyed them a couple of times suspiciously when they asked the would-be silly questions. Bayode responded saying, "You're not permitted in the basement or CPU room."

"No problem," Sara replied.

That day in Nigeria the team gathered information on Noah Constructions and RWI Haruna designs from their wireless Internet laptops. After all day figuring it out like a puzzle, how the Obelisk Building was constructed, the data was forwarded to Matt.

Turning off his goggles, Matt eased the ceiling tile just enough out of the way for him to drop down in the center of the room. He was as agile as a cat. Landing on top of one of the many computer components like a feather hitting the ground, he repeated the move by now landing on the floor between the machines. He did this in one motion like an apple dropping from a tree. All the while he kept his eye on the five surrounding individuals. They never looked up from their terminals.

Moving slowly among the small maze of computers, he found the backup CD drive. It was easy inserting his portable hard drives into the computer, for it was previously functioning and he was already positioned behind it. The occupant operating the terminal never knew he was there. He moved so silently and nimble, Matt couldn't hear himself breathing. Matt noticed the only thing the occupant saw was that his screen flickered about five or six times in the last ten minutes. That was enough time for him to fill his two hard drives. This time, he had to look at when a small light on his drives finished flashing, to tell when it was complete.

Before pulling his last drive out, he noticed the guy at the terminal was touch screening the air at digital data. A hologram of data floated five inches from the computer screen. Gee, he said to himself, now that's something he'd only seen in movies. These Nigerians are stepping up. I bet the Japanese don't have that yet. I take that back; they're probably working on it.

He moved back to the center of the machines quietly and looked up from where he dropped down, identifying the crack opening he left. Scrupulously and unwearyingly, he watched the five people in the room. He was waiting for them to all simultaneously look away from his target.

One guy decided he had to go to the bathroom, and Matt made his move. With only four in the room, he climbed into the ceiling again in one motion like a bobcat climbing a tree. He was almost perfect. Making it inside the ceiling and turning around to close the tile, he hit his foot on a beam.

One of the IT's looked up in the exact spot he just entered. Matt stood still for a minute as he watched from a hairline crack in the tile. The technologist stared at the ceiling for about a minute, shrugged, and went back to his numbers in the air.

Wednesday the SOF team flew back to Abuja to finish their investigation. That's when Matt flew into Lagos and met his friend Ezequiel. After getting himself acquainted with his buddy, the Lagos night life, and the data forwarded to him, he wasted no time. He was on the job. He and the SOF team called this operation In and Out.

Climbing from the ceiling, he stood again on the desk in the business office. Stepping down from the desk again he peeked from behind the door leading to the well lit hallway. This time he watched the man who had to go to the bathroom walk back into the CPU room using a green pass-card. Matt then closed the office door and locked it.

Taking the backpack off his back, he opened it on the desk and took out a cement gun full with water. He sprayed the edges of the rectangular glass he cut out of the window. As he sprayed, he made sure the extra water sprinkled onto the floor. He then sprayed down the circumference of the hole in the window. Putting the water gun away, he took out another cement looking gun. In this gun was a clear polymer resin that he put on the glass edges as he did the water. Putting the backpack on his back, he climbed on top of the desk and slipped out the window.

Finding the looped rope on the wire outside, with one hand he hung from it and the other reached back in the cut open window for the missing piece. Like a door, using the suction cup as a handle, he closed up the rectangular hole slowly for a seamless fit. The resin mended the cut glass to where it looked as if someone scratched a rectangle in the window.

Matt took out another carabiner from his belt pocket and attached it to the rope and his waist. He dangled now so that his hands were free and his one arm didn't have to hold the weight of his body. He then placed a clear adhesive tape-like patch around the rectangular scratch.

He was like a mountain climber, he thought, as he had to wait a little for the tape to dry. He eyed his watch—time 3:35. At 3:40 he removed the tape and suction-cup and placed them in the sack on his side. There, the window looked as good as new.

Matt then twisted his right hand in the rope supporting him, making a knot. With his left hand he yanked hard three times at the grappling-hook anchored in the windowsill above him. It gave, and he immediately swung back into the opposite building he originally came from. As he swung into the building he made sure he hit between the windows so that he didn't crash through them. He hurt his shoulder a little, grunting as he crashed into the wall. Using the rope he then began his climb up the building to the roof. He was on the thirtieth floor, thirty-first—now thirty-second.

The streets below were pretty much vacant now as he still went unnoticed. Climbing higher—twenty more flights to go before the end of this mission, Matt said to himself. He accelerated his pace up the wall of the building.

Thursday, Matt had now transferred the stolen data through a special e-mail account to the SOF team. The team told Matt that they interviewed more executives of the Livenal Company in Abuja while secretly studying the data. They didn't get back to him until about eight o'clock that night.

After taking a long warm shower he laid on a white soft bed in a luxurious five-star hotel called The Rezidor. In his underwear covered in a navy silk bathrobe he felt good and safe with his .45 under his pillow. He was about to check the cartridge again when he heard a bell ring on his Sager laptop that he was receiving an e-mail. He got up and sat at a gold-looking desk and opened the computer.

He was registered in the royal suite on the seventh floor going by the name Mr. and Mrs. Austin. He didn't need all this space and attention of a dining room, living room, balcony, twenty-four hour butler service, and private masseuse. It was just the ideal cover, and he wasn't going to give up its pleasantries. He had every intention in indulging himself, but first business.

Opening his e-mail, he clicked on the new message in his inbox titled INO.

So far, nothing. Just job salaries, employer names, money movements of imports and exports around the world. Information on building plans, takeovers, acquisitions, and projects past and present.

After reading this, he hit reply, then typed: *You wizards couldn't find anything. Give me something. Give me anything that sounds weird, you know, out of the loop.*

He then hit *send*. In two minutes there was another e-mail.

Okay, there was one canceled project called Denisova in the mountains of Gotel. Why and what project did they start to build in the mountains? Denisova has something to do with Neolithic man. What that means is anybody's guess. That's about as strange as it gets.

Thank you. Tell Brian I said stop holding back.

Brian said whatever.

Okay. Send me the coordinates to that project.

Not a problem. The location is a bauxite mine now in use.

Matt knew the SOF team was going home first thing tomorrow morning. He wasn't going home. Of course, being the inquisitive man he was, he was going to check on the dead lead. Using the Internet, he found a map of the Gotel Mounts. He found the disregarded project, now quarry, resided in southeastern Nigeria and stretched to the border of northcentral Cameroon. It was going to take him to a place called the Adamawa Plateau.

Turning off the computer, he sat back and thought on how he was going to execute this new solo mission. First, he was going to go on a vow he made with himself to get a massage from the pretty masseuse he paid for. What was her name again? Oh yeah, Abebi. She'll ask about his wife again. He'll continue his story on how they're going through a bitter divorce and how they're trying to reconcile differences on this trip here in Lagos. Mrs. Austin will be meeting him here in Lagos tomorrow, so his story goes.

Matt smiled as he put on his wedding ring that sat on the table. "So what's that to say about us?" Abebi will probably say again as she said the first time. This time he wasn't going to turn her down. Besides, he had one more free day before his wife comes, so the story goes.

FRIDAY, MATT FELT GOOD and refreshed after his night out with Abebi. His body was well prepared for today's task after she ironed out a few kinks.

He made it to the Adamawa Plateau by dusk dressed in his custom-made suit.

Ezequiel had guided him to a place to rent an inexpensive charter plane. Using an alias name, he rented it and flew himself here, the place of interest. The bauxite mine, owned by Livenal, sat at the side of a mountain called Gotel.

It took twenty minutes to crawl to the fence that enclosed this facility. The green savanna made it hard for him to just sneak up to the fence. He also stayed clear of motion detectors, making sure he was about ten feet away from each one. They were embedded in the ground about twenty feet from one another. Moving close to these things will end his trip here real fast he thought. Making a flimsy carpet out of grass attached to his back, he went unnoticed as he cut the fence at the bottom with pliers, just enough for him to wiggle through.

Matt felt the place was a bit secure for an aluminum mine. The barbwire fence went a mile around the whole front of the mountain enclosing the main part of the mine. In the lush green mountains overlooking the facility were watch towers, five in all. Each had two government soldiers in brown and green camouflage uniforms, armed with machine guns.

Right outside the fence on the north side was a field about five miles wide of nothing but coquelicot dirt craters in the ground. Bulldozers, cranes, and dump trucks littered this landscape grinding and churning the red soil. It was like a replication of a full scale excavation of planet Mars.

He knew mines like this needed protection from domestic terrorists, but he felt it was a little over-protected. The little aluminum this country produced he was sure didn't bring that much interest to fanatic groups.

The machines were winding down, and people in orange helmets were getting in their vehicles and going home. Good, the less people, the better, Matt thought. Snaking through another grassy field he put on his night-vision goggles as dusk became night, pitch black. It was now easy for him to move through the field even with the tower spotlights on.

The air was dry and warm to the point he could hardly breathe, making him sweat. It took another twenty minutes to reach small stagnant wooden houses and large trailer-houses positioned around a dirt field. He wasn't timing this mission—it was purely motivated by his speculation, so he had all the time in the world.

Standing, he now crept past the mobile homes toward the mountain. He could still hear workers going home for the night. Probably the foremen—they're always last to leave.

He found a large steel door built into the side of the mountain. He would have never found it if it wasn't for his goggles. The door was covered in grass, weeds, and hundreds of leafy twisted vines. Out of the many trees that grew out the side of the mountain, one covered the door with its' drooping branches.

Moving to the entrance, he examined it. It was rusted and filled with moss. The door not only had a huge lock, it was chained shut with a corroded padlock. Remarkable, Matt said to himself, as he took out his electronic master key. Whatever was behind this door was probably locked up for some time.

After unlocking the door and padlock he took off the lawn carpet from his back and placed it next to a patch of grass. The door squeaked a little as he squeezed through into its darkness. He closed it the best he could so that the chain didn't hang loose, making it seem as if the door was still tightly sealed. He took out his .45 just for precaution.

The concrete tunnel he walked through was jet-black but he moved through it as if bright green lights guided his way. The passageway spiraled downward for about a mile until he came to another locked steel door.

Now what part of the mine was this? Matt thought. He had the biggest notion that this had nothing to do with the mine. What are you hiding, Livenal, or better yet, what have you hid? Looking around the tunnel, he could tell the place was well lit and wired at one time with miles of piping and hanging lamps.

A wire for a camera was positioned over the door, camera now long gone. Using his master key, he made it through that door into a hallway with an elevator in front of him and a dusty desk to the left. He found more holes for cameras. Easily he pried the elevator doors open and peered into the shaft. The shaft went down about five stories. There was no elevator car, only an abandoned badly soiled and corroded chasm.

He climbed down into the abyss using foot holes imbedded in the wall. Making it to the bottom floor, he cracked open the elevator doors and emerged into an empty hall. This hall had offices on his left and right. The offices no-longer had doors. Now nothing but barren chambers. What interest him most was the huge plate-glass window ten feet across from him. He slowly crept to it, to see what was beyond.

Beyond the transom was a wall to wall, floor and ceiling metallic auditorium. The window he looked through was the middle point of this underground theater. It went down twenty feet and up twenty feet. A steel balcony went around the hall, and many aluminum conductors and pipes twisted all kinds of ways across the ceiling and floor. He counted three metallic doors that almost blended into the walls. Eight metal sockets lined the floor an even distance from each other, like light bulb outlets that could screw in ten foot bulbs. To the left of this arena, behind another window, was a deserted laboratory.

Obviously something big happened here long ago as he saw globs of collected dust and cobwebs everywhere. Besides all this, it was desolate and void of sound. But his thoughts seemed to echo. Holstering his gun in his shoulder holster made a loud noise. Taking a digital camera from his pouch, he started taking pictures of the huge room.

He then noticed something flashing in one corner of the place. If he didn't have his night vision, it would have flashed red, but he only perceived it as a twinkle. Crap. A live camera, he said to himself.

He moved to one side of the window and looked around for more cameras. There was only that one that faced a door in the arena. Good, he said to himself, it wasn't facing him. He could have been spotted or walked right up to it. He felt it was time to leave. He overstayed his time with curiosity.

Leaving from what he liked to call a steel tomb, he made sure he closed elevator doors and locked other doors the way he found them. What was this place? Why was it built? What did this place have to do with the mines? Matt felt he already knew some of the mystery. It was first clearly obvious Livenal had all to do with this. Next, this had to be the abandoned cloning lab of 2000. He didn't believe Livenal had fully forsaken their cloning capabilities. He couldn't confirm nor deny the truth here. He had to first show the SOF squad the photos.

After locking the outside door, he found his grass carpet and strapped it on his back. His watch read eight o'clock. He spent about two hours out here, but wasn't out of the woods yet. It took a half hour more as he crawled through the shrubs taking the same path he made the first time. He had to stop every now and then as spotlights washed over him.

He found the fence where he cut a hole in the bottom earlier and squeezed through. Crouched low, he jogged to a small hill. As soon as he made it over the hill, an alarm went off. The blaring noise blasted through the air across the savanna. All the spotlights moved in his direction in an instant. Damn! Matt shouted almost out loud as he lay flat and still on the ground behind the mound. He must have tripped a motion detector near the fence. He managed to avoid them on his trip in, but forgot about them on his way out.

He then heard the dogs. He again pulled out his .45. He heard the safeties of machine guns being clicked off. He heard the dogs' barks getting closer and men shouting. It sounded like maybe three, no four, men. He stayed as still as he could. He knew the soldiers couldn't see him in the night camouflaged like he was, but he knew he couldn't trick the dogs. Should he wait until a dog bit him, or right before to shoot? Then he knew, if it came to that, all hell was going to break loose.

A German-Shepherd to be exact, appeared over the hill about five feet from his head. The only thing stopping this growling, snapping canine from biting his head off was that it was chained to its master. He could see the soldier now on top of the hill searching in his direction with a flashlight practically shining him in the face. Then another soldier emerged with a dog. This officer pointed a finger straight at him. It had to be impossible to see him unless one of the dogs attacked, Matt thought.

He gripped his gun tight, tense, and ready to fire. Sweating, with his finger on the trigger, he decided who he was going to shoot first. He also decided which way he was going to scurry. He supposed he was going to zigzag on this flat terrain with no trees for cover.

Then he heard a sound behind him. It sounded like a long, low persistent moo. The ground trembled as a herd of cows moved behind him. He then heard the soldiers shouting in their custom language, angered at the herdsmen. They lowered their guns. The ordeal lasted about five minutes before both parties dissipated.

Matt, perspiring still, laughed to himself, saying over and over in his head, I was saved by cows—saved by cows. You could lose weight doing this job. He thought to himself. Easing his finger off the trigger, he slowly looked over his shoulder. He counted about forty cows and six herdsmen in traditional flowing robes and holding staffs moving away from him across the flat plains. When the sounds of the barking dogs became distant, he moved.

Chapter 15

HE KEPT HIS WORD and let his partner stay home for the weekend. Allen strongly insisted that he was going with Joe to Chicago, but Joe ignored him. Joe said, "Look, it's early in the case. All I'm getting is a little information. Spending time with your girl on your anniversary is the right thing to do." Besides, Joe said to himself, don't be like me. Divorced and without a life—cranky and wearing the same damn dark blue or black suits every day.

Driving into this city, Joe got a glimpse of the Willis Tower with other skyscrapers about in the Chicago skyline. Nice, Joe said to himself. It had that huge metropolis feel.

Larry and Rachel came together ten minutes late this early morning at ten minutes after ten. Joe called them the day before, and they agreed to meet him at the Ralph Lauren Restaurant on Chicago Avenue near the Hancock Building and landmark Water Tower. Joe knew why they picked this spot. They were away from the CBA Law Firm Building that was closer to the Willis Tower on Franklin Street.

Larry wore a white shirt and blue dungaree pants. Rachel wore a blue shirt and black slacks. He spotted them quickly when they entered the restaurant. He and Larry locked eyes, then Larry guided Rachel to a table in the back where he sat.

"Hi, Agent Clay," Joe said as the two sat across from him at a decorated table. He flashed his badge in front of them, especially Rachel. "Thanks for coming out. You must be Rachel?" Joe shook Rachel's hand, then he shook Larry's. "Thanks again, Larry."

Rachel was about five feet, five inches, thin, natural long flowing blonde hair—he could tell by her eyebrows, light blue eyes, and pretty. Allen would have liked her; she was his type. She favored his girlfriend. Rachel looked about twenty-five years old and had a nice smile, showing her perfect white teeth.

"I already ordered breakfast." Joe then asked. "You guys want anything, my tab?" He sipped some coffee already served to him about five minutes ago.

"Yeah, I do, I'm starved," Rachel said.

Outspoken and not as shy as Larry, Joe noticed. All Larry ordered was a coffee. By the time Rachel introduced herself as Rachel Danes and what she did as a attorney for CBA International, they were eating. Joe had pancakes, eggs, home-fries, and orange juice. Rachel had the same, but with bacon and no pancakes. Larry had his second cup of coffee. The restaurant was crowded as the Saturday morning rush came through.

"I admit I was a little nervous when I first heard you on the phone," Rachel said. "The FBI and all. I thought all week about this, like how to tell the whole story."

"I know a lot of the story already," Joe said, "Maybe you could full in a few pieces."

"I'm glad, but surprised you guys responded so soon. Larry and I, for some years, only saw all this as our own little conspiracy theories."

"Then it hit home in my company some months ago," Larry spoke and sipped some of his fresh hot coffee.

"Getting right into it," Joe said and ate his last piece of pancake. He sat back and looked at Rachel. "What do you see your company doing next?"

"My department executive keeps complaining about how the I Company is turning down deals the Chelsea Corporation keeps offering," Rachel spoke. "He complains about how the Vice President, who partly owns I, doesn't want to sell to Chelsea. If Chelsea was to own I, their bonuses would skyrocket—big golden parachutes and all that."

"I'm starting to see a pattern here," Joe said, raising an eyebrow. "Let me understand what I is. I seems to be a company that owns electrical grids that power mostly New York and Los Angeles. I've seen the commercials." He spoke, trying to sound like the deep voice on the commercial, "I—I light up the city, I light up planes and trains, I light up your life—I."

"Very good, Mr. Clay," Rachel said. "Yes, that's the company Chelsea's trying to own."

"The full name is the Illumination Corporation based in Buffalo, NY,"

Larry spoke. "They're also trying to push owning electricity in Florida and Ohio. They have headquarters in England, France, and Spain."

"Hum," Joe said, and took out a pad and pen from his brown overcoat on the back of his chair. "That's interesting. Do you know the name of the vice president of I?"

"I think it's, it's . . ." Rachel had to think for a few seconds looking up at the ceiling. "James . . . James, Wash, or something like that."

"I'll look it up. I'm sure I'll find the correct name." Joe finished his orange juice. "So how do you know what your executive is angry at isn't a rumor?"

"True, this very well could be a rumor," Rachel answered, "but you see a pattern here like we do. You yourself could check with Tony, my department boss, and find out in more detail about Chelsea trying to buy out I."

"You might not have to do that," Larry spoke. "I think they mentioned it in last week's issue of *Businessweek*."

"Oh," Joe said and watched Rachel finish eating her eggs. He then scribbled some names down on his pad and put it away. "Unless there's anything else, I must say you guys have been a great help."

"Yes, there is," Rachel said and smiled. "To confirm our theories, will you call and tell us if we're right?"

"It'll be my duty. And if you guys have anymore theories, I'd like to know."

Rachel gave a warm, pretty smile that made Joe smile back. Yeah, Allen would have liked that smile, Joe contemplated. Joe shook both of their hands again and handed them business cards with his name and phone number.

"If you guys have any problems, give me a call."

Joe found last week's issue of *Businessweek* in a small nearby Chicago library on a computer. He read a one-page article titled, *I Want It All*. The first sentence read, *I want I, says the Chelsea Company*. It read exactly what Rachel had told him, and more. First he learned that the vice president's name was James Walsh—Rachel was close. Next he learned that, not only did Mr. Walsh not want to give up his company to Chelsea, but he took her for a joke. Mr. Walsh was quoted, *"The offer of currency is good, but there's no way Chelsea can juggle the world. Chelsea can't seriously think it can maintain managing I and every other company they're controlling. I'll not see the day that I will fall into mismanaged hands."*

The article gave the latest major companies Chelsea was juggling, like the CBA Law Firm, WCBH-TV network, and a soon to be merger with an advertising agency called Alona. It also told of her telecommunication network businesses in Nigeria, Japan, Australia, India, England, and Brazil.

What are you up to, Ms. Chelsea? What are you doing? Joe kept those sayings in his head on his day long drive home to Washington. He felt like calling Allen about the new information just fed to him. Joe knew Allen would be ecstatic. No, let him enjoy himself with his girlfriend. He'll meet up with him Monday afternoon. Besides, he needed a little rest himself.

They'll evaluate all this in the J. Edgar Hoover Building two days from now over some coffee where he'll be able to think straight. One thing was for sure, and that was Mr. Walsh just might need protection. The painting the Chelsea Company was making for itself was starting to become clear.

IT WAS A DAY WELL REMEMBERED. All the big shots of both companies were here. Maddox sat at the far end, in an enormous tan conference room on the fortieth floor of the East Impeding Tower.

Nzingha stood in front of a huge beige oval table. She was dressed in a black pants suit and red blouse.

"I feel as though this was a quick merger, like back in the late eighteen hundreds," Nzingha spoke as she held onto a wine glass full with water. "The transaction value at fifty-two million United States dollars is good. We'll all soon definitely grow rapidly in the near future."

They all applaud before she finished talking. On the right side of the table with Maddox was the Chief Executive of Alona, Thomas Garnett, and Chief Executive Assistant Jason Culver. On the left was the Chief Executive of the Chelsea Designing Department Aaron Lerman and Assistant Executive Gregg Reid. The men wore black or blue three-piece designer suits and wine glasses full with red wine sat in front of them.

"I have to thank Alona for implementing our company's joint endeavors together. I'd like to call this a merger of equals where new company stock will be issued. Some may call this an acquisition, but I feel it's too positive to be called that. Mr. Garnett and I have agreed this is in the best interest for both companies. In the interest that we'll be making a lot more currency." She was stopped again by more ovations. "Though this merger is already known to your board of directors, employees, and shareholders, we'll still have confidentiality agreements on some things as discussed.

"As we in this room know this will increase consumer surplus, cross-selling, and any loss your company has will reduce our tax liability. This, gentlemen, will generate a vertically integrated firm that'll be profitable." Everyone clapped until Nzingha sat down, then Mr. Garnett stood, taking the front of the table with wine glass in hand.

"I first have to thank Ms. Chelsea for this smooth transaction," Garnett said, "and finally meeting Ms. Chelsea was more charming." As he looked her way, she smiled. "I have to thank Chelsea for letting us keep our company name, where usually smaller firms in merger and acquisitions don't. We agreed to call this a merger rather than an acquisition because of the complex process with many acquisitions whereas fifty percent of them don't work.

"This merger will now help Alona and Chelsea remove duplicated departments, lowering costs but maintain the same revenue stream. By Chelsea absorbing us, we now become a major competitor on the market which will increase our market power as we maintain a set price. Now our conservative investors will have more confidence in investing in our company. You see, guys, it's all about stability and the authority to control our company's future."

So it's all about survival. That's why his company finalized the merger, Maddox thought. After Garnett finished his speech, everyone clapped, then stood.

"A toast," Garnett said, as everyone raised their glasses. "To immovability, continued existence, endurance." They all hit their wine glasses together and drank.

Food of all kind was in the front of this windowless room. The executives helped themselves to still warm spaghetti and meatballs, slices of chicken, macaroni, rice and beans, tossed salad, sandwiches of all kinds, and drinks of bottled water and soda. After getting their plastic plates full and drinks of their choosing, they sat at the table and ate in low, exciting conversations among themselves.

A large canvas over the food reminded Maddox of a city, though the painting relatively were a bunch of colorful abstract squares, rectangles, and triangles of all sizes.

Nzingha came and stood next to Maddox as he was last to get his food. He filled his plate with spaghetti, rice and beans.

"I had your CEO make sure you were present during this merger's final deal," Nzingha whispered, just out of ear shot of the others. "If you're wondering why you're here."

"Thanks," Maddox said in a low voice, then smirked. "And I thought it was just because they liked me."

"If they appreciated you or not, doesn't matter. I know your potential."

"Thanks."

"Do you still want to see the technology we spoke of?"

"Of course." Maddox grinned.

"Tomorrow morning your boss wants to take me to a restaurant to discuss future planning about our stocks and all that stuff. After that I'll be free. How about you see me at my house in the afternoon, and I'll show you the formalities. My assistant will call you tomorrow on the particulars of time and where I reside."

"It'll be an honor, and long awaited. I can't wait."

Nzingha smiled at him before she went back to the table with the executives.

That two-second smile to Maddox seemed to last forever in his mind, like a photograph. The dimples on her grin were stunningly beautiful. Her radiant high cheekbones reminded him of fresh peaches. He noticed she didn't see him smile back as she left him.

AmI wasn't a technology to take lightly. It was a move into the future the world might not yet be ready for. His company was now part of something big, something innovative. If only the executives of Alona knew what they were getting themselves into. When they do find out, they'll probably gloat in the technology's magnificence and seek higher wages. But it'll be too late. They would have only agreed to a deal done now.

Then what did that have to say about him? Was Nzingha going to take care of just him or did she have other plans? He was keeping quiet about all this. Did she truly have an interest in him just because he dug her fancy technology? It was not only her equipment he liked, but it was her equipment he *liked*, if you know what I mean, Maddox said to himself as if he was talking to a bunch of guys.

What was he doing? He couldn't mix business and pleasure. Still, he couldn't help but notice she was a woman; a woman he admired. Her hourglass figure showed through the two-piece pants suits she wore. She had that average petite shape that he liked. Maybe it was just her smile he couldn't get out of his head.

CHAPTER 16

HER BLOOD FELT AS IF IT WAS BOILING, and this was no dream. Her body temperature was one hundred and nine point two degrees Fahrenheit. It was a little high from her normal one hundred and nine degrees. Maybe her temperature remained so high was because her body thought, as she did, that one day she was going to freeze to death. This was no dream. She was sweating profusely in her silk gray Chinese button down loosely fitted gi uniform. Nzingha looked and felt as if she jumped in a pool of warm water.

Her female doctor told her that her temperature was a rare condition. She called it controlled hyperpyrexia. The doctor at first when she was a child gave her antipyretics, but they never worked. The private doctor, who kept things confidential, always wondered would she spontaneously combust. To science, this was a proposed phenomenon, but the doctor doubted it would ever happen and didn't believe in such things.

It was strange and a spectacle Nzingha thought, that she could walk around at that temperature all these years and not drop dead. She could remember being this way since she was five. Today, and for years, she practically forgot about it.

She slowly moved about her inside homemade dojo in slow motion routines of chopping and punching. Her bare feet twirled about repetitively on the shiny wooden floor. She moved to and fro slowly across the wooden panel square room in many postures and forms. She pushed the air around her as if trying to escape some kind of imaginary boundary.

Her form was of perfection. Her mind was that her body was the center of gravity. Keeping her knees bent throughout her many flexible forms, she moved fast, then slow. She moved in small circles, then large, squares, then round. She practiced more open-hand strikes, kicks, and rolls. She was breathing hard, but controlled. She inhaled long deep breaths through her nose and exhaled slowly out her mouth.

She then sat in the center of the room in a lotus pose and closed her eyes. Nzingha cleared her mind of everything; her only thoughts were of a black ocean of nothingness. In her calm she could actually feel her temperature gradually go down, just a little. She was now breathing normally.

After about twenty minutes of thinking about nothing, she then thought about her technique of Tai Chi Chuan. Tai Chi means supreme ultimate fist. Pushing hands, was the name of an exercise of Tai Chi. She learned the art of blocking and yielding before attacking. She must meet softness with violent force, she thought, follow its motion, and safely redirect it away from her until the attack is exhausted. If she used hardness to resist violence, both sides are certain of injure. I'm the center of gravity, she thought.

MADDOX, AFTER LAYING HIS HEAD in a downtown Columbus, OH hotel, rented a two-door black Dodge Challenger and drove to Bratenahl. The directions Nzingha's main assistant gave him were easy to follow. Nzingha resided in northeastern Ohio near Lake Erie. Figured so, Maddox said to himself. It was damn cold up here near the mammoth lake, especially in November. She lived about as far north as he could go in Ohio. Maddox figured he was going to take her out to dinner. The assistant said Nzingha will be ready by six o'clock.

Though the sky was dark blue, he still got a good look at Nzingha's home from the outside. It wasn't a mansion. It looked more like a huge white two-story million dollar home with many huge arches. At the center front of the house, which sat on a hill, huge wide white marble stairs began from the driveway and ended in front of a long portico. The porch had white marble pillars on the left and right securing its' canopy. Large palm and Chinese Pistachio trees mixed with bushes surrounded the house on this hill.

A valet parker dressed all in black stood waiting for Maddox as he drove onto the driveway leading to the front of the house. The young male valet then took his car and drove somewhere toward the back of the house, following the red paved round-brick driveway. Maddox was left alone in front of the house to climb all those stairs, leaving behind him a fifteen foot brown marble basin fountain. The fountain, which stood in the middle of the driveway, was surrounded by all types of colorful flowers.

After opening and moving past glass doors, he stepped into the brown vestibule. A man in black suit and tie approached from a door to the left.

"May I take your jacket, sir?"

Maddox took off his lambskin jacket, stripping to his taupe-gray Brioni shirt and black slacks.

"She'll be right with you, sir," the man said as he quickly disappeared with his jacket through the door from which he came.

A small chandelier high over Maddox's head gradually brightened until the whole atrium was fully washed in white light. He then heard a pleasant female voice from the wall speak.

"Welcome to the Chelsea estate." The voice didn't sound like Nzingha. It was more mechanical. "Mr. Mathews, Nzingha will be ready in ten minutes. Please come this way." A door automatically on the right opened, and Maddox walked through.

The house is talking, Maddox said to himself and smiled, cool. This must be AmI at work. Nzingha was showing it off already.

He walked down a long well-lit white hallway. Another door opened leading to an outside small square white cement yard.

The courtyard held a white stage in the center. On the left and right of the yard were small thin trees growing out of gray round rock-looking gravel. Above were two white ceiling beams, probably to cover the yard for extreme weather, Maddox thought.

On top of the center platform was a large black pot that seemed to grow out of the stage. Also on stage was a twelve foot long cigarette-looking purple, black, and white crystal rock. This chunk of crystal levitated three feet over the stage. There appeared to be no stand or strings. Was this a huge magnet? He touched the rock to see if it was real. It was. Some kind of illusional art, Maddox deliberated. He was about to feel under the rock until he heard the house talk again.

"You can proceed straight ahead through the glass doors. Please remove your shoes before entering."

Maddox moved to the tinted large windows across the yard and removed his shoes. On the right side of a glass door, numbers and photos floated five inches off the window. Three-dimensional, blue numbers read: Today's Weather, Monday, High 48 degrees, Low 42, winds 6 mph. Next to the chart readings were depictions of animated clouds, rain, and wind. It also showed the weather from this day to Sunday. The time now was 6:15

PM, and fog will be coming from the lake. Nice, Maddox said to himself, as one of the windows automatically rolled aside.

He stepped into a dojo, and the window rolled back shut behind him. It felt like forty degrees outside as in the dojo. Maddox hoped the whole house wasn't like this for he shivered.

The dojo was the size of an average empty square bed room. The floor and walls were made of light-brown wooden paneling. Five foot straight swords hung on the walls on his left and right. He counted twenty in all. Though the lights were low, he could still make out the beautiful Japanese and Chinese designs of the sword cases and handles. He could smell sandalwood incense that probably had been burning a long time. He could tell from the look of burnt-out incense holders imbedded in the walls.

Then Maddox saw Nzingha sitting in the center of the room in a yoga position that looked extremely painful. Some of her hair spiked in the air and some mat to the rivulets of sweat on her face. She still looked alluring.

He put his hands behind his back and waited for her to open her eyes.

"Sorry to disturb you, but your house guided me here," Maddox said.

"Yes, that's her alright," Nzingha responded ever so calmly. "She's always interrupting me, always telling me what I need and want. But then I couldn't blame her. I programmed her."

"Not bad." Maddox folded his arms in front of him. "So the house is alive?"

"Alive in AmI."

Maddox smiled for a second, and so did she.

"I see you like collecting swords. It's my guess you know how to use them?" He looked around.

"Maybe," she responded, smirking.

"No, you wouldn't happen to just be back here sweating, doing nothing."

"You could leave your shoes in the yard," she said. "I'll meet you in the living room in about twenty minutes or so." Nzingha then pointed to the back of the dojo. "You could use this back door. Make a left, then another left. There are two big black doors in the hallway. Entering there is the living room. Make yourself comfortable."

"Sure thing." Maddox quickly left for the living room.

Maddox found the black doors. The doors had one connecting huge round ivory doorknob. Pushing it open, he entered the colossal living room. It took Nzingha thirty minutes to join him, so he had plenty of time to snoop around.

Entering the room, Maddox saw a large rectangular black table with a four-foot silver African-style vase on each side. That looked expensive, he said to himself, as he gazed at his reflection in the jugs. Smaller white tables with lamps sat on both sides of the bigger black table. The lights brightened as he walked more into the living room.

The room had four white leather couches, all facing each other, making a perfect square. Two fluffy black pillows lay on each couch. A black table sat in the middle of these sofas with a three-foot copper statue of the Lady of Justice. An enormous chandelier hung directly over from a high ceiling.

On the left wall of the room was a twenty by twenty foot mirror with paintings on both sides about half that size. One painting was of the right side of a man's face close up. His chubby features simulating defined gray marble. The other painting was a defined depiction of the inside of a simple 1800's style kitchen. The huge photos were illuminated by lights in the ceiling. Small white futons sat beneath both paintings.

On the right of the room the ceiling was a few feet lower and had a white spiral staircase. Past the stairs he could see into the well designed and furnished lounge and dining area.

The remaining wall was of glass leading to the outside pool area. Enormous plain brown drapes covered the glass obscuring the view.

Maddox moved to the far left side of the wall with the paintings. Blue numbers and words like a hologram hovered a few inches from the wall. It read: *Food Menu* and *Music Menu*. No way, Maddox said to himself. He looked around the room to see if anybody was watching him like a child would do before doing something naughty. The truth was, he didn't want to look stupid in doing something, and it didn't work out his way. But, like magic, it did work.

He touched the music menu that hovered in front of him. The menu quickly changed into categories. *Rock, Jazz, Classical,* and *Rhythm & Blues* words appeared. Maddox scrutinized the wall behind the words, then glimpsed at the floor and ceiling. He saw no holes. He scratched his head. Where were these words emanating from? He questioned himself. He pressed jazz, then the words out of thin air changed and read: *Find by artists or song.* He smiled like a child playing with a new toy and pressed artists.

Out of about thirty jazz artists displayed, he chose, Duke Ellington's song, "Mood Indigo." The song filled the living room with its sounds. He pressed thirty percent volume and the music gave a nice background feel to the place.

"One of my favorites, too," Nzingha said, standing five feet behind Maddox with arms crossed in front of her. She startled him, and he turned around quickly.

She looked stunning, Maddox thought, even though he noticed she wasn't dressed to go outside. Her face seemed to luster; he figured she just had taken a shower. Her hair was now fresh in neat waves. She wore a white nicely fitted blouse and gray slacks with no shoes. He saw her bare feet feeling the wall to wall tan carpet.

"It's like seven o'clock." Nzingha then demanded more than asked, "Let's eat here."

"Sure."

She quickly moved to stand next to him in front of the floating menu. "Sky's the limit," she said then asked, "What do you want to eat?"

"You have any seafood?"

She touched the food menu, moving her fingers like a professional secretary at work. The menu then showed all types of seafood dish names with a clear picture of what it displayed.

"Take The A Train" then played as Maddox and Nzingha put their order into the floating computer, then together sat on the couch with the mirror behind it.

"Music," Nzingha said, loud enough for the house to hear, Maddox figured. The music changed to Beethoven. "This is AmI voice command. Already programmed to play my favorite music. Soon the food will arrive from an excellent restaurant in the area, and my butler will serve us. So, what do you think?"

"I'm impressed. This may be a little rich for most."

"No, it soon won't be. We're going to commercialize it."

"How do the words just hover in mid air? What's operating so that when you touch the words, they obey your commands?"

"That's nanotechnology and ambient intelligence at work together. There're pinholes built in the walls that access the visual and sensors. This could also be put into your television and make it three-dimensional without the glasses. This is already up and working on computers in some countries like Japan and Nigeria."

"Other countries already huh?" Maddox scratched his chin, then his eyes searched the room. "So the computer is built into the walls?"

Nzingha nodded.

"What about hackers and viruses?" Maddox asked. "If they get through, they could invade your most private endeavors. Easily control and steal from the very sanctuary of your home."

"Good question. You're right. Nothing is fail-proof. Remember what I said to you before. You could also walk around with this technology. With your cell phone or any computer online you'll be able to monitor your security system. It'll be like any other system that alerts you to viruses and such."

"Of course, you'd have the answers to all of my questions," Maddox said. "It's your baby; you built it." He showed an over-exaggerated sad face, as if he was beaten.

Nzingha smiled, showing her high cheekbones again that reminded him of peaches.

They both decided to eat in the living room when the food came. After a butler dressed in black set black trays in front of them, he served them their hot plates of food. Nzingha then excused the butler for the rest of the evening. The music then switched to Brahms, giving the atmosphere a calm, romantic feel, Maddox felt.

He ate a dish called Swordfish Milanese. It consisted of four steak-looking pieces of meat, a small portion of yellow rice, and salad. Nzingha's plate was lightly portioned with herb and spice steamed vegetables with mushroom gravy. Maddox stared at her plate, scoping what looked to him like carrots, squash, and brussel sprouts. The other stuff he couldn't make out. They also both had full glasses of water.

"I wouldn't eat that if my life depended on it," Maddox said, pointing at her food.

She looked at his food. "Likewise."

"Tell me," Maddox said, after eating a small piece of fish from his fork. "What's that?" He pointed to the distinctive copper Lady of Justice on the center table.

"It's the Lady of Justice," Nzingha responded and took a couple of bites of her food from her gold utensil.

"I see that, but why is she standing on an ancient globe map? I've never seen that before. If I had to guess, she's bringing justice to the world. Why not the new world? Why the old?"

"Very observant, Mr. Mathews. I see you're really into your art."

Nzingha took a sip of her water. "You're the head of your designing department. Art is your baby." She stayed quiet for another minute as they both ate. He looked intently at her in a way that he seriously wanted her to answer his curiosity.

"The globe is the first full world map made by a Belgium man named Abraham Ortelius," Nzingha spoke with seriousness. "The Lady of Justice's real name is Ma'at, and she's the predecessor of the Greek successor Themis the Lady of Justice that we see today, adapted by the western world. The meaning of this statue here is that the new world order is not working. It would be wise to go back to the old."

"I figured you'd have something philosophical to say."

"I figure you wanted to hear it."

Maddox laughed and Nzingha smiled as they ate more of their food.

"How much do you know about that Tai Chi stuff?" Maddox asked. "I bet you're a black belt. You're not the type to settle for anything less."

"There's no belts in this style. Simply when you're ready to do arduous things is when your ready."

"Well, how about you?"

"I do okay. I primarily use it for exercise."

Maddox made a face as if to say, yeah, right, sure you do. I'm betting you could whip somebody's ass, Maddox said to himself.

"It feels about sixty degrees in here. Is it always that cold?"

"Yes," Nzingha answered seriously. "Would you like some tea to warm yourself? I make very good herbal tea. It'll warm you right up."

"Sure, and some blankets."

He watched her gave him a smug look acknowledging his sarcasm.

She's been out to sea too much, Maddox thought. He knew he wasn't imagining things when he was on that boat. He wondered why she liked the cold. She had a philosophy to everything. He wondered what her philosophy was to that.

The classical music then changed to Mozart, and Nzingha took away the trays of finished food. Maddox then quickly dug into his left pants pocket and popped a Certs mint in his mouth. You never know, he thought. You have to always maintain good smelling breath, especially after eating. She disappeared through a hallway on the right of the living room, probably the kitchen, because she came back five minutes later with some tea.

More relaxed this time, they both again sat next to each other on the sofa. As Nzingha folded her legs underneath herself, Maddox got a good look at her fair camel-colored feet. She had beautiful toes, he thought, and pedicure clear toenails. All women should have nice feet.

He sipped the leafy tea from the yellow small bowl she handed to him. He then made a face as if to say it was good.

"The green tea leaves are straight from China, laced with a freshly squeezed lemon and some honey," Nzingha said, enlightening him.

Maddox sipped more of the hot, steamy beverage. "Okay, so besides taking over companies, you can make tea," Maddox spoke as he almost spilled his tea when she lightly kicked him in the thigh.

"What's that supposed to mean?" she asked with a smirk.

"I'm just saying . . . You're a pretty powerful woman. I mean, there's no denying that. And much deserved from your works—"

"What about you, Mr. Mathews?" Nzingha interrupted him. "You moved up fast in your company for someone hired about eight months ago, chief executive. I talked to some of your co-workers and your boss recently. They tell me you had a perfect record before they hired you. Nobody has a perfect record."

"Is that good or bad?"

"Good, if you convinced your employer and know how to continuously toil with his system. First impressions last. Bad, when they find out the method you used to obtain perfection and exploit it. You know the invisible rule. Never give them your all or expect to be used. What did you do before Alona?"

"I want to know what co-worker of mine was talking about me." Maddox speculated and took another sip of his tea before setting it down on a green saucer on the black table in front of them.

"Don't evade my question," Nzingha said still smirking. She was about to kick him again when this time he caught her foot. He didn't let go. "Did I say you could touch my foot?"

Maddox smiled. "Did I say you could kick me?" She pulled her foot back, but he held on firmly. She gawked at him with a straight face for another second before responding.

"Okay, *mi casa sue casa*. You're allowed to rub my foot while you tell me a story."

He was already rubbing her foot, feeling her tiny round toes. Still smiling, he spoke, "I guess I'll be nice."

She held a straight face as if to say *you better.*

"I used to own a chain of privately owned retail stores called M and M groceries for eight years," Maddox explained. "I also owned a couple of supply stores nationwide; you know, like merchandising warehouses. Then five years ago I met an old friend who hooked me up at a small-time company called Media Group Studio 1 also known as MGS-1. The company was about to go under. I turned it around within a year, and they made me vice president."

As Maddox told his story, Nzingha slowly and subconsciously put both her feet on his leg, and he caressed them. Her feet were smooth and perfectly shaped. He thought by far the most flawless feet he ever saw or felt, but he noticed something was strange about them. They weren't clammy, but were incredibly warm, almost hot, like heating pads. He actually liked it. Her feet were practically massaging his hands. Strange, he thought.

"What does M and M stand for?" she asked.

"It was stupid. The man who started it made up this silly slogan called, more and more. He started ordering things on the Internet and claimed the demand was so great that he had to order so much more stuff. It was to the point that the saying just stuck in his head, more and more."

"Who was the old friend? An old college friend?"

"Hey, why all the questions?" he asked surprised. "I feel like I'm being cross-examined or something." Maddox caressing moved his hands ever so meticulously from her feet to her pants.

"Maybe that's because you are." Nzingha grinned. "So who was this friend who hooked you up?"

"Peter DeLay was a top executive at the MGS-1 firm, and yes, he was an old college buddy of mine. We were always competing with each other in our younger years."

Her legs were also well shaped, stern. His hands then leisurely moved to her small precise mannequin waist.

"He must have been livid when he found out you were going to be VP?"

"Who?" Maddox moved closer toward her. His hands were slightly pulling her by the waist nearer to him. She folded her legs under her rear again and he moved in closer.

"Your friend . . ." Nzingha whispered.

Maddox didn't respond. He moved his head closer to her head, steadily. He could see the tan pin-size freckles on the bridge of her nose. Staring into her eyes, he finally defined the exact color. Of all the colors he saw in her eyes before, he now knew they were midnight-green, the darker green of the spectrum. They were dazzling, he thought. Maddox and Nzingha didn't say anything for a few seconds as the piano sounds of Mozart played on, more distinctively in Maddox's head now.

Pleasure before business, Maddox thought. Wait a second, wasn't it business before pleasure? Was he falling for this woman? She was beautiful, which made it easy for any man to give in to her. No, he couldn't give in. He couldn't give her his heart. She'd probably take it, chew it, and spit it out.

He felt there wasn't much of a future with no kids. So then you never know.

He leaned in and kissed her on the mouth for a few seconds then pulled away observing her reaction. She reacted by kissing him back on his upper lip, then smiled showing her dimples. It was like a dream come true Maddox thought as his heart raced. Her lips were warm, soft, and moist. With his right hand he felt the back of her head. Her hair felt like the softness of velvet as he slowly used his fingers to caress through the waves.

He watched Nzingha close her eyes and open his lips with hers. Slowly at first. Then they moved their heads every which way, going for a deeper, faster kiss. With his eyes closed, his other senses became keener.

Her tongue and lips still tasted like strawberries. She must have also put some kind of mint in her mouth when she went into the kitchen, Maddox thought. That meant that she wanted this to happen. Peeking, he saw that her eyes were still closed and she grabbed the front of his shirt and arms moving him closer towards her. He then found an opportunity to kiss her on the neck. Naturally, she moved her head, allowing him to do so.

Mmm . . . he said to himself. Her fragrance today was a mixture of vanilla and citrus. He wanted to bite into her soft ochre neck, but then again he noticed something strange. Her neck was practically stinging his lips. It was like touching a new hot cup of tea or coffee for the first time.

Maddox pulled away and gazed at Nzingha. No, she didn't look sick. She wasn't sweating. He felt as if she was having a fever. Nzingha opened her eyes, moving them about making a face like—what?

"You're hot."

"Thank you," she said, then smiled.

"No . . . I mean, you're burning up," Maddox said and almost laughed. "I mean, yes, you're hot, but I mean you're literally hot, like you have a fever or something. Are you okay?"

"I feel fine."

"You don't feel sick or anything? Do you?" Maddox asked, with concern in his voice.

"Well, maybe I'm a little tired," Nzingha responded and yawned. "It's been a long day. Tomorrow I have to go to another meeting. I don't mean to cut this short, but I'm going to turn in. I enjoyed our early evening together."

"Really? The night is young," Maddox said. "I'm sorry if I embarrassed you. It's just that you were so warm."

"We must talk some more, Mr. Perfect, *savior* of companies."

"Well, I had a great evening," Maddox said. "I hope we can meet like this again."

SURE YOU WOULD. The mood was gone, Nzingha contemplated. She had to end the night, but she wasn't finished with Maddox. There was a slight discrepancy in his college friend story.

She accompanied him out to the front door after retrieving his jacket and shoes. She then made sure the valet brought his car around. She told Maddox that she wanted to meet with him again for dinner sometime at the end of the week. He obliged with a cheerful yes. She lightly kissed him on the lips, and he was gone. Nzingha hoped she didn't discourage Maddox and he'd come back to her on a talking-friend level. If she was going to get into any type of serious relationship, she had to know more about Maddox Mathews.

She was fond of his smooching though. She hadn't been kissed like that in two years. It kind of sent electric currents through her. Phew! She said to herself, it's been so long she almost forgot how it actually felt.

Nzingha made more of her leafy green tea and sat again on the couch in the living room. She let the steam from the hot beverage crawl up her face as she placed the small yellow bowl to her chin. Composed, she stared into the air in deep thought as the music changed to John Field.

Nzingha had sent one of her employer friends a week ago to MGS-1 to talk to Mr. DeLay, to be a spy, so to speak. Mr. DeLay admitted going to school with Maddox, but beyond that he didn't seem to know Maddox. Maybe DeLay was angry or envious that Maddox excelled so quickly and didn't want to talk about him much. Still, she was going to investigate like she did all her would-be dates.

She had to be cautious. What was she doing anyway? Nzingha said to herself. Mixing business with pleasure was never her thing, but if she stuck by every rule, she would have never made it to where she was today.

An old boyfriend had told her that long ago. Too many rules was probably why she was by herself for so many years, though, she had to abide by some principles. I have to stand for something or I'll fall for anything. People were trying to set her up, sabotage her. There was a price to pay with great wealth. She had come this far. She was up for the challenge whatever path she chose.

She sipped her tea slowly.

CHAPTER 17

JOE AND ALLEN SAT IN FRONT of Assistant Director Kordey's office desk with open folders on their laps.

"So what do we got?" Kordey asked from behind his desk. Joe knew Kordey was talking to him, the veteran in charge.

Jacob Kordey was a tall man who wore thin slate-gray glasses on his long, shaven face. His clean-cut look matched his neat straight silver hair. He wore a blue suit and tie and, sitting behind his desk, he still towered over it. Joe saw Kordey as one of those messy organized persons.

"Nzingha Chelsea, today a self-made billionaire," Joe said, reading some things from his notes and some things he knew off the top of his head. "In 1990 was the head of a Cleveland black militant group called Crescent Enterprises. She became leader after the pending leader was assassinated. Saturday I made some calls to the Cleveland detectives on the case back then. They told me the case went cold, unsolved, but Nzingha raised great suspicion, person of interest. This, sir, was the beginning of recurring events for the misfortune of others, and fortune for the Chelsea Corporation."

Joe started late this Monday. Kordey told them he was backed up in paperwork, but he wanted to hear their case. At about nine tonight Joe collaborated with Allen on what they were going to tell their boss. Kordey then had them meet at his office at ten o'clock, here in the J. Edgar Hoover Building.

"Since 1999 the Chelsea Corporation has been growing from takeover after hostile takeover. Most seem legit, but a few are suspicious in foul play. Some witnesses came forth from the CBA International Law Firm and Ohio TV Network. They declared, before Chelsea owned them, the accidental deaths of their bosses were no accidents. In late August of this year the president of a real estate firm, Clive Inspirations, died in a boating accident. Land the company was going to purchase is now owned by the Chelsea Corporation."

Joe looked through his notes and found pictures of Mark Douglas and his friends. He laid four separated photos in front of Kordey. "These are the pictures of Mr. Douglas and his friends, drowning victims of the vessel the King. If you look closely, you can see the same pin-hole abrasions on each of them." Joe showed Kordey with the back of his pen the tiny holes on each of the victims. "This brought us to a conclusion of foul play of some sort. Though we found no drugs in the victims except that Mr. Douglas here was drunk."

"Interesting," Kordey said, as he played with a pen, twirling it between his fingers.

"A week ago we just got information from witnesses that Chelsea wants to own the Illumination Corporation. The Vice President of the company James Walsh doesn't want to sell. Well, we know what happens to executives who don't want to sell to Chelsea. They have a bit of an accident. So we're starting to see a pattern here."

"Is that the I Company that makes those commercials about electric energy?"

"The very one."

"Do you have a name yet for this case?"

"Sure do, sir," Joe said. He smiled and glanced at Allen. "After an hour of putting this case together, to present to you, Allen here actually came up with it. We're calling it Fortunes and Misfortunes."

"Good, it's done then," Kordey said as he wrote his signature on a document in front of him. "Case 12457, Fortunes and Misfortunes. Good title, young'n. It's your first one?" Joe saw that Allen knew Kordey was talking to him and Allen responded proudly.

"Yes, sir."

"Good," Kordey said. He folded his hands and looked back at Joe. "So do y'all have anything directly linking Chelsea to any of this?"

"Of course not, yet," Joe answered. "This might take some time."

"Y'all might need some informants and stuff like that, right?"

"Yes, soon," Joe said. "First I need to build evidence, research a little more." He then spoke as if he forgot to mention something. "Oh, earlier today I alerted the Buffalo PD to keep a surveillance on the Walsh home.

I don't want anything accidental to happen to our friend before I question him about anybody threatening his life and such. We're probably going up there tomorrow."

"You're going to be the lead in this, so y'all know me, whatever you need."

"Well, sir, there's one thing I might need."

Kordey spread his hands out in a gesture to say, what.

"In our science department there are some classified things on the Chelsea and Livenal Companies," Joe said. "I'd like to know about that, if you know what I mean."

"Classified?" Kordey asked, puzzled. "This case is becoming more appealing by the minute. I reckon I never heard of this female billion dollar Chelsea Company. I'll see what I could do. Y'all know, pull some strings like I do."

"Great." Joe stood, and shook Kordey's hand, and Allen did likewise. Kordey also stood and handed the four photos on his desk back to Joe.

"I'm glad you're on this case, son. What is this, your twentieth?"

"Twenty-second."

"We're getting old, son. Good luck on this one. I reckon you won't need it. Your record is flawless."

"I'll take the luck anyway, sir," Joe said and smiled.

"Be good, young'n," Kordey said, looking at Allen. "Make sure you keep this guy's record unblemished."

"Sure will, sir," Allen said before he and Joe left the office.

Joe left in good spirits. The case was fully underway. He rested for a day and a half, and Allen wore a Yale-blue suit and tie, to impress the boss, no doubt.

"Nice suit," Joe said to Allen as they walked down a long white hallway on their way to exit the building. Allen responded by smiling and putting on his Versace shades. It was his way of telling him, *whatever, man.* "We were so busy preparing our case I forgot to ask how your anniversary went."

"It was good. She took me out to this expensive restaurant, then we went to an AC\DC concert. Johnson rocked!"

"I personally like Bon's, but Johnson's okay."

"Yeah, and what do you know, geezer?"

"I was young once. That group goes back since 1973."

"Yeah, I guess you'd know then," Allen said as they both laughed.

SHE HAD WAITED LONG ENOUGH. It had been an hour already, and finally Mr. and Mrs. Walsh came home. Her mission now was estimated, thirty minutes. She had premeditated it three weeks ago. Three weeks ago she studied Mr. Walsh's movements on where he worked and hung-out. She read some things about him on the Internet, and she seldom liked to read.

She found out Walsh worked at the I Command Center in Western Buffalo-Niagara Falls Metropolitan Area. He would take a thirty minute drive to his home every day to the suburbs of Southtown. On the weekends he'd play bridge in the city and golf nearer to home. She also found out he attended a lot of empowerment seminars around the country and business meetings.

Two weeks ago she actually kept him under surveillance. Sometimes she simply walked behind him and his friends or spotted him from afar with powerful ultra-bright marine binoculars.

She found a great deal more about Walsh stalking him than reading about him. He was fifty years old, no children, and his young twenty-eight-year-old wife, always complaining, was an unsightly looking individual, in Suraksha's opinion.

When she peered into their house she heard Walsh quarreling with his wife many times and saw him belt her. Once last week Mrs. Walsh must have called the police. The Buffalo PD came and went in twenty minutes. They did nothing. This could have been an occurring thing or the first time, but nothing came out of it. She must not have pressed charges—Mr. Walsh was rich. Mrs. Walsh who was young, no doubt wasn't going anywhere.

Suraksha had broken into the Walsh two floor million-dollar home through the back door and circumvented the security system a couple of times last week, then studied the house. She surveyed the beautifully decorated rooms, garage, and foyer, not for its splendor but for familiarity. She was a predator, an invader, and she wasn't going to make the mistake again of gloating at the beauty of things as she did when she was under the sea.

She found some guns set neatly in a case on the wall in the study area. Perfect, Suraksha said to herself. This was going to fit into her designed plan of Mr. Walsh killing Mrs. Walsh, then he's going to commit suicide.

Today Suraksha had already snuck in the back door as she did before. She bypassed the Shield home security and picked the lock again, then locked it behind her. Of the six brand new hand guns in the case, she had already grabbed the Smith and Wesson. She had already placed bullets in the gun. She was already upstairs in the master bedroom where she was going to make her move.

Today she was dressed in a black jogging suit with gloves and made sure some bamboo blades were secure in her sleeves. You never know, she said to herself, things could go wrong. They were her back up.

This time she brought along a black ski-mask. On many of her assignments she never needed one because most of the time when her victims saw her face, they died. Though her new victims were about to receive the same fate, it was still a somewhat pedestrian area. Someone in this little town might recognize her face if she had to flee.

Her hair was neatly in a firm bun which made it easy for her to slip on the ski-mask. She glanced at the two watches on her wrist. It was 11:15 in the night. Finally her targets were home. Patient. Calculated. She was on a schedule, as usual. Time was her everything.

The Walshs had three cars. The chrome BMW was the car they usually paired up in and left together to the dinner. That car just turned onto the driveway. The Jaguar, Mr. Walsh's car, was already in the lot. The Audi A5 that belonged to Mrs. Walsh wasn't there. Possibly it was in the shop or at a friend's house, Suraksha thought.

Today the Walshs were coming back from a beneficial dinner, celebrating the fiftieth anniversary to an administrator who had been with the I Company that long.

Suraksha stood by the red curtain and blind window in the master bedroom waiting for her victims to arrive. She could hear the front door open and close. A voice followed. It was Mrs. Walsh's voice. She was rambling on about something Suraksha couldn't make out.

Closer now, Mrs. Walsh was climbing the stairs. Suraksha sensed not so much that something was wrong, but something was out of place. She perceived two footsteps instead of four. Mrs. Walsh had to be on her cell phone. She was saying things like, "Yeah, yeah, I like that, too. It was a beautiful night, especially when Roy almost fell into the cake." Then a laugh followed.

Did Mrs. Walsh come from the dinner by herself? Did Mr. Walsh walk off to another part of the house instead of following his wife upstairs as he always did? Suraksha thought. She also knew it didn't matter. The victims were going to meet their fate. This also had to go in a timely fashion. Time now, three minutes into the mission.

Closer, Mrs. Walsh finally made it to the top of the stairs and down the hall to the master bedroom.

Suraksha saw that, without much thought, Mrs. Walsh turned on the light to the room. She then punched Mrs. Walsh in the mouth. She fell to the floor, and Suraksha turned the light off.

Suraksha noticed Mrs. Walsh was in a red Betsey Johnson ruffle dress, and her small red purse and cell phone dropped on the brown rug without a sound.

Suraksha straddled Mrs. Walsh and grabbed her by the throat with one hand. She could see Walsh's bottom lip was bleeding as she squeezed her windpipe just enough for Walsh to answer questions.

"Where's your husband?" Suraksha inquired, purposely making her voice deep. Suraksha could tell her voice was frightening to Mrs. Walsh, who shuddered when she uttered the words, besides the fact that she was totally caught off guard. Suraksha could also tell Mrs. Walsh's adrenalin was pumping from this surprised home invasion. Her own adrenalin, on the other hand, wasn't high, for she had done this many times. She was calm, always thinking. This mission had to end in twenty-five minutes.

"What? What do you mean? What do you want?" Mrs. Walsh asked, pleading.

Suraksha smacked Walsh across the face, making her nose bleed.

"Where's your husband?" Suraksha asked, in the same calm tone as before.

"He . . . He's . . . He's coming up now. You better get outta here!"

Suraksha released her strangle-hold on Mrs. Walsh and picked up her phone on the floor. A female voice on the phone, like a broken record, kept saying. "Hello? Hello? Barbara, are you there? Hello? Hello?" Suraksha pressed *end* on the cell phone, broke it in half, then dropped it back onto the carpet.

To Suraksha's surprise, Mrs. Walsh pushed her off, jumped from the floor, and took a chance for the bedroom door. After Suraksha rolled off to the side, she effortlessly grabbed Walsh's long blonde hair and dropped her back onto the floor. Mrs. Walsh screeched at the top of her lungs. Suraksha cuffed her again across her right cheek, cutting her shriek short.

"Where in the house is your husband?" Suraksha asked calmly.

"He's . . . He's . . ." Mrs. Walsh began to cry and tremble in fear as she held the tender red right side of her face.

"DID YOU SEE THAT?" Officer Terrence Cohen asked and then took another bite out of his hero ham sandwich.

Terrence and his partner Michael sat in their white squad car for only six minutes now. The Chief called them out here a half hour ago, but he had to go to the deli first. He was hungry; he hadn't eaten since breakfast.

"It looks like someone grabbed for the blinds and was snatched violently back," Terrence said. "On the second floor." He stared again out the passenger-side windshield, from the driver's seat.

They were parked across the street a half block from the Walsh home. With a perfect view of the house on their right, Michael looked up at the second floor. Terrence looking again, now viewed a piece of blind out of place, and his partner saw it, too.

"Let's check it out," Michael demanded more than asked and unlocked his door.

"Hey! Wait a minute! Can I finish my sandwich first?" Terrence asked, somewhat frustrated, but knew his partner wasn't trying to hear him.

"Come on, man, let's do this. You said you saw something, and we already got here late." His partner was out of the car now.

"Damn!" Terrence said out loud and folded his half-eaten sandwich back in its wrapper. "They're probably up there having sex or something." After laying his sandwich on his seat, he climbed out of the car. He wiped his hands together and crumbs fell onto the street.

"Or he could be beating her again," Michael suggested.

Terrence glanced at him in a peculiar manner as if to say *not again*.

The street of the Walsh home on both sides had five other exclusive houses a block from each other. Enough trees lined the sidewalk, and parked cars were about so that their police car was obscured, Terrence thought. Their car wouldn't stand out. The night and not a lot of streetlamps definitely helped, though he wished he'd parked closer, so when this false alarm becomes a false alarm, he could get back and eat his sandwich.

Soon, as they walked on the attractively paved crimson brick pathway to the front patio, the Walsh estate, headlights almost blinded them. A red Audi cruised the street, then came to a stop in the driveway behind the BMW.

The engine purred off and headlights gradually joined the darkness. Even in the dark, Terrence could see it was Mr. Walsh who stepped out the car. Mr. Walsh, dangling his keys about, shouted, "What can I do for the boys in blue tonight?"

"Ah, nothing," Terrence spoke quickly. "Just checking the houses in the neighborhood. Making sure everything's safe." He then whispered to his partner. "He's definitely not beating her."

"They're definitely not having sex," Michael whispered back.

"We saw something suspicious in the upstairs window, so we just came to check it out," Terrence continued talking to Mr. Walsh. "You know, make sure everything's okay."

Mr. Walsh was a tall man, black hair, blue eyes, and wore his royal-blue three-piece suit perfectly. Someone could have easily mistaken him for President George H. W. Bush in his younger years.

"I assure you everything should be fine," Mr. Walsh said, now standing in front of them. "That's probably my wife who came home before me."

"Did your wife come home with someone?" Terrence asked.

"Not to my knowledge. Why? Did you see two people enter the house?"

"No. We weren't here when she arrived."

Then Terrence contemplated Mrs. Walsh was cheating on her husband, but hoped he was wrong. He didn't want to deal with this now, because he was so hungry. "Um, I'd like to stick around for a second just to make sure everything's okay?" Terrence inquired more than demanded.

"Sure," Mr. Walsh said. He fumbled for the right key to his front door. As they walked to the patio, Mr. Walsh spoke, "We were just coming back from a dinner celebration, and I had to drive some friends home. A friend was holding my wife's car so why not pick it up now, then my wife said she was tired, so she came home a little earlier." He smiled as he went on. "She's not into these types of dinners and such, so she begged me to let her drive home by herself without me tailing. I never let her drive by herself. But, hey, I did drag her with me to this. She was good to me tonight, so I said why not." Mr. Walsh opened the door and yelled, "Honey, honey."

Terrence glanced at his partner in a way to say, here goes nothing. Michael sighed, took his hat off, and stepped into the house after Mr. Walsh.

DAMN! SHIT! She cursed over and over in her head. She hated abandoning a mission. Time now was 11:30. She got all the information from Mrs. Walsh that she was going to get before she had to knock her out. Mrs. Walsh attempted to evade her again by reaching for the window, but failed.

Suraksha remembered the last time this happened. About six years earlier she had to ditch a mission she did in Nigeria. The assignment was carefully conspired, but at the last moment of initiating it, it was canceled. It would have worked beautifully, too. Never did she have to stop in the middle like this. Someone had to have known about this or was just damn good in hunches. Although, this could have been a fluke.

As she walked down the main stairs to leave the house, the lights turned on, washing her in brightness. Mr. Walsh and two young looking cops no more than in their late twenties blocked her way. To leave, through the back door, she had to walk around the stairs, exposing her to the front.

"Honey . . . Honey, are you up—" Mr. Walsh's shouts were cut in half, and his jaw dropped when he saw her.

They didn't have time to react. Suraksha was way too fast. They were stunned that she nonchalantly but briskly walked up to them. It was as if she was comfortable and knew the house. It was as if she'd been through this dance before. It was as if she said, *here I am, come take me if you dare.*

"What type of home invasion is—" Mr. Walsh said, but was quickly cut off with a straight kick to the face.

"Stop! Get down on the—" the cop who seemed the lead said, and he also got a swift kick in the face. As the first two men fell, the youngest officer managed to release his gun, but to no triumph. She twisted his right shooting arm, and they both watched the Glock pistol fall into her hands. She quickly flipped the gun in her hands so that the handle was sticking out and hit him across the temple with it. He fell like a sack of potatoes to the floor.

She also hit the cop she attacked first with the butt of the gun across the temple, for he was still moaning on the clean fresh brown carpet. Suraksha then dropped the second officer's gun by his still body sprawled on the floor.

Leisurely, she walked into the study area, emptied the bullets from the Smith and Wesson and put them in her pocket. Neatly she put the gun back in its case. She walked out the back door and locked it again from where she came. She then jogged three blocks down a bushy back rode to astride her ride, a black Ducati Desmosedici.

Time now 11:35, her assignment was stopped in full flow. Mission failed. Though she devastated everyone in the house, including those amateur blue clothed police, she wasn't angry at them. She was furious at whoever fouled the hit. Someone in Nigeria was going to be pissed when she had to report back to her contact. Who made those cops come to the house tonight? Was her connection trying to set her up? No, they wouldn't have brought such amateurs. Someone just had a damn good hunch that Mr. Walsh might be in danger or there was a hiccup in her timing.

TUESDAY LATE AFTERNOON CAME FAST, Joe felt, as he sat in the extravagant dining room of the Walsh estate. It took seven hours of driving to get here, but he wasn't tired.

He got the call last night about the break-in and couldn't sleep since. He tossed and turned all night in anticipation of this meeting. They were going to interview the first eyewitnesses to this phantom assassinator and possibly the same one who killed Mark Douglas and his colleagues. They left eight o'clock in the morning to make it here by three o'clock to a four o'clock meeting, as promised.

All the way to Buffalo he and Allen evaluated the investigation again. This was sure to be a breakthrough. He was also sure about one thing, and that was that Mr. and Mrs. Walsh were going to need around the clock protection.

Everyone decided to meet here at the Walsh home, including the officers who were attacked. They sat around the dining table.

"I heard from the authorities, you guys got pretty banged up and checked into a hospital last night," Joe spoke. "I'm happy everyone made it out okay," He sat at the front of table with pad and pen out. "To capture this assailant, we're going to need a bit of information." He then looked at Mrs. Walsh. "The best as you can, can you describe your attacker?"

Mrs. Walsh was dressed in shorts and t-shirt covered in a loosely fitted huge purple and red bathrobe. She sat on Mr. Walsh's lap with a face as if she had just finished crying. Her arms were wrapped around his neck holding on for dear life. Her head and jaw was swollen and bottom lip was cut. She looked as if she hadn't had sleep for days.

"I'm sure the attacker was a she," Mrs. Walsh spoke. "She had a deep voice. A chilling deep voice. She was dressed in a jogging suit, all in black, gloves and ski-mask, and kept asking where my husband was."

"You guys concur with that description?" Joe asked any one of the officers on the left side of the table.

Officer Terrence Cohen, plain clothed, wearing blue jeans and a heavy gray sweater, seemed the lead to his partner Michael Sachs. Michael also wore blue jeans, but a black sweater. Terrence had knots on his head and black and blue marks around his eyes and nose, and Michael's right arm was in a sling and his head also had some protuberances.

"Yes, we do," Terrence spoke. "She was skilled. She knew some good karate and all that stuff."

Mr. Walsh and Michael nodded.

"This one unarmed woman took out three men, two of whom were armed," Joe stated. "This was definitely a professional hit."

"Apparently so," Terrence said, and the three men chuckled. "She could have easily killed us, but she didn't."

"I had a feeling she knew my house well," Mr. Walsh said, dressed in black shirt and white khaki pants. He had a bandage around his nose and right eye was black and blue.

"How so?" Joe asked.

"I don't know exactly. It was the way she moved down the stairs toward us, I suppose—without hesitation. It's just the feeling I had."

"How tall was she? What was her build?" Allen asked. Today he was dressed in black suit and tie. Finally, Joe said to himself, Allen is dressing like a fed. But he was sure it was just momentarily.

"She was about the size of my sister, five-six, average build," Terrence answered. "Not fat or skinny. In pretty good shape, of course." The guys chuckled again.

"Can you remember if she said anything else?" Allen asked, scanning the officers, then Mrs. Walsh.

"No, she didn't say anything to us," Terrence confirmed.

"She just kept saying over and over again . . ." Mrs. Walsh blurred out. "Where's your husband, where's your husband?"

"Okay then," Joe said, looking at everyone. "Today I'm going to order the Buffalo Crime Scene Investigation Unit to dust for fingerprints in specific places. I know she was wearing gloves, but you never know. I'm also going to order round the clock surveillance for you and your wife." Joe looked directly at Mr. Walsh. "Some agents should be here in an hour or so, so I wouldn't go anywhere yet."

"I'm not going anywhere now," Mr. Walsh said, and he gave his wife a hug.

"Do you know anybody who might want to harm or threaten you, Mr. Walsh?" Joe asked. "Like someone in your company who's jealous, a family member, another company?"

"Well, there's my Cousin George," Mr. Walsh said dryly and smirked. "No, just kidding. There's really nobody I can think of at the moment."

"How many other people know about this incident?"

"I'm not going to lie. Just about everybody at the company. It's already in the Buffalo press. I don't know about major news stations yet."

"It's alright, they know little at this point, but it might rattle some cages." Joe glanced at the two officers. "I don't mean to be rude, but I'd like to talk to the Walshs in private."

"Not a problem," Terrence said.

Joe shook the officer's hands. "After all that's happen, thanks for meeting like this so soon, guys."

"Thanks," Mr. Walsh said to the officers, and they all shook hands and nodded.

"Can I get your numbers in case we need anything else?" Allen asked.

"Sure," Michael and Terrence said, and they both uttered their numbers as Allen wrote it in his E-Keeper pad.

Mr. Walsh saw the men out, then sat next to his wife again in the dining room.

"I know you're aware of the company called Chelsea?" Joe inquired, staring at Mr. Walsh.

"I am."

"We're investigating and have reason and suspicion that the Chelsea Cooperation is assassinating top executives in companies of interest."

"Really?" Mr. Walsh said, in a tone of resentment. His wife began to cry, and she laid her head on his shoulder. "A couple of weeks ago, or sometime at the beginning of this month, *Businessweek* published some stuff I said about this company. I practically called the Chelsea Company incompetent. I didn't know by saying this, I was playing with my life."

"Someone in Chelsea might be killing high executives who don't want to sell," Joe said, "but we don't have conclusive evidence yet. I wanted to personally tell you and your wife about this, so that you're aware that you might have another company out for your blood, in the literal sense."

"I knew that company was growing too rapidly in this weak economy," Mr. Walsh said, balling up a fist.

"Remaining subtle about this for now would be appreciated. So going around saying that the Chelsea Company wants to eliminate you wouldn't be to forthcoming."

"What do you mean, using us as bait would?"

"No," Joe responded quickly. "I want whoever is doing this to think we're off balance. Blaming anyone would also do us justice.

"Two scenarios present themselves here. One, the assassin might move on to another target that would be beneficial to the Chelsea Company, strengthening our case. Two, the assassin might make another attempt on your life, but we'll be right there when it happens."

"The number two scenario sounds like a worst case scenario," Mr. Walsh said, with a matter-a-fact face of nervousness.

After Joe assured the Walshs again that they were going to be safe, he sat in his Lexus LS with Allen. His car was parked on the street in front of the Walsh house. He promised them that he wasn't going anywhere until the FBI surveillance team arrived.

"So what do you think, sport?" Joe asked Allen.

Allen sighed before responding. "We might need an informant."

"Might? We will."

"We should have a four-month surveillance on Mr. Walsh. Interview low level people in the Chelsea Company here and there. You know, trouble Chelsea slightly. Like you said, rattle the cage a little."

"I like your style, kid," Joe said, smiling. "You might make a lead agent yet."

CHAPTER 18

MADDOX GOT A CALL FROM NZINGHA, sensing worry in her voice. She asked, was he staying with anyone this Thanksgiving. His answer was no, then he found himself here at the Marriott Hotel on Lexington Avenue on the eastside, 49th Street.

She explained to him over the phone that she was in Manhattan for three days, this Thursday being the second day. Yesterday already and tomorrow she had business with Alona. She said she was lonely and wanted him to accompany her for dinner at nine o'clock on the top floor of the hotel. He felt her solitude, for he was a bit of a loner himself.

He made it there nine o'clock sharp in light-blue shirt, black tie, blazer, and slacks. On the thirty second floor, the reservations-only, jacket-required Le Bon restaurant was where she said it would be.

Le Bon, in neon red scripted letters hanging over two huge glass doors was what Maddox saw as soon as he got off the elevator. He opened one of the doors and entered an almost pitch black world. Right away he saw the maitre d', a tall elder man with white beard and white suit.

"Good evening, sir, and welcome to Le Bon," the maitre d' said in a deep voice behind a white podium. "Reservations for . . ."

"That would be for Nzingha," Maddox said.

The man adjusted his bifocals and scrutinized a list on a clipboard in front of him. The maitre d' had to also use the small gold lamp built into the stand.

"Ah, yes, here it is, Ms. Nzingha Chelsea." He looked up from the clipboard. "I don't believe she's arrived yet. Do you care to wait here?"

"Sure, sure," Maddox said, and nervously crossed his arms and stood off to the side.

Nzingha talked to him cagily over the phone. He wondered what she was up to now. It was almost as if she needed to talk to him. He moved out of the way as a young couple walked to the maitre d'. They were laughing, breaking Maddox's concentration, both handsomely dressed and full of cologne and perfume. The host saw them in after finding their names on the list.

Then he saw Nzingha come from the elevator and walk toward the Le Bon. He'd never seen her so stunning. Two things flashed in his head. One, he felt he wasn't worthy to walk around with such beauty. The other, he was the lucky man tonight.

Nzingha wore a tan Patagonia Eva Luna dress. It was a long sleeve deep V-neck dress that tucked at her shoulders and bosom. It had a split in the front and draped more in the back, exposing her clear tan legs now and then as she strutted. She also wore tan open-toe high heel shoes, held a tiny purse, and her short black, and brown highlighted hair didn't move a bit out of place.

Maddox held the door open as she walked into the restaurant. She quickly with one hand feeling his bicep held under his right arm as if she was trying to hold herself up.

"You absolutely look beautiful," Maddox said, inspecting her face and noticing her highlighted ochre eyelids and mahogany lips.

"Thank you," she said, as the maitre d' came back to his post.

"Ms. Chelsea, you've arrived and guest," said the maitre d'. "Please, follow me."

Maddox glimpsed at the old man, smiling at Nzingha as he led them deeper into the diner.

The restaurant took up half of the top floor, making it larger than Maddox had thought. There were twenty-five well dressed white tables evenly spread out across a brown and white spherical marble floor. Though the lights in the round dome ceiling were dull, his eyes adjusted.

A huge black round table sat in the center of the restaurant full of yellow marigold and white tulip flowers. Directly above was an enormous painting of Sappho and Phaon, the legendary Greek poetess Sappho and her lover Phaon. Maddox knew the artist, Jacques David.

The host led them to a table for two near the window and spread his hands out for them to sit. "Please enjoy."

As the host left, Maddox pulled Nzingha's chair out for her to sit. As she sat, he noticed today she was an inch taller and wore a new perfume that smelled sweet and possibly to the taste, tangy.

When he sat across from Nzingha they placed white napkins on their laps. A young waitress in a white suit skirt approached them right away. She handed them both a menu and introduced herself.

"Hello, I'm Kelly. Welcome to La Bon. I'll be your personal waitress this evening. Would you like a cocktail to start?"

"Green tea, please," Nzingha answered.

"I'll start with a Chardonnay," Maddox replied. As the waitress left, Maddox looked around and noticed most of the tables were occupied with couples and businessmen. Beyond the open white draped vast window he was washed in the skyline lights of midtown Manhattan buildings. Soft Jazz played. Nice, Maddox thought. The place must be new. He'd never seen this on top of the Marriott before.

"Nice," Maddox said. "I've been to the concierge deck but I don't believe I've been here."

"First time for everything," Nzingha said.

"Yeah, and the first time I've seen you wear make-up. What are those?" Maddox leaned over and observed Nzingha's ears. He saw that she wore small square gold earrings.

The waitress came back with their drinks.

"Thank you," Maddox and Nzingha replied.

"When you're ready, just raise your hand," the waitress said and walked by the flower table in the center of the restaurant. A few waiters stood there waiting on other tables.

Quietly they stared at the menu for three minutes. Maddox nodded toward Nzingha for if she was ready to order. She was ready, and he waved the waitress over. He ordered a meal called La Poitrine de Poulet Cordon bleu, and Nzingha ordered a crudités platter. The waitress took their menus and left again, promising their meals when she was to return.

"I definitely wanted to see you again," Maddox said with a smirk. "I'd like to believe you wanted to see, me, too. This time I sense you really wanted to see me. Anything wrong?"

Nzingha sipped some of her tea from a white cup before she responded. "I remember once someone came to me and asked, did they look how they sound on the phone. I responded that they were handsome. You're handsome Maddox, in appearance and intellect. I know how you see me. How do you think people perceive me?"

Maddox took a sip of his white wine in his half full wine glass. He didn't like that she evaded his question of her push to see him this evening. It made him feel as though she was hiding something. Something big.

"Obviously, people perceive you as a resilient corporate woman whose private life is enclosed in mystery. Like, what family setting did you have? What type of recreation do you like? I recently read in *Forbes* that you were an orphan who grew up in Ohio. That must be interesting. You attained a career specific scholarship and graduated with a masters in business administration, arts, and science from MIT at seventeen. I know you were given a large sum of money when you were younger. I wonder if you wonder who's your real family? I think that's what people want to know."

"I don't know why. I find other people more interesting. Like you, Mr. Mathews. What do you like? What are your interest and motives?"

"Nobody cares. I'm not as rich or smart as you."

"Then maybe you want to know these things about me?"

"I might. It would be nice to know."

Nzingha slowly sipped more of her tea and smiled before speaking. It was a warm smile. "The truth is, when people look at me, they think I'm on the arm of some rich tycoon. They wonder why I'm getting on a private plane by myself or in the front row of a basketball game all the time. I must be an R & B singer or something.

"Then, to move on to my private life, I believe in courting nowadays only for the sole purpose of getting married. Not many guys like that true commitment. Usually when men find out my wealth, they're intimidated.

"To sum this all up, when people find out your private life, that's when the scandals come out, then the media tells you how to live your life."

"True, very true. Oh, um, not to change the subject, but I heard you visited Alona yesterday. How was it?"

"Yes, I did. It went well. That was the first time I was in your building. I gave a speech on the finalization of the merger and how my company is going to take everyone to the next level. Like the rise in our stocks. We talked about how to run a clean and respectable, but flourishing, business in an immoral world."

"Yeah, well, I never knew business today to be moral," Maddox said, then sipped more of his wine. "That's going to be a hard task."

"Are you a God-fearing man, Mr. Mathews?"

"I would say that I am."

"I absolutely don't believe a conscious God in any way is helping humans in the strives of life. I do believe, though, in an intelligent being that continues to breed life, but then stepped aside. Humans then created rules to govern themselves to survive. This concept, a ploy of survival of the fittest, one must master. That's my God. That's pure. That's moral. That's business."

"Stay within the rules, in the game of business and life," Maddox said. "That's an interesting concept, but I think I'm going to stick with God."

The waitress approached their table balancing two large hot plates of food.

Maddox had pieces of chicken breast stuffed with ham and cheese on his plate. Nzingha had small portions of steamed raw asparagus, carrots, broccoli, mushrooms, and snow peas. Nasty, Maddox said to himself, but healthy. He guessed it was her way of staying within one of the rules of life.

"Would you like more to drink or a different beverage?" the waitress asked, smiling from cheek to cheek.

"Some water, please," Nzingha replied.

Maddox raised his glass and nodded at the waitress. The waitress nodded and said happily, "Sure."

Maddox and Nzingha ate silently for two minutes until the waitress came back. Managing a pitcher of water, ice, and a bottle of Chardonnay, the waitress poured their drinks. "Anything else?" the waitress asked. Maddox glanced at Nzingha. She shook her head no.

"That'll be all, thank you," Maddox replied. The waitress left. Maddox and Nzingha ate a little more before Nzingha broke the silence.

"I do have a couple of important things to talk to you about."

I knew it, Maddox shouted in his head, and he listened closely between bites of his chicken.

"There have been rumors floating around my company that we're killing off our opposition to advance our cause of making more money."

"What do you mean by killing off?" Maddox asked innocently. "Isn't that good news?"

"No," Nzingha said, and she smiled, for he sensed she caught his naïve understanding of the matter. "They're saying I'm literally murdering my competitors so that I'll advance in owning land and takeovers."

"Really!" Maddox said, surprised. So this was why he sensed tension in her voice on the phone. "Who's saying these things?"

"It hasn't hit the media yet," Nzingha said, staring at her half-eaten plate. "But it will." She then looked up from her plate and directly at him before reverberating, "the FBI."

"How do you know this?"

"I have my sources."

"How did this come about?"

"To make a long story short . . ." She drank some of her water before she went on. "I'm a woman, strike one. I'm a woman of color, strike two. I'm immensely successful, strike three. Someone has breached my main headquarters in Ohio and has stolen classified files. I don't know how long this professional phantom has been doing this, but clearly someone is setting me up. Our very government or some secret organization is slowly trying to discredit my company.

"Someone powerful is trying to dismantle my passion for righteous aptitude. But I'll not falter. I'll not bend. I love the truth, Maddox, and love makes the wildest spirit tame and the tamest spirit wild."

"So how are you going to handle this?"

"For starters, truth will prevail. There're adversaries about-externally and internally that I feel are trying to bring me down. I had faith and trust in a person once, but I fear it's been shaken." Nzingha frowned at him with eyes that read suspicion. She glared at him for a few seconds in silence. Maddox, for that moment, figured out why she was staring at him.

She didn't trust him. She had her qualms about him that he himself was setting her up, an informant if you will, he thought. Her eyes turned black with—he almost sensed hostility in Nzingha for the first time. He was the betrayer.

"What are you trying to say?" Maddox said with a tense smirk.

"Your friend Mr. DeLay and yourself attended Columbia and graduated with a masters degree in nineteen-ninety, is that correct?" Nzingha asked, her stare not wavering.

"Yes, but where are you going with this?" Maddox stopped eating now. He lost his appetite. He felt her interrogation was unnecessary, and she was becoming paranoid, though he couldn't blame her. In her position she probably felt enemies everywhere.

She ignored his question and pressed on. "I found your photo online in the Columbia yearbook of nineteen-ninety. Nice picture, by the way." Nzingha paused for him to respond with a natural thank you, but he didn't react. "Anyway, actual textbook photo albums don't lie."

"What do you mean?"

"Other people graduated in ninety, Maddox, and your picture is neither in their graduation book photos nor your name on the list that you even attended the school. Interesting, don't you think?"

"You don't trust anybody, huh? Do you investigate all your friends?" Maddox stared hard at Nzingha. Nzingha blinked a couple of times, but remained silent. "Okay, I have a small confession to make." He drank the rest of his wine. "I look like a nerd in those days, so I never bothered to take a graduation photo. Later on, I fixed it online. My birth name is Mathew Mathews. I never liked that name. I have my graduation diploma. Would you like to see that? There. Now, you exposed my secret that I've been trying to hide for years."

"I don't believe you, *Mathew Mathews*," Nzingha pronounced his name sarcastically. The waitress came back with a bottle of wine and pitcher of water. Maddox nodded, and the waitress filled his wine glass again. She poured more water into Nzingha's glass, then left. "I don't believe you look like a nerd then or now," Nzingha continued, then gave an anxious smile. She ate more of her food, then wiped the corners of her mouth with her napkin.

"You're cautious, no doubt," Maddox said. "I like that."

"If you're an informant, I'm guiltless of any human beings' untimely fatality. I run a clean and respectable business. I'll fight for the truth like the ancients. First with arrows, then with chariots and spears. Then if that fails, we'll fight close up with swords and daggers."

"I'm no informant. I must say, though, you're . . . interesting."

"I think I like you, Maddox, but then I don't know." Nzingha sipped some of her water. She looked down at her plate as if she lost her hunger, as if she lost a friend.

Maddox leaned across the table and lifted her head with his hand, touching the bottom of her chin.

"I like you, too. I always liked you." Maddox inclined more across the table and lightly kissed her on the lips.

Nzingha never closed her eyes or puckered up when he kissed her, but she didn't pull away. She then looked back down at her plate beaming, showing her dimples.

"That kiss was like a polygraph test," she said. "I detect you're hiding something more, Maddox. I don't know what it is. It's just how I feel."

"I'm sorry, and deeply hurt you feel that way."

"If I'm to trust you," Nzingha said, "and you want to know about me, we first have to start with our names."

"You're right, and I'm sorry."

"I have a collection at home of religious artifacts I'd like to show you. It's some art that might be interesting to you."

"I'd like to take a look at it."

"I don't know *Mathew Mathews*, it's hard to trust people these days."

"Please, Maddox," Maddox insisted. "Call me Maddox."

Maddox all of a sudden had the sense of an epiphany. The whole meaning on why Nzingha wanted to see him was to question him. Some kind of dreadful events were taking place in her company or about to take place, and she was suspicious of everyone. He guessed she very well should be.

He tried to talk to her more about the FBI probing her company, but she refused to talk about it. He felt the evening went sour after the interrogation. He had the strangest feeling their already short relationship was getting shorter.

Then again, what the hell was he thinking about in dating such a powerful woman? Nzingha Chelsea was no feeble woman in any way or form. She was actually quite complicated, but well rounded and dignified. He couldn't say he had met many women like her.

He was glad he kissed her again, even though she seemed to have no affection toward the act. Maybe she never had any feelings for him? Maybe she just flat out was using him? He felt a bit sad inside that she had no feelings. Maybe she never had feelings for anybody. It was because of her position and line of work, he came to realize the reason of her lack of sensibility, though he felt he always knew this. At least he got to kiss those soft full lips, one last time.

CHAPTER 19

HE WAS USED TO THE COLD of Washington DC around now, the second week of December. He didn't complain that the temperature here, which was far from home was in the high sixties, and it was around eleven o'clock in the morning, almost noon. The U.S. Bank Tower loomed over the many large skyscrapers of the Financial District of downtown Los Angeles. He couldn't remember the last time he'd been in Los Angeles, California, the second largest city in the United States. It was probably when he was on some case early on in his career.

Joe followed his surveillance team who flew out here trailing Mr. Walsh to California. Today Mr. Walsh was giving an important speech about his company's goals in future energy. It was to take place in the forty story I Building on Wilshire Boulevard.

The FBI surveyed the Walshs for three weeks, but Joe and Allen didn't join them, too boring. Watching them go in and out of the house, visit relatives, friends, and know their recreation and work schedules was a thing for the rookies. What made him and his partner fly out to this event was the magnitude of it.

Invited to the lecture were big company executives of Basin Power from North Dakota, Power Electric from Utah, and Dominion Electric from Virginia. The media was going to be there in full force, so Joe figured he shouldn't miss all the hoopla and excitement. Joe read in the *Los Angeles Times* that this meeting was talked about all week. One of his agents also informed him on the chitchat the journalists were conjuring up. *The Investor's Business Daily* had a small article yesterday titled, "I Invites All the Big Shots but Chelsea Not Invited."

Joe again briefed the five agents who worked with him on how they were going to protect Walsh as he entered, delivered his speech, and departed the building.

In a four-star hotel called LA Luxurious, Jo and Allen resided in a suite across from an executive double suite where Mr. Walsh was preparing his speech. This hotel was seven blocks from the I building. Nobody, and especially the press, knew he was here. There was a huge well known hotel across from the I building called the Wilshire Grand Hotel which would have been easer to work from, but not safer.

Joe wore his usual blue suit, as did the rest of the agents. Allen wore a dark gray suit, out of character as usual, Joe thought. They had argued earlier in the day about what to wear. Joe said, "look, everyone is wearing the same thing to blend in with the crowd that's sure to be there."

Allen retorted, "Please, we stand out. We look like a bunch of secret service men." Then Allen not only put on the gray suit, he put on a dark blue tie and shades. "Hey, it's California."

Joe tightened his lips and gave him a look that it wasn't funny. The kid's a glittering, blind target. He was going to get himself—he didn't want to think about it. Joe let it pass. I have this case to solve and a man to protect. I guess I have to let these petty things out of my head.

They went over the formalities of their soon executed task. In his room, Joe spoke to field agents David, Lisa, Glenn, George, and Carlos. He spoke about why they were here today.

"Reviewing our purpose, the Chelsea Corporation is hiring assassins to murder important executives in companies of interest for financial gain and development. There's little evidence of this, but much motive. So far the assassin or assassins have been elusive. We examined video surveillance on our possible first victims and fingerprints of the last surviving victims, the Walsh incident, and have come up with nothing." He handed each of them manila folders labeled, Case File: Fortunes & Misfortunes.

"Take this and look it over again, if you will. The little evidence that we do have is matching prick marks on the Mark Douglas incident victims and the masked attacker at the Walsh residence. The attacker, of course, failed, but wasn't caught, so the Walshs are on a twenty-four hour watch every day.

"Though we've not yet spoken to anyone at Chelsea, the small press in Buffalo, has taken it upon themselves to say we're investigating foul play amongst the two companies. And, of course, it's reached here in LA."

NOON HAD COME, and the Walsh entourage was ready to move for the one o'clock speech. Joe had also briefed the navy-blue uniformed LAPD in the hotel lobby for a half hour before their departure.

Talking mainly to the Chief of Police, they set up a perimeter to where they were mostly going to be inside and outside of the building. Joe's people were going to walk and stand with Mr. Walsh, dealing with him in a close vicinity. All the while Joe said he wanted his people and the uniformed police in constant contact with him over the radio earphones.

Joe then rode down Wilshire Boulevard seven blocks to the I Tower. The LAPD were already at the building in their places. Joe set up Agent Carlos to drive Mr. Walsh and three of his executive directors from other states in a black four-door rented Cadillac Escalade while Agents David and Lisa escorted them in their rented blue Ford Taurus. Joe and Allen drove in a tan vehicle behind them. Glenn and George drove in their car, following.

The entourage is complete, Joe said to himself. Everything was in its place. The lecture should go smooth and calculated. He was informed that this whole ordeal should last about two hours, then it was back to Washington to go over more details of the case, perhaps talk to old leads like Larry and Rachel, and see if those two conspiracy theorists found anything new. He hated surveillance and protection work. He was more of a solve-it guy. Give him a mystery or riddle, and in a couple of days he'd solve it.

A puffy arsenic-looking mist slowly engulfed the sky, creeping in like huge gray fingers of God trying to say, *I alone have the power to obscure the sun.* Some clouds dispersed, shot beams of light to the earth now and then. He remembered earlier someone say it might rain later, but he hadn't given it much thought. The weather wasn't important to him at the time. Nobody had umbrellas. Now he hoped, if it rained, it would hold up at least until they got Mr. Walsh inside.

Two blocks away now, in light traffic, they all stopped at a red light, and Joe glanced up at the sky. The clouds seemed to bring along a rose-quartz haze throughout the city. He wondered, was it low clouds or pollution? He really didn't want to answer that. He had confidence that the rain would hold up as the light turned green. The scattered clouds gave him more assurance that they were going to make it.

They were now in front of the almost all glass I Tower. The front of the building was cleared by the police so they all parked right behind each other. Next, Joe and his team got out of their cars first, then Mr. Walsh and his executives.

When Joe got out and looked around, there weren't as many people as he thought. Maybe forty, maybe less, mostly reporters. Some onlookers were there, but they were easily held at bay by eight scattered officers.

Mr. Walsh emerged from his car, followed by his executives in dark blue three-piece suits. Mr. Walsh wore a brown three-piece suit and started his climb up the wide block-long white hundred steps in front of the entrance.

Mr. Walsh never made it to the top without getting almost stabbed with at least five microphones in the mouth and chest. It was childish and somewhat arrogant of him, Joe thought. Mr. Walsh made the reporters almost chase him up a few flights of stairs, then come to a complete stop to answer one of their questions. This guy really believes he's in Hollywood.

From the reporters' tags and cameras, Joe picked up that the *Los Angeles Times, Los Angeles Business Journal, LA Weekly, ABC,* and *Fox* media networks were there. As intended, Joe said to himself, Mr. Walsh was supposed to walk slowly up these stairs and keep going as he answered as many questions as he could during that time, not this herky-jerky movement of fast and slow. Joe figured it to be his normal every day time with the press. His federal men, though, stayed in perfect formation.

Lisa walked with the press, David strolled behind with the executives, Glenn paced in front, and Carlos moved behind the reporters who were mostly on the left of Mr. Walsh. Allen stood at the top of the stairs next to open glass doors waiting for them to enter the lobby. George walked with Mr. Walsh and Joe tottered backwards up the stairs in front of Walsh, kind of edging him to keep moving.

The reporters spewed a barrage of questions almost simultaneously; "What are you about to say to the world about clean energy? When was the last time you gave a speech like this? What's mainly going to be said today? What's the future for I, Mr. Walsh?" Mr. Walsh answered some of them.

"We hope to expand our technology in every state in the U.S.. The future for I, is of course, to bring us as a nation into . . .."

Joe that very second became aware of his sixth sense. He didn't know if he ever believed he or anybody could predict events, but at this very moment he had. Maybe it was just his repetitious nature as a detective. He did, most defiantly, believe in an inner-voice. His inner-voice was telling him something was wrong. It was at that moment when Mr. Walsh was answering questions his voice faded. It seemed like everyone's voice faded away, and everything was moving in slow motion.

For a second the sun peeked through huge accumulating clouds. It was a flash of light like a camera, visual at about the twelfth floor window level of the Wilshire Grand Hotel across the street. With everyone's back to the hotel, only Joe and Allen who were facing it could have seen the glint. Joe had a feeling Allen didn't see it and decided to take action by himself. He saw the flicker again and reacted as easy as a carpenter operating his tools or a baseball player using a bat.

He tackled Mr. Walsh, knocking him to the floor, and they together rolled down a couple of stairs. They almost knocked over the executives behind them like boiling pins. Mr. Walsh glared at Joe, who was now on top of him with a distorted face as if to say, *what the hell are you doing*? Mr. Walsh then changed his expression to utter surprise as a female reporter screamed. She didn't screech because Joe pushed over Mr. Walsh; it was because a male reporter for *LA Weekly* was bleeding profusely from his right shoulder. His white shirt just made it more obvious.

Then Joe professed everything in real time. The woman shrieked again as the male reporter dropped, landing hard on the stairs. Everyone simultaneously ducked, kneeled, and laid down, though no shot was heard. All the agents pulled out their weapons. Joe spotted Allen stooped low, looking around wildly. After they locked eye contact, Joe yelled at him. "The hotel across the street! I believe it came from there!"

"I'm on it!" Allen yelled, ripped his shades from his face, and ran down the stairs to meet Joe, all the while looking up at the hotel. "What floor?" Allen asked, kneeling next to Joe and Mr. Walsh. "Did you see?"

"I think the tenth, eleventh, or twelfth floors," Joe responded. "I'm not sure."

"The sniper has to come down," Allen said, "I'm on it." He took off running down the rest of the stairs.

"Allen, wait!" Joe shouted. "Shit!" Joe then grabbed George's arm. "You and David stay with Mr. Walsh, no matter what!" Before George could say yes, sir, Joe was gone.

As Joe ran down the stairs he had to jump over someone's leg and almost tumbled down the rest of the way.

"Paramedic!" someone hollered. "We need a paramedic!" The crowd dispersed, some hid under trees that lined the sidewalk.

"Chief Brooks, come in, do you read? Over." Joe bawled into his earpiece walkie-talkie as he watched Allen disappear into the hotel lobby.

Joe juggled crossing the street and working the radio. A car honked, just missing him, as he made it to the other side of the street. Through static, Chief Brook's voice came, faint.

"Agent Clay, is that . . . I heard all the commotion out . . . What's going on?"

"This is Agent Clay," Joy spoke as clearly as he could into the radio headset. "I don't have time to explain. I need all your men to surround the Wilshire Hotel across the street. Over."

"I read you loud and clear," Brooks said, his voice coming in clear now. "Is everyone okay on—" Joe cut him off.

"I need that ASAP. We have to surround and lock down the Wilshire Hotel, now." Joe purposely didn't shout. He spoke stern and in a professional manner, trying not to disrespect the Chief. He found long ago people moved quicker that way.

"Read you, I'm sending officers now." The Chief answered.

Joe stepped inside the hotel lobby and found it to be lavishly decorated. Bellhops, couches, chairs, wall to wall carpet, and civilians were scattered about here and there. Allen was at the registration desk vigorously talking to the well dressed clerk in black. When Joe approached the desk, Allen spoke.

"Tyrone here says there are two major entrances, this side and the 7th Street entrance on the other side of the hotel. There are also two side doors that kitchen personnel and maintenance use."

"I have the LAPD surrounding the building," Joe said. "We're going to need to talk to the manager in charge. This could turn into a catastrophe. Hostages could be involved."

"I already asked for the manager, and he's coming. The police might take a minute to lock down the hotel. I'm going to the 7th Street side and make sure nobody leaves. You know, see if I see anything suspicious." Allen then left.

"Yeah, sure," Joe replied and knew Allen didn't hear him as Allen vanished out a back door. Two minutes later Special Agent Glenn and Chief Brooks stormed into the lobby.

"Amazing!" the Chief said, surprised but out of earshot of the clerk. "Your agents whisked Walsh back in his car and drove away. As soon as you jumped on him, a reporter was shot in the shoulder. I think he'll be alright. You're a—"

"Thanks," Joe said, cutting him off. "Where's your men? We have to lock down this hotel. Nobody can leave."

"I have four men in the back of the hotel and two marked units."

"I'm also going to need men on both sides of the hotel, east and west. Please talk to the manager when he arrives about our situation. Nobody leaves—"

"Right, I got it." Now the Chief cut him off. "Nobody leaves the hotel."

Joe grinned; eureka, he's got it, he said sarcastically to himself.

"I'm going to check the 7th Street entrance. I'll be right back." Joe motioned with his head for Glenn to follow. As they turned to leave, they saw a man in a dark blue suit approach the desk. Probably the manager, Joe thought, but he had to go. His sixth sense was bothering him again.

Was his partner qualified enough to handle a full-scale hostage situation or shoot out? Was he himself ready? Joe thought. No matter what, Allen was going to need his help.

Joe opened the snap-on on his right hip and checked his SigSauer P239. He clicked off the safety. His sixth sense sensed more danger.

WHO WAS THAT AGENT IN BLUE, or was it gray, who pushed Mr. Walsh out the way? No matter, she was given new orders. The instructions were, just send a clear message. She believed she did, though she meant to hit Mr. Walsh in the shoulder and not the reporter. How in the hell did that agent see it coming? How did he know where to look? She knew that they knew to head toward the hotel because she saw the agent in gray running across the street in her scope. Then it dawned on her. The scope. Her lens must have twinkled when the sun came from out of the clouds. No matter, the mission was over, and it was back to Nigeria for good.

Suraksha, in the elevator of the Wilshire Grand Hotel, waited to arrive on the first floor. She looked at her two watches. It was 12:40PM. The mission was over, but it was going to take until 1:30 for her planned escape. She had an airplane to catch at 1:40. Being late wasn't an option.

Today she wore loose black slacks, long sleeve shirt, and gloves. Strapped on her back was a long carrying case—her rifle, which was dismantled. Her hair was up in a bun and face exposed. She figured it didn't matter; this was the last time she was going to be seen in this country anyway, alive or dead.

Like a cow bell the elevator dinged once and opened on the first floor lobby. Suraksha nonchalantly walked toward the glass doors to exit the building on the 7th Street side, passing a few people standing around mumbling something that made them apprehensive.

She noticed two cops outside walking leisurely about and one empty police car. She would easily take them. Her black Ducati Desmosedici was parked across the street between two cars. Her skills at using the motorcycle would be overmatched by any cop trying to catch her. But out-running them was not her plan. If they were to chase her, she would only use it as a deception. In a sense she wanted them to chase her, for she wasn't going to be seen here ever again anyway.

Touching the glass door to open, she almost made it out the hotel undetected. She probably could have made it past those two silly officers, too, until someone behind her spoke.

"Miss, miss, I need you to step back inside. It's dangerous."

She ignored the voice and swung the door open. The man was right behind her. She misjudged where he came from, and he put his hand on her shoulder.

"Miss, I'm a federal agent. I'm going to have to ask you not to move." The voice was more demanding now.

When she looked over her shoulder, she saw the man had a young looking face, maybe in his mid-thirties, brown slick hair, and good smelling cologne. Was this the agent in the loud gray suit who interrupted her objective? She was glad to meet him. Young man, she said in her head, I'm Suraksha.

With his hand on her shoulder she glared at him with a scowl that read *how dare you touch me.*

JOE MADE IT TO THE 7ᵗʰ STREET LOBBY with Glenn trailing him into what he described as a shit-storm. Concurrently they took out their guns, placing it at their side, and evaluated the scene.

Police sirens could be heard in the distance. Five people murmuring crowded around someone at the front door. A uniformed cop outside on the ground in front of the hotel kept yelling over and over again, "My arm! My arm!"

Joe perceived everything moving fast now. He had to make decisions quickly. He had no time. This case could be solved right here and now or it could get away from him forever. Decisions, decisions, he had to make them quickly, Joe deliberated again and again. This was what separated him from the average guy. This was what got him to solve all his twenty-one investigations.

Then he saw who was laid out at the inside front door of the lobby. No, it couldn't be, Joe thought, sweating now. One of his worst fears came true. Damn, not the youngster. These youngsters are so fast. He should have waited for me. He should have waited. The 7th Street male clerk was holding a bloody bundled up towel over Allen's abdomen as he lay on the brown now stained carpet.

"Damn, kid, what happened?" Joe asked, his voice shaking. He kneeled over Allen "Are you shot?"

"It . . . a woman in all black . . . uh . . . motorcycle." Allen winced in pain as he responded and kept pointing outside.

"Try not to talk," Joe said, and Allen extended his right hand. Joe dropped his gun on the carpet, and they held each other's hand tightly, as if they were arm wrestling.

"Sir, I already called," the clerk said. "An ambulance is on the way."

Joe nodded in acceptance.

Allen took a deep breath and spoke a little clearer now. "Joe, go! The assassin we've been looking for just hightailed outa here." He coughed violently.

"You should have waited for me," Joe said with sadness in his eyes. "Where are you hit?"

"Joe, go! I'll . . . be alright! Go . . . you'll never catch her here talking to me!"

"Are you sure, kid? I could stay here—"

"Go, Joe! Get that bitch!" Allen blared out cutting him off. He coughed, grimacing. "For . . . me."

"Okay, okay, I'm on it!" Joe then looked at Glenn. "Stay with him!"

"I'm not going anywhere," Glenn said as Joe picked up his gun, holstered it, and ran out the hotel.

Outside in the street he could hear a loud motorcycle, distant now, and fading. There were two cops sitting on the sidewalk. One officer was holding his arm moaning and the other holding his bloody nose.

"Is this your vehicle?" Joe asked, pointing at a police car double parked in front of the building. He showed his badge, talking to the officer holding his nose who seemed in less agony.

"Here, take the keys and hurry." The officer sounded like a man only talking through his mouth. "We have a marked vehicle pursuing her now. Use the radio; you'll find them. They're headed west."

"Thanks," Joe said quickly. The officer handed him the keys and he climbed into a black and white Dodge Charger.

Adrenalin made him think fast. He somehow remembered where to turn on the sirens, then he peeled out onto the street like he owned the squad car.

"This is Agent Clay I'm in pursuit right behind you on that motorcycle. What's your position? Over." Joe asked into the car radio, holding the receiver in his left hand and the wheel in the right.

"Nice of you to join us, sir," came back an excited voice, and the sound of tires screeching over the dispatch transmitter. "We've just turned onto Olympic Boulevard. Wait! Now turning onto Venice Boulevard."

Joe honked his horn, making sure his opposite traffic stopped when he didn't have the light. These crazy people here in LA still didn't seem to want to stop even though his marked car with sirens was obvious. He almost felt young again as he darted in and out of traffic.

He noticed that the tires were screeching more as he made sudden turns. It was drizzling, and the sky remained gray. Damn, he thought, this light rain wasn't going to help.

"We're on the Santa Monica Freeway, going west! Over!" the radio almost screamed.

"Copy that," Joe said and picked up his speed, though he was already going seventy-five miles per hour.

With the help of the GPS-system, Joe made it onto the freeway and right away knew something was wrong. There weren't that many cars on the highway, and they were going incredibly slow, about twenty to forty miles an hour. He could also see the lead pursuing police car's sirens ahead of him. He judged the chase to be about three or four miles away. The cars on the highway were already parted right down the middle like Charlton Heston divided the Red Sea in the movies. Joe almost brought the pedal to the floor as his car exceeded ninety miles per hour.

"She's getting off the freeway and heading down La Brea Avenue," the transmitter rang out.

"I see. I'm right behind you," Joe spoke into the radio as his car started to lessen the gap between the lead police car. He eased his foot off the gas pedal. Now their sirens gave an echoing whine and tires squealed as they both made sharp continuing turns exiting the highway.

Joe saw her now. Through the confusion of civilian cars stopping in near collisions with the motorcycle or police cars, he saw her. It wasn't so much as her face he saw, but her skills. She glided that bike in and out of traffic like it was scripted for her to do so. She moved like she was on a pro racing track. She wasn't moving fast enough to get away; she was like, just, gliding.

She took out two officers and Allen at the hotel single-handedly. This had to be the same one who attacked Mr. Walsh the first time. This quite possibly was the same marksman in the Mark Douglas incident.

He felt like killing her, but he needed her alive. He needed to interrogate her. Was she connected to the Chelsea Company? Is she acting alone? Why? She couldn't have been acting alone. What would she gain by killing these people? She had to have received some sort of side deal. Only Chelsea would prosper big from this. There could be easy jail time if she was to talk. Nine out of ten, criminals talked.

"If she keeps going this way, she'll be heading toward the LA International Airport or the beach," the officer said from the radio. "If I was to take a guess, it would be the airport."

"We might have to alert—" Joe said.

The officer cut him off. "Wait! She's turning off!"

Joe saw it, too. The woman on the motorcycle turned into a vacant lot in front of a white warehouse. She parked the bike in the lot, calmly dismounted, and walked toward a steel door on the left side of the building. The lead police car parked next to the motorcycle, and Joe parked next to them in unison.

The two officers emerged from both sides of their car, guns drawn. Meanwhile, the lady, like they weren't there, took out a key, unlocked the door, and disappeared inside. Joe got out his car with his gun at his side and walked to the two cops.

"Good job, fellas." Joe looked around at the grassy field beyond the huge storehouse. "What is this place?" He asked.

"We're on the edge of Kenneth Hahn State Park, sir," the African American officer spoke, who was on the driver's side.

"I don't want you to go in, but cover the door," Joe said, checking his gun and hoped it didn't jam. "I don't want her doubling back."

"I already called back-up," the African American officer said, then asked, "don't you think we should wait for back-up?"

"What's your name, son?"

"Danny."

"Good idea, Danny. But I'm afraid this culprit is too smart for that. I have a feeling it's going to be over before backup arrives. But that's exactly what I want *you* to do, is wait for back-up."

Rain sprinkled down, dampening the gray parking lot tarmac. Joe and Officer Danny crept to the steel door where the lady in black disappeared.

The other officer stayed behind, his gun still drawn over the top of the police car at the warehouse door.

The warehouse was about the size of a major supermarket with no windows. Besides this one entrance, there were two aluminum large garage doors in the front. Those doors made big enough for a truck to off-load, were bolted down from the outside, so once he was inside, there was no getting out.

Over the doors were yellow hazard signs that read, *Danger NH4 NO3* and above that white signs read, *Trespassers Will Be Arrested and fined $800.*

"What kind of place is this?" Joe whispered to Danny. Danny shrugged.

"You got me, sir."

"Okay, I'm going in. Just watch the door and watch your cover fire." Joe opened the door. Entering, the door slammed behind him, giving off an echo. He held his gun with both hands in front of him. His palms touched as his hands wrapped around his SigSauer and right index finger was off the trigger, but ready.

Inside, high dangling floodlights were dull because not all of them were turned on. No time to look for a light switch, Joe thought. Crates full with green potato-looking sacks ten feet high cast long shadows on the floor. Walking deeper into the area, he smelled something unpleasant. A strong manure-dirt stench filled the air finding his nose. Joe noticed white writing on the bags, *promote plant growth*, *organic* or *inorganic*. Fertilizer, Joe said to himself.

The sounds of crashing metal reverberated throughout the vicinity, and Joe cautiously moved through the maze of crates. The sounds seemed to come from the center of the building. As he gradually crept toward the clatter, there would be a pause every few seconds, and he could hear the rain slamming into the ceiling.

After moving through the enormous auditorium-long labyrinth of fertilizer crates, he finally appeared at the source of the resonance.

The path he took led to meeting her face to face. She looked African American with Asian-like features. She also appeared young and attractive. He kept his gun pointed at her as she turned over another steel cylinder barrow.

Six barrows were already dumped around her. White crystal looking sand in huge mounds surrounded her, the substance she was dumping out of the cylinders.

172

Now Joe knew why this woman was victorious against so many officers. She was well trained in some kind of karate, and now she was attacking him. Not giving him time to think, she moved inhumanly swift. She glanced at him and blindingly quick threw the container's round steel top at him.

He shot at her, but the bullet slammed into the floor and bounced somewhere else. With perfect precision, that round metal top flung through the air like a frisbee bullet and crashed into his chin and neck, almost knocking him out.

She was for a half-second, five feet away—now she was in front of him after he got off the shot. Dazed, he tried to go for another accurate shot and fired wildly. She clutched his firing arm, twisted and whacked his hands, knocking his pistol clear across the gray cement floor. He yipped as she then knocked his feet from under him, and he slumped on his back to the floor.

By the time, only a second, Joe came to his wits, the woman already straddled him, and they remained locked in a struggle with her gun. Her silver Beretta's muzzle was inches from his left temple.

She was young, strong. He was older and a bit shocked, but he still had the strength to barely hold the gun away from his head.

"Do you know what you're doing?" Joe grunted. He started recuperating his strength, moving the gun more away from his head. "I'm a federal agent." As he sensed that she knew she was starting to lose the battle with the gun, he watched her smirk. It was a devilish grin from cold blue eyes.

"It's unfortunate you'll never know why," she whispered in his ear.

What happened next was a flash to him. He managed to get his legs under her and kicked her back with all his might. She flew backwards through the air and at the same time fired her gun.

She could have easily killed him. Instead of shooting him, she fired about five shots into the ceiling. One thing he knew about her, was that she was an excellent marksman. Her bullets smashed into the hanging thin metal beams and wires that held a lit huge flood-lamp. The lamp flickered out and came crashing down onto the center piles of white sand she'd dumped. Sparks and metal drizzled onto the sand. She herself went crashing backwards into a crate from his momentum, then stumbled to the floor losing her gun.

A flash of lightning blinded him for a second, then all the white piles of sand went up in flames instantaneously ignited from the still hot flood-lamp. He saw her one last time through the flames that separated them, and it looked as if she was in agony. Getting up, he moved behind a crate because the heat was so intense. Then the first explosion went off, knocking him back onto the floor.

He had to get up and get out. Coming to his senses again, he realized how badly he wanted this assassin and how far he was willing to take it. But now he misplaced his gun. This was suicide! She had come here purposely, luring him in, to probably kill herself and whoever followed her, like an ancient samurai who failed a mission. This was as far as he could go. He got up and ran back from where he came.

Rushing for the door, he knew from his long experience as an agent that fire and fertilizer were a dangerous mix. He ran faster for the door as the crackling sound of the blaze filled the entire warehouse. He could also hear pipes slamming onto the floor, falling from somewhere high in the ceiling from the first blast.

Bursting out the door, Joe saw Danny was now about ten feet away and drew his gun. Joe didn't bother to say don't shoot, it's me. Instead, he shouted, "Run! Run! Get clear of the building!" They ran together toward the front of the building to warn Danny's partner.

"When I heard shots, I thought you—" Danny spoke as he ran, but was cut off in mid-sentence when the building erupted again.

The blast pushed them face-first onto the hard parking lot asphalt. Joe felt the last time he was pushed from the back like that was when he was twelve years old by a bully named Bud. He also watched Danny's partner, who was still standing by the police car, get knocked backwards, legs high in the air as if someone pulled the ground from under him.

The building's entire roof blasted into the raptures about forty feet high, engulfed in a fireball of the same height, but wider. The large aluminum doors in the front ripped open like someone sneezing snot into a tissue. Two white bricks were thrown into the windshield of his police car, making it halfway through.

Dazed again and bleeding somewhere on his forehead, he felt Danny lift him. Danny put his arm around his waist and pretty much carried him about fifteen feet to his squad car and dumped him behind it. Danny's lips were moving as he shouted at his partner but Joe couldn't hear any sound, only a ringing in his ears. Joe then saw him run to his partner. He lifted his partner who lay flat on his back on the ground and dragged him behind their squad car as debris from the building fell around them.

As Joe lay in the grass on his back, he barely heard sirens in the distance. He was sure the arriving cops saw the fireworks as he dozed in and out of consciousness.

There was darkness. Then regaining his hearing he heard what sounded like sand, metal, and rocks pounding onto the earth like enormous boulders falling from the sky. He felt intense heat, as if the sun was shining directly in his face, but there was no sun, only a continuing orange and red glow. He heard an explosion, followed by another and another and another.

There was darkness. The ground seemed to oscillate. Then he heard voices, confusion in what direction, where to go. Sirens. Then he felt the rain. The drops bashed into his face, soaking him. Normally, if someone threw water in his face, he would have woken up, but he liked it. It was soothing. Maybe he was in his shower and this was all a dream. He felt cold now, and his head was stinging.

He managed to sit up and look across the parking lot from behind a dirty and wet police car. Damn, Joe said to himself, this was no dream.

The warehouse didn't look like a warehouse anymore. The back and right side wall was still intact, but the rest of the building was demolished, with the center a black and brown crater. Shredded like paper, steel, white-brick, and black soot littered the floor around him everywhere he looked. A stale-dry smell filled the air. Flames still shot out of the cavity, followed by choking thick white, black, and gray clouds of smoke that reached forever into the already gray sky.

There were five more police cars now in the area and one fire truck with red and white lights flashing. Officers seemed to be rushing about frantically.

"Thank God it's raining," Joe heard one fireman say.

CHAPTER 20

MORE RAIN. Today, it fit the scene. Gloom. The rain hit the ground hard, and lightning flashed. It was what Joe felt inside. Bitterness; he felt like crying. It was a sad day. It was a cold day. It was a poignant week since the Los Angeles catastrophe. On this gray cloudy day he stood across the Potomac River from Washington D.C..

A section was roped off and reserved for about four hundred people with open black umbrellas at the Arlington National Cemetery. Pipes and drums were played by the DC Police Corps, their blue uniforms appearing bluer saturated from the rain. An officer played *Taps* on his bugle. In a three-volley salute, three officers fired three shots into the air from their rifles over the gravesite.

Two FBI Agents in dark blue suits each held a twenty foot flagpole. One held the FBI navy-blue emblem flag and the other the United States flag.

Joe was asked to join, but declined. For some dumb reason he said he just wanted to watch. Six agents, three on both sides, carried the coffin covered with another American flag to the gravesite. One of the men was Kordey, and he seemed sad, but this wasn't the first time Joe saw him like this.

The six together folded the flag into a triangle to where they only saw the blue and some stars. Kordey, who held the flag last, handed it to FBI Director Barry Bishops, and they saluted each other. Director Bishops handed the flag on one knee to Allen's mother, who was in an all-black dress. She was a small woman of about sixty years old. This was the first time Joe ever met her.

Allen's girlfriend, Petrice, looked young and attractive in her black dress. She was taller than he remembered, about five feet eight inches, blue eyes, dirty blonde hair; she could have been a model. He only met her about four times, this being the fifth. She cried, as did many friends and family. Though Joe couldn't tell from all the rain, but expressions said everything.

You're in a good place son, Joe thought. Presidents, military service people, and notable civilians were buried here; John F. Kennedy and Joe Louis, for starters.

A priest dressed in all-black with white collar said a prayer. "In the sweat of thy face shalt thou eat bread, till thou return unto the ground; for out of it waste thou taken: for dust thou art, and unto dust shalt thou return." Then for a second Joe thought about God and Heaven, questioning himself again. Was he in a better place?

Lightning flashed again, this time followed by a roar of thunder. Everyone slowly started to disperse back to their cars as the rain came down harder.

A week earlier after spending a few days in a LA hospital from a slight concussion, many things of culpability came into his head. Should he have forced Allen to just wait for him? Should he have stayed with Allen when he told him to go? Would all of this have made a difference or would there be two bodies being buried instead of one? No, maybe his youth was to blame. Youngster was moving too fast for his own good, anxious to catch this assassin as I. He did catch Allen's murderer, didn't he? But she killed herself, didn't she? There was no way she escaped that explosion.

FBI Director Berry Bishops and Kordey were among some of the people who spoke at the church services, but Joe didn't speak. It was because he felt too choked up and emotional about funerals and possibly would break down crying before he got anything out of his mouth. In his opinion, being a man, and crying wasn't a good look. He guessed it was just a man thing. His father was a strict military-type man and told him before he died, "Don't you cry for me, don't you dare." Though he wanted so badly to cry, he just didn't. So he'd show little to no emotion at ceremonies or just didn't participate. Indeed, though, he did weep inside. He always did.

Later that week after he left the hospital and before the funeral, he found out a great amount of things. It was alleged Allen put up a good fight with the assassin and that's why he was shot. Allen was shot with a single bullet in the stomach, and the coroner said it traveled to his chest, flooding his lungs in blood. When the examiner recovered the bullet, they found it was fired from a 9mm Beretta. That wasn't a surprise, coinciding with the fact that the assassin tried to kill him with the same Beretta.

The LAPD did an excellent job with the forensics at the exploding warehouse site with a little push from Kordey, of course. In the hospital, he got to thank the cop Danny for saving him, moving him away from the blast.

Forensics found out why the blast was so intense. It housed tons of ammonium nitrate and only needed a spark to ignite. Everyone, police and agents, called it ground zero. Even though Kordey gave him the week off, he demanded the files from ground zero. The week off helped him think clearer, steering him away from the LA media who had a field day.

Mr. Walsh made his speech two days after the incident, still protected by the five field agents assigned. The media's story had it that a young female assassin made an attempt to assassinate the I Company VP James Walsh. Unsuccessful, she escaped to a fertilizer deposit warehouse where she was tracked down and killed in an explosion heard and seen for miles. Nobody else was hurt in the explosion for it happened in a remote area in Baldwin Hills, LA's Central Park.

Unfortunately, when all the smoke cleared, an agent was shot by the assassin's bullet in an earlier incident and died later in the hospital from complications.

Field Agent Lisa Rivera kept feeding Joe the forensic reports from ground zero even though he was on leave. This, Joe felt, was the true story of what happened, the behind the scenes story, if you will, the stuff he was used to. The media got it right, except one thing bothered him.

Yes, forensics recovered the body of a young female in her early twenties, charred and burnt beyond recognition. They couldn't tell, though, if she was African American or Asian, but she wasn't Anglo-Saxon. Her dentist had lost her dental records. Now how did that conveniently happen? Joe wondered.

The bullet recovered at the stairs of the LA I Tower that had gone through a reporter's shoulder belonged to a Remington 700 M24 rifle with scope and silencer. That was also found dismantled next to the body of the charred female.

Yes, they even found his SigSauer, *and get this,* recovered the two bullets and shell casings he fired.

What worried him most, though was—where was the 9mm Beretta that killed his partner? They never recovered that, even when he pressured

Rivera to pressure the forensic team. Did that just get vaporized alone? Did that alone get blown so far that it might be found in another field miles from the area? Could take weeks or months to find.

The media wasn't done. Later that week the major television news networks across the country stated, *Chelsea Company head of security blamed for assassination attempt on Mr. Walsh. There has been an ongoing FBI investigation that Chelsea wants to own the I Company. VP Mr. Walsh, a strong influence on the board of directors for I, convinced them not to sell, a cause for the attempt on his life.*

The Chelsea Company denied all allegations. They denied wanting to take over the I Company and cooperated with the FBI by releasing all information on the female head of security. The female head of security name has not been released, but we do know she was a Nigerian-born immigrant.

"This person clearly acted on her own and no parties of the board have or had any knowledge of this person's motive or actions until now," quoted a man named Kaleem Nastafar the speaker for Chelsea.

The behind-the-scenes-story, from a file Rivera brought Joe, was about Special Agents Glenn and George's visit to the Impending Towers in Columbus OH. After tracking the rented motorcycle, they found out the Nigerian immigrant's name was Suraksha Using. She'd been working for the Chelsea Company for five years and had just made captain a year ago.

After interviewing all security in the building and apprehending her records, they found out she was a lot different from most immigrants.

Most immigrants had large related families or at least knew a lot of people in their community, she knew nobody. Her green card said Nigerian, but she neither spoke, had an accent, nor had Nigerian friends. Most of her co-workers through the years said she hardly talked at all.

To most of her associates, she spoke well, when she did speak. She acted so American that all of her co-workers never knew she had a green card until now. They always knew she used a fighting style called Kenjutsu and probably the reason for her promotion. She even taught some of them some of her moves. She soon became part of the CEO Nzingha Chelsea's personal bodyguards.

Agent Rivera retrieved six months of Using's cell phone records and handed them to Joe. Reading the transcripts, she only made calls to people at her job, about her job. There was nothing incriminating, like calls to a top executive, Nigeria, or Nzingha herself about a deal of murder—a contract killing so to speak. She was too smart for that Joe assumed, she apparently would have used different phones and then thrown them out.

Though her immigration papers said she came from Nigeria, she looked Asian or Korean to be exact. Was Using a Korean last name? She'd been in the States for six years and five months, roughly the same time as the accidental deaths. Strange, Joe thought, it was as if she popped out of nowhere and began a mission. A mission, Joe kept pondering in his head.

Well no one was going to close this case until he decided it was over. He was the lead. It was now Sunday, the day of the funeral, and tomorrow he was back from leave.

He had known him for four years and served with him three. Goodbye, Special Agent Allen Valentino. Your death has become my X-wife's nightmares about me long ago. Not to sound cruel but your girlfriend will never have to experience long-term suffering, hoping, and wondering if you'll come home safe every night. You're the only partner I've lost. I cry inside because I liked you, youngster—too young to pass away. Joe felt that was his prayer, his only prayer. Amen.

Revenge for Allen boiled inside him, but he knew he couldn't let those emotions cloud his diligence toward this case. Revenge on whom? The Chelsea Company, who claims to know nothing? Suraksha, who is dead? Something more was behind this Suraksha Using. Her death seemed too cut and dry. Give him a riddle and he'd solve it, echoed in his head. He didn't have solid evidence that it was *this* assassin who murdered Mark Douglas and his crew. He couldn't even prove that she was the one at the Walsh home, though she obviously was the one. For now Fortunes & Misfortunes was going to stay open.

THE THURBER CONFERENCE ROOM was full with managers and top executives. The room, half the size of an auditorium, was dark. A projector housed on a long rectangular table played on the front wall.

A strong beat to a fast-paced instrumental song played. A burly, deep, and loud voice spoke words of excitement. "And you, too, could own this. Protect your friends and family. You shall enter a whole new world. A whole new meaning for life." Words flashed and slid across the action scenes on the screen saying, *easy to control, tailored to your needs, security systems, a new intelligentsia for a broadening new world.*

The action on display showed a smiling man in suit and tie coming home from work. The camera in front of his house recognized him and automatically opened his front door.

Inside his house now, he sat on his comfortable blue sofa. The house's pleasant female voice spoke, asking him, would he like to watch TV? The man answered, yes. His favorite television sports channel automatically came on with the latest news of the world three-dimensionally scrolled across the bottom. On the side of the screen was a three-dimensional menu. It was an immediate full report and route to exactly where and when his children were getting ready to come home from school and if his wife was finished grocery shopping.

Everywhere he went in the house, the lights came on automatically. The thermometer moved routinely by itself, making the room temperature how he liked it. His wife's flowers and the lawn were mechanically watered.

A menu with tasks were listed on a wall, its words floating in mid air. The man touched the words, programming his favorite music, and it played.

"C. A. I. embrace the future." The deep voice presented itself again. The words CAI and a phone number showed on the screen before the commercial faded away.

Lights came on in the tan-colored conference room, and everyone clapped loudly. Seated around the long rectangular table were fifty-five managers in mostly different shades of blue suits and ties. They were from Alona's and Chelsea's many different business branches.

Seated in front of the room at another rectangular table facing the managers were Maddox and his two assistants Benard and Charles. They were joined by Alona's Chief Executives and their assistants. Also present was the Chelsea Company's three Chief Administrators and their assistants with Nzingha. White cardboard name tags were in front of each of the individuals in the room.

The only media Nzingha allowed in the hotel was the *Columbus Dispatch*. They were there to observe, but she specifically told them she wasn't taking any questions. The five reporters agreed. They wore plain clothes and stood off to the right side of the room with digital cameras, pads, and pens in their hands, quickly jotting down notes.

Nzingha stood and moved toward a podium in the middle-front of the room. She called this seminar here at The Westin Columbus Suite Hotel to not only promote her new technology, but to inadvertently clear her company's name of business travesty.

She wore a black pinstripe business suit with a lavender shirt. The media flashed some pictures from their cameras as she stood behind the podium. The room grew quiet, and she cleared her throat.

"I have to thank Alona for our first couple of commercials, the advertising of Chelsea Ambient Intelligence. I especially like the one when the man gets up a little from the toilet to reach for the toilet paper and it flushes for him. And he says, hey, I'm not finished yet!" There was a resounding noise of giggles throughout the room as Nzingha glanced at Maddox and his crew and smiled. "CAI will be controversial at first and criticized, but that'll all wither away in time. This system will soon be operational in millions of homes, giving people new means for comfort.

"Other companies around the world will soon be seeking CAI to better their communities and surveillance systems. We've already made this technology easy to handle at your fingertips. The great thing is that this system is already up and running. We already have over a hundred thousand pre-ordered customers in line for this product, mostly American business owners. Now we need to spread this publicly. So I'd like to give another round of applause for the commercials created by Maddox Mathews and his team."

The room erupted in claps, as did Nzingha, and she glanced again at Maddox and his assistants. Now she waited fully for the room to become silent. She cleared her throat again and stared into the sea of managers before her with a face of sternness.

"I'll always believe my company is pure. That's why I'm here to share technologies with the world and make it a better, safer place. I'd like to help the world embrace positivity. But first you must be an example of it. That example is the Chelsea Corporation." Some people began to clap, but Nzingha put her hand up to stop them.

"Some people in the I Company, and especially the media, believe that my company wants I so bad that my company literally wants to kill someone for it. The farthest I'll speak on the matter is, yes, we offered to buy them out or have a mutual merger, but they refused and that was it. The only thing I can say is that *they're* missing out.

"Chelsea, starting in a year and a half from now, will be powering this entire State of Ohio. We won't need the I Company or any other power company to achieve this."

There were mumbles of excitement and confusion throughout the room, particularly from the top executives at the front of the room as they glanced at each other.

"Soon electric power and oil companies will be out of business, and they'll seek me out to kill. Chelsea has invented a new way to burn power called M.E.G., a matter, energy, and gravity module. It works much like an anti-matter machine except this new energy is clean and diminutive, making it cheap. This M.E.G. energy has already been tested and is up and running. The technology is ready to take on Ohio, then the world. It's the red tape of the bureaucrats slowing the process down.

"In closing, the religion of my company. Being real and positively imaginative is the key to the mysteries of the universe. Thank you all for coming out today. Those who are visiting Ohio, enjoy. The day is young."

Everyone stood and clapped as Nzingha went back to her table. The five reporters couldn't help themselves. They attacked Nzingha with an onslaught of questions before they were escorted out by three big bodyguards. They shouted, "Is this new technology real and working? If so, where? Who in Ohio State will be giving you permission to launch M.E.G.? The Governor? The Mayor? If M.E.G. is like anti-matter, isn't that energy dangerous?"

Everyone else in the room exploded in group conversations, and some gravitated to the back where there were many trays of food. Some walked up to Nzingha, shaking her hand, giving her small talk about her new technology.

Nzingha noticed a man in a brown suit and cherry tie. He seemed out of place at the front door. Maybe it was his tie, because it didn't match his suit. The white guy had a gentle look to him, she thought. He looked about in his late forties, neat brown graying hair, medium build, and curious light brown eyes set in a long head.

One of her bodyguards kept shaking his head after the man showed a badge. They were both in a little shoving match at the entrance. Through all of the chatter around her, she couldn't make out what they were saying. A detective, no doubt, Nzingha figured. The guy seemed persistent, but calm, as if he dropped something of importance behind the bodyguard and just wanted to pick it up, trying to explain the situation, that was all. She figured the man was most likely looking for her. Nzingha walked to the door.

Why would a detective be looking for her so unrelentingly? She felt she had nothing to hide, especially from the authorities. She had always done everything by the book to dotting all of her I's and crossing her T's. This detective, or whoever he was, had nothing, but she was up for the challenge of indulging his curiosity. She was going to make any of his attempts to tarnish her company fool-hearted.

"Is there a problem?" Nzingha asked, behind the back of the security guard in black suit. The guard glanced over his shoulder, seeing it was she.

"Yeah, this guy here—" security began to speak.

"That's a federal agent," the man spat back at him, but smiled at Nzingha.

The security guard said this purposely, irritatingly slow as if he went over and over the procedures to keep officers like him out. "He says he wants to set up a meeting with you anytime at your earliest convenience. I asked him for a warrant or something stating his interest. He doesn't have anything."

The agent gave Nzingha a dumb smile as if to say this is a shot in the wind, but I'm trying.

The guard was surprised when Nzingha motioned with her head for the agent to pass. The agent smirked at the guard as he passed him to stand in front of Nzingha just enough away for the guard not to hear their conversation.

"Hi, I'm Special Agent Clay," the agent named Clay said, flashing his badge, and Nzingha got a glimpse of his full name.

They quickly shook hands. "I don't mean to infringe on your conference," Agent Clay began, "but I just want to talk to you about some things that I'm curious about. This could happen anytime you want. It's just that I'd like some closure on some things, and I think you'd be a great help. I know how the media is, and I heard your speech. Maybe your company and the FBI got off to a bad start. You know what I mean?"

"I'll meet with you, and just you, in my office at the Impending Towers in two hours, Agent Joseph John Clay," Nzingha said and smiled at him. "Give your name at the front desk." Agent Clay thanked her and seemed relieved as he left out the front door from where he came.

Maddox glanced at her from about six feet away through the crowd, as if to say, *who was that*? Nzingha shrugged at him.

Part of her felt it truly wasn't important. Another part said, just for a precaution, to make a phone call to a long-time old friend. Her friend knew a friend at the FBI who just happened to work at the Washington DC branch.

Nzingha knew that DC Federal Agents were protecting the Vice President of I and investigating her company when they stormed into

Impending Towers demanding to see their employee, Ms. Using's records.

It was strange, this single agent wanting to see her personally. Authorities don't usually do that unless she was a person of interest. This had happen to her before many years ago. They would generally start from the bottom and work their way up. Did they find something suspicious in her company? Like what? Like maybe there might be more assassins?

She felt a lot of unanswered questions were building over some of her company's takeovers and buyouts. After Mr. Wells' accident her company takes over his television network, something she'd been looking for, for a long time. Then Mr. Douglas had a misfortunate event, and real estate firm Clive Inspirations gives up land to her company after years of trying to give them a sweet deal. This didn't look good. Was Using hired by someone to do all this? How long has Using been doing this? Could this date back to the Chicago incidents? Was there somehow a connection with this and the espionage in her company?

Nzingha needed answers, too. If Agent Joseph Clay was investigating these things by probing her company, she was going to do some inquiring of her own, see what he knew; in a nice way, of course. He was sarcastically smiling at her, so she was going to do a little smiling back. Don't worry, Agent Clay, this is going to be a clean fight. No, I mean debate. You did bribe your way to meet me, and I accepted. Bring it on.

KORDEY WARNED HIM not to talk to any of the executives at Chelsea. "You did good, son," Kordey's voice echoed in his head. "You caught the assassin to where she committed suicide."

But here Joe was, at the Impending Towers, not only talking to an executive, but talking with Nzingha Chelsea herself. Kordey said, "I know this was your first loss of a partner, but you might have to let this one go." Kordey questioned him because he hadn't closed the case.

He tried to explain to his boss that the assassin wanted someone to follow her into that explosion. She was dumping all those chemicals purposely to set it off. He tried to explain to his boss that there was something not right about her suicide. It was to cut and dry.

"They found her body," Kordey said, "though there could be more assassins. But until then, snooping around Chelsea won't be a good look." That was all Kordey had to say. He didn't force him to close the case, just strongly suggested it. Kordey trusted his judgment, even if his vision was a bit blurred from Allen's death. Hey, Kordey had to somewhat trust him.

He had resolved all his cases. Joe had to admit that this was at the top of his list for odd cases. His partner dies and his lead suspect commits suicide.

What did the suspect mean when she said to him, too bad he'll never know why? Did she simply act on her own? Why would she?

His instincts had brought him here on the twenty-first floor of the east tower, Nzingha's main office. Goodness gracious! Joe thought, nice office. So this is how you billionaires live? Spacious, marble floor, oil paintings, Bamboo plants, and sixty-inch flat screen television—amusing office. Nzingha sat behind a brown-ivory desk, and he sat in front of her in the middle of the room.

They shook hands before they sat. Strange, he thought. She had a warm hand shake. Was she nervous already? He hadn't even said anything yet.

She was a lot more attractive in person than the pictures he'd seen of her. Pretty eyes, and her short hair seemed to fit her perfectly. Her features were Brazilian looking, she had no accent, her English was clear.

"I've cleared the room for twenty minutes," Nzingha spoke and folded her hands on top of the desk. "So, what do you have for me, Special Agent Clay?"

"I know you're a busy lady, so I hope I can get this all out in twenty minutes," Joe spoke.

Nzingha spread her hands out and skewed her head a little in a gesture to say, it is what it is, she doesn't have all day.

"I better get straight to the point then," Joe suggested then asked, "Do you believe this assassin, Suraksha Using, might have been doing this for some time?" He took out a pad and pen.

"No, I didn't believe or know if she was doing this for some time. I met her once a year ago when she was promoted captain of security."

"Her being captain of security and being your personal bodyguard, wouldn't you have an extensive background check on her? Wouldn't you know her pretty well? She was your *personal bodyguard*." Joe leaned more toward Nzingha mockingly in the ready position to write down on his pad what she was about to say.

She grew a slight smile before she answered, "Yes, an extensive background check was done on her, and now you have all those records. So you know as much as I know about her. So I won't squander any time going over all of her details.

"Who wouldn't promote her, after having a perfect record in the company for four years? As far as me knowing her on a personal level because she's my personal bodyguard, you're a little wrong."

Joe scrunched as if to say he didn't understand.

"I have many personal bodyguards, some I know more than others," Nzingha continued. "She's only been on my bodyguard squad for about a year. I have personal security that have been with me for about five years plus. They're David Heim, Ryan Alexander, and Adam Stuart. Mr. Stuart is right outside that door." She then looked down at his pad toward the things he was scribbling down and contemptuously said, "Did you get that? Stuart." Her smile extended.

"It would be my guess then that she won't be one of the security you would know more than the others?" Joe asked with a silly smirk, and Nzingha continued to smile. "Have you ever heard of Mark Douglas of Clive Inspirations, Mr. Wells, who used to own WCBH-TV, and Mr. Walsh of the Illumination Corporation?"

"Of course, I heard of them."

"Do you know what happened to them?"

"Of course. Mr. Walsh was almost killed, and I found out through Clive Inspirations and WCBH-TV's own board of directors that Mr. Douglas and Mr. Wells had unfortunate accidents."

"All this doesn't strike you as a little suspicious? Red flags, so to speak?"

"You know, it did. At first I figured it to be one of their company's own board members trying to insure that the deal went through, and it was a good deal. You see, Clay, most of the time when I merge with companies, it's a sweet deal for the both of us. So I pretty much don't care if they do or don't merge.

"In the case of this assassin, Using, who's now dead, for whatever reason why she did what she did, don't you think we solved our suspicions?"

Okay, Joe thought, now she was asking him questions. Who's in control here? Okay, he said to himself, back off a bit. She was a graduate from the Massachusetts Institute of Technology, and at seventeen no doubt. She definitely wasn't stupid or naïve. He came to grips with himself that she wasn't in court. This wasn't a trial. He had thought in the beginning that she was going to be nervous. He was wrong. Warm hands usually, to him, meant the person was sweating or had been sweating nervously. Okay, Joe said to himself, change the subject, then get back into it.

"I'm curious," Joe said. "You don't talk much to the press, if at all. Why? You seem well read?"

"I talk to the press all the time, Agent Clay. Through my works," Nzingha replied, still smiling. "I'm curious, too. Did your wife give you that tie? It doesn't seem to fit you."

"Let's just say I got it from a good, bright partner of mine. It's sort of like a lucky charm." He chuckled a little, straightening it. She leered at it.

Joe hated her sneer. It was a cocky grin that made him hate everyone who had dimples. He went back to his pen and pad. "So, how long has Using been in your company?"

"You have the records, Agent Clay. You already know it was five years."

"I know you said you weren't close, but can you imagine why she would take out these high executives? Knowing she wasn't getting the profit, but your company was? I'm sorry, I don't have much time, and these questions are just what I wrote down."

She nodded in acceptance of his apology. "I can't imagine why someone would kill and not profit from it themselves. If you want me to stretch my imagination, though, I will."

Joe nodded ironically in the same way as she bobbed at him a second earlier.

"Maybe she's trying to set me up," Nzingha recommended. "Maybe another corporation hired her to do so. Some months ago, some private information from our company computer mainframe was stolen. This could be part of some kind of industrial espionage from a rival organization."

"Really?"

"Really. You got that down?"

"Do you have any suspicious executives who might have wanted to hire an assassin?"

"I have a couple of suspicious rivalry companies I'd like to report. Like, there's this executive in the Bilderberg—"

"No, no, I mean executives here," Joe said, interrupting her. Now he smiled. "Here in your company."

"Oh," Nzingha said sarcastically, surprised she supposed the wrong thing. "Oh, my executives?"

Joe nodded pleasantly with a grin.

"I can't say," Nzingha said raising her eyebrows. "But then one could never be too sure. I think I'll leave that up to you guys. You guys are far more trained than I in suspicious people."

"Oh, so if I could interview every executive in your company, that would be okay?"

"Sure, you can interview every last one of them." Nzingha's smile widened. "If there's a turncoat amongst us, I want him or her sorted out."

"I guess you know I'll be back if you're hiding something that you should be telling me." Joe stopped smirking and glared at her seriously.

"You know, I hope you investigate my espionage case with the same fire. Whenever you decide I really have a case, and you will." She remained smirking. "You shouldn't let your emotions get the best of you, Mr. Clay. It could cloud your judgment on dealing with the essentials of an investigation."

So she's giving me advice now, Joe thought, and she's still grinning. He glanced at his watch. "Look at how time flies. I got five more minutes. Ah, one more question."

Nzingha nodded for him to go on.

"I'm curious," Joe asked. "What's your affiliation with the Nigerian company Livenal? Is this an associated company, opponent? Maybe they hired this assassin? She was a Nigerian citizen."

Yes! Nzingha stopped grinning. He invisibly slapped that smirk off her face. She was as serious as she was going to get since the beginning of the conversation. Too bad he didn't ask the question earlier. He couldn't. He had to warm up first. He couldn't show his hand in the beginning of a card game. He had to save the high-hand.

"Livenal?" Nzingha repeated.

Joe tilted his head ever so gently for her to proceed.

"Livenal is a huge automobile, oil, and agricultural worldwide corporation," Nzingha explained. "Yes, as you already know, based in Nigeria. I've dealt with them on many occasions, like currency transactions and such." She breathed hard in and then out. "But if they have anything to do with this investigation of yours, I say good luck, because you're dealing with a giant."

"Giants fall, too, you know. You ever heard of Jack and the Beanstalk, David and Goliath?"

"Fairy tales, Mr. Clay. If Livenal is involved, and I hope they're not, you have your work cut out for you."

"Maybe *you* hope they aren't. But I'll do my job no matter how big the company or how far they reside."

"I hope so, for your sake," Nzingha said, with a tone of seriousness.

"You'll be dealing with many developing eager nations, a network of powerful corporations."

What is she trying to say? Joe thought. Is she trying to scare him? This woman is something else. "Let's not detour on what I asked you. What's your exact involvement with Livenal?"

A black phone rang on her desk, and she quickly picked it up.

"Okay, send him in," she spoke into the phone, then hung up. "Sorry, I have an important meeting with a portfolio manager for investment strategies and sorts. To answer your last question, Livenal and Chelsea have exchanged donation funds for two sole objectives of charity and non-profit organizations."

A man in brown three-piece suit came into the room with a black suitcase. He looked European, Joe thought, as Nzingha rose from her desk and they shook hands.

"*Bonjour et bienvenue*," Nzingha said, transforming her voice into a perfect French accent.

"*Bonjour, merci*," the man spoke back with a nod.

"Thank you for coming, Agent Joseph Clay," Nzingha spoke to Joe, extending her hand for him to shake. "Perhaps I shed some light on your curiosity and closure to the case."

He stood and shook her hand lightly. "Hardly," he responded with a miserable grin.

"Well, I'm sure you'll do your homework." Nzingha's smirk came back.

Joe left the towers as he figured he was going to feel, unsatisfied. These billionaires are something else. They think they own the world, they're above the law.

Nzingha was a lot smarter than she looked. Being the richest woman in the world he assumed she had to be witty. She went by the three corollaries. Admit nothing, deny everything, and launch counter accusations. She wanted him to come; she knew he had nothing.

He felt, he was forming a pattern here. Livenal started in America before it moved to Nigeria. The assassin Using was Korean-looking while Nzingha had a Brazilian look, and both behaved very American, yet had strong ties in Nigeria. Maybe it was nothing, Joe thought, but then again he didn't believe in coincidences. Many things were planned. What were those non-profit organizations? Did that have something to do with those unclassified files Allen found?

Allen was talking to him from the grave. He was right. He always was right. Chelsea and Livenal were definitely somehow working together.

CHAPTER 21

THE BATTLE OF THE LAPITHS AND CENTAURS by William Adolphe Bouguereau, oil painting of Greek mythology by Homer hung high, wide, and bright over their heads. Walking slowly, the three stared at other gigantic oil canvases that imitated what the tiny nameplates titled them. Moonlight Marine by artist Edward M. Bannister, White Mountains by Jasper Cropsey, and Three Ladies Making Music by Benjamin West were suspended on the wall with many other paintings in the American Art section.

Central Intelligence Agency Director Edward Grass was a big round fellow, five feet, seven inches and two hundred and fifty pounds. He wore his blue suit and tie comfortably well. He had neat combed silver-gray hair, and thin wire-like spectacles hid his light-brown profound set eyes. His square jaw was cleanly shaved, making him younger than his age of sixty-eight.

Brian wore a gray shirt, tie, and black slacks, and Matt wore a dark-blue shirt and pants. They leisurely walked with the Director, their boss. Matt didn't add much to his disguise today, only contacts and a curly wig.

It wasn't crowded now at 4:20 in the afternoon. The Virginia Museum of Fine Arts closed at 5:00, and people, mostly coupled up, moved quickly past them every now and then, mumbling to each other on what to see next.

The only one of the three who brought extra people with them was Grass. He had two plain clothed bodyguards, one to the left of him and one on the right. They were sufficiently out of earshot, but not that far to survey his slow walk with his associates.

"Sorry we had to meet like this on such short notice," Grass began with his hands behind his back, pretending to take interest in the pictures on the pure white walls. "Powell and I have agreed we have to step up our efforts. The President will be back next week from Europe, and he's going to want results. I want to tell him, sometime in January, we should have a resolution. This technology mustn't reach another country. *Put A Bag On It.*"

Matt knew *Put A Bag On It* meant their next operation was a go. The mission now was set in motion for attaining the target's agreement of their demands or taking the target out.

The target will be forced to handover its technology to the DOE, Department of Energy. As soon as that's established, the target won't be able to give the secrets to another country or else be tried for treason.

Or the target just refuses all together, resulting in elimination. Either way, this chapter of the mission, Masters of Fire, will be over. Usually, in the end, the target, no matter which side they're on, is eliminated anyway, for the government trusts no one individual. They've done it many times before, Matt thought. Their most illustrious act went back as far as 1943. Nikola Tesla, a man who invented new ways to channel electricity. In debit and alone, he died in a hotel in New York of heart failure—was he alone?

"Just curious, sir," Brian spoke, choosing his every word vigilantly. "I trust this isn't too soon. Were we able to duplicate the technology?"

"They say yes, but it's never been tested," Grass answered.

"This could be a loss of a giant leap into the future if we eradicate the target."

"Then I'll leave it up to you guys on the particulars. However this goes down, you just remember that our scientists, I assure you, have obtained the technology. Now we have to contain it. Initiate, *Put A Bag On It.*"

"As you wish, sir," Brian said with a nod.

Grass turned to Matt. "You've been on this for some time. How do you feel about the decision?"

"It's time," Matt said with inspiration. "The target has stepped up and made it known to the world. Now we must raise our stakes if we value our future."

"I like you, soldier, I really do." Grass developed a wide smile.

Brian gave a frown. Jealousy, that's all that is, Matt thought, as he glanced at Brian. He forgave him, though. He was young in this game.

Matt also knew Grass wanted to say his name instead of calling him soldier, but there were protocols. Their names were classified.

Not many people made the Director smile. Hey, he was no ordinary guy.

BEING HERE TRULY BROUGHT BACK MEMORIES, flashbacks. Who do you think the U.S. gets when it's time to spy behind enemy lines? They get me. Why do you think Reagan had the Marines leave Lebanon? It was because he killed the main terrorist who caused the death of two hundred and one Americans. He remembered being the main one who devised the plan on how to invade Grenada and joined in with the battle they won.

He reminisced creeping into Libya behind enemy lines to make certain U.S. air strikes hit suitable targets. He went into Panama obtaining information on where and how to ensnare the military dictator. This was weeks before the U.S. captured Noriega. He was the key one who foiled the plot to assassinate Clinton when he went to the Philippines. He fought in the battle of Mogadishu in Somalia, saving soldiers, and killed important leaders of al Qaeda in Afghanistan.

Matt had also been on many clandestine missions not known to the world. Nobody knew he had assassinated the notorious terrorist UBL six years earlier. If the world knew about this, some Muslim extremist would make Osama a martyr. If he had to tell anyone about these operations, he'd have to kill them. That's how he lived. That's how he always lived. He was proud to work for the SOF; they were his family.

Today, he went to see Jeremy Taffy, not to converse on his heroic past, but to discuss quitting. Most people would have considered him too young to quit anything, but they didn't know the half.

He'd seen the world and had basked in the light of the most powerful country man has ever known. What else was there to accomplish? He knew human geography, was exposed to different religions, politics, and the entangled fabric-webbed secrets of the world.

He was void of one thing—Love. He never thought of the so-called ideal American dream of a wife, house, car, and dog, though when he really thought about it, in hindsight, he saw peace in the American vision. Wasn't that what everyone on earth wanted, peace in some kind of way or another? What better time to do it while you're young. Hell, he more than served his country. It was all pious insight from here on.

What does a man gain by controlling the whole world, but lose his own soul? An Indian man told him long ago, "The soul was soothing, strengthening, cleansing, and healing. That's why the old Indian still sits upon the earth instead of propping himself up and away from its life-giving forces." That saying stuck in his head for years, now more than before.

Jeremy Taffy was in his late seventies. Matt wasn't sure; he never told his age. Former Commander of Forscom, former Director of the FBI, and former Director of the CIA, to Matt he was a legend and forever his first and last real boss, his father figure, so to speak.

Matt sat across from Taffy on a multicolored couch and watched him light his dark-brown hand-crafted Ukrainian pipe. He simulated a college professor. He wore a full gray and black highlighted beard that was neatly trimmed, glasses, and his peach face was almost always stuck in a pose of an intriguing thought, like he was always thinking. His tan shirt and pants also made him replicate one of those archaeologists from the early nineteen hundreds.

The library of books built into the wall and fireplace behind him where he sat, in his brown sofa-chair, defined his image.

"I know you didn't come all the way to Beaver Falls, PA to tell me a story about your latest escapades with the Agency," Taffy spoke in his deep voice.

Matt looked out neatly blue curtained windows before he spoke. He realized the last time he'd been here there was snow. Now snow was all around the house, in the windowpanes, and on the glass itself, made by wind that he could slightly hear still howling. He'd been here five years ago when Taffy retired.

He sipped tea from a white china-teacup Taffy offered to him when he came in earlier.

"That's yes and no," Matt answered.

The smell of tobacco filled the air as Taffy gave a puff from his pipe. Taffy's right gray-black bushy eyebrow rose slightly, examining him. "That would be a yes, something is deeply troubling you at the job. No, you're here to seek advice again, or no you came to give me an early Christmas present? You're not into presents, so I suppose I'll rule that out. So what can I do for you today, my dear boy?"

Taffy had a dry sense of humor and never laughed at his jokes. It made him even funnier in a dark way, Matt thought.

"I'm thinking about chasing that dream, sir," Matt spoke. "I think I've become like that athlete who just keeps winning and has become bored of the game. I know what happens when that fire is gone. You start to trip up. You start losing. In my profession it could be your life. You start hating the lies you've created. You start losing reality, and soon you don't know who you are."

Taffy inhaled deeply on his pipe and puffed out a cloud of smoke before responding.

"Old age is more than white hair and wrinkles, the feeling it's too late the game is over, and that the stage belongs to the upcoming generations. The truth is not the weakening of the body, but the realness of the soul. You know The Company just doesn't let you go?"

"I've been thinking about this for a year now. My heart's not in it anymore. To just spell it out for you, I think I want peace."

"Don't think, my boy, don't think." Taffy kind of shouted it out as if he was scolding him, teaching him. "You better know very well what you want. A doubtful friend is worse than a certain enemy."

"Then sir, yes, I want to put in for my renouncement." There, he said it. Now what? Matt thought. "I suppose I came here to hear how you did it and what you suggest."

"Well," Taffy said, then puffed more smoke. "What are we doing now?"

"We're on that same project when you left."

"Um, Masters of Fire. Is that what the old General is calling it now?"

"That's classified, but I won't ask how you managed to attain that."

"I'm retired. I'm not dead." Taffy played with the bud end of the pipe with his teeth. "So this has been going on for at least five years now. Any hopes of resolve?"

"I'm glad you said that," Matt answered, and then sipped more of his tea. "Yesterday Grass has just okayed the lid on the operation."

"It's simple," Taffy said excitingly, but still held his serious persona. "Make this your most flawless performance, then quit. Who's going to question you? You've served your country many times over, I'm afraid. Sure, they'll taunt you to stay, your so-called associates. You just remember, my dear boy, don't think, and know what you're doing.

"You said something before. You said you wanted peace. Nobody can give you peace but yourself. Remember, peace isn't something you wish for, it's something you make, something you do, something you are, and something you give away. I once sought peace myself, and I found it. That's why I divorced my wives."

Matt chuckled, watching if Taffy was going to laugh but, of course, he didn't. He kept his serious look, staring straight ahead.

"Come," Taffy said, getting up from his chair. "Let's get some drinks in celebration of your soon departure of The Company. Then let me teach you the subtleties of retirement."

Matt saw the man finally give a little smirk from the corner of his mouth as he got up and followed him into the kitchen. Taffy was going for his wine collection. Matt wondered if he was going to age like Taffy, like fine wine and full of wisdom.

CHRISTMAS AND NEW YEARS HAD COME AND GONE. It was the same as the other years, Joe thought. Colorful lights, cheerful tunes, Times Square ball dropping, Christmas trees, presents exchanged, people going to church, vacations, cheering, shouting, and drinking emulated the end of the year. Then you'd have a New Year's resolution, break it, or not do the things you promised yourself. Now everyone is back to work, some people will have domestic disputes and some will go as far as committing murder. That'll happen in January, and guess what folks? The world is back doing the same thing they had been doing all year around. Humans are creatures of habit.

Joe listened to himself in his head. His idea of the end of the year sounded facetious to most, but he was dead serious. It was his actuality. That being said brought his attention back to the reality of the case.

"So what are you going to tell your boss about the case?" came the voice of Pete out the speaker of the office phone.

Joe had his feet up on his desk and sat back in his chair. "I suppose, Pete, for now, I'm going to have to close the file. I guess we'll never know the real motive. I figured time would have its way with bringing more evidence forward. I presume I was wrong."

"I'm glad you caught that sniper. I knew giving this to you and only you, you'd solve it."

"Yeah, well, I didn't really kill the sniper. She took her own life. Funny, I don't feel I solved the case."

"Hey, you're too hard on yourself. It is what it is. You stopped the deaths of possibly more innocent businessmen." Pete then cackled. "Though I think half of them are crooks anyway."

"Yeah, maybe you're right." Joe looked around his office. His office was neat, as usual. Orderly file cabinets to the right, fax machine, clean, picture of a beach on the wall, straight, and the billboard behind him full with papers tacked to it in precise categories.

It was his desk that aggravated him now. It was a mess, with files of the

Fortunes & Misfortunes case sprawled all over the place. On top of that were erasers, pencils, pens, paper clips, and staplers. Then there was Allen's E-Keeper pad holder next to his computer screen. Joe closed his eyes and focused on his phone conversation.

"By the way," he changed the subject, "you never told me what you got your daughters for Christmas."

"Oh, man! If you could only see their faces! I helped my oldest, Jane, get a new red 2012 Nissan Sunny she always wanted, and Jackie got another faster computer. She's fifteen years old and knows a lot more than me about computers. It almost makes me feel stupid."

"No, you're not stupid. It's just a different era, my friend."

"Yeah, well, you know. Information is so fast these days. You now have access to the library in your very home. Kids of this era suck that up like a sponge. So what's going on with you? Any lucky ladies I should know about?"

"None, I can't think of—" Joe was cut off by a knock on his door. "Hold on, Pete." Joe turned the speaker off and picked up the receiver, putting it to his ear. All the while he took his feet off his desk and sat up straight. "Come in," he shouted at the door.

The door cracked open, and Agent Rivera peeked in, smiling. "Sir, Kordey wants to see you."

"Sure, thanks," Joe said, returning a smile, and she left as fast as she came. "Pete, let me go. I gotta go. The boss."

"Okay, good luck on whatever you do with that case," Pete said.

"Thanks. It's always good to hear the voice of an old friend."

"Hey, I do what I can do. And Joe, I'm sorry again about your partner."

"Thanks."

Joe took a long walk through the many hallways in the J. Edgar Hoover Building to find Kordey's office. On his way there, he thought of many things to say on why he held the case open so long.

If Kordey was going to close it, let him close it. Joe felt he would just have to move on. If that did happen, he knew this case would probably linger in the back of his mind forever. In his book it was his first solved case on paper, but unsolved mystery of motive and loose ends.

Then he asked himself, was he getting old, was he getting rusty? I guess I can't solve all the riddles of the world. This will go down in his book as one man down, one enigma lost.

He arrived at the Assistant Director's office and knocked.

"Come on in," Kordey's voice sounded from behind the door. Joe walked in looking around as if he was guilty about something. "Lock the door behind you, son." Kordey waited for Joe to close the door, lock it, and sit comfortably in front of his desk. "How ya feeling son?"

"I'm fine," Joe responded with a sheepish smile, "and you?"

"I'm just dandy." Kordey placed a closed folder down in front of him on his desk. "I want you to know I went through a lot of trouble to attain this file."

"The classified file," Joe said knowingly with excitement, life coming into his poignant-looking eyes.

Kordey nodded.

"The only thing is, this file can't leave my office," Kordey said. "This file is not authorized to be read by anybody but the Director, my boss—for his eyes only. I'll give you time to read, then we'll discuss it here and leave it here. You know what I'm saying, son? This could be both of our jobs, so after you read it, keep a lid on it. I trust you, and I know how you feel about this case. After I destroy the documents, we walk out of here knowing nothing."

"It's that deep, huh, sir?"

"I reckon so."

Kordey slid the file across the table in front of Joe. Joe took a deep breath and opened the file.

There were nine pages with the word *confidential* in red written across them all. Reading as fast as he could, he read that it was a report from the Science and Technology Division of the FBI, signed by a name scratched out in black marker. There were many dates, starting from 1999.

Chelsea gives millions of dollars to Livenal in Nigeria supporting human reproductive cloning. Livenal was forbidden to practice the procedure. Chelsea then stopped giving funds. Lead Special Agent Hagberg monitored Livenal and found nothing until 2007. In 2007 suspicion of human cloning reactivated.

Joe then read five pages of jargon about irrepressible technology. Names of the technology were blotted out by a black marker. Hagberg stepped down, then the CIA obtains control of the whole operation.

CIA Director Edward Grass, who has jurisdiction of project MOF, now active, one page read. *Livenal now giving money to Chelsea's M.E.G. program. Caution: Do not initiate. Active CIA informant in place.*

"I don't understand something sir," Joe said, looking up from reading. "This seems to have nothing to do with my case."

"You wanted the file, you got it," Kordey said. "Look deeper, son. Do you think the CIA wants to make anything obvious? There's something shadowy working here. Clear the smoke, son. What do you see?"

"You may be right." Joe calmed himself. "Obviously the CIA doesn't want us to place an informant in the Chelsea Company because they already have one in place. So Nzingha wasn't lying when she said she might have a mole or espionage case.

"Livenal is giving money to Chelsea toward a new technology called M.E.G. and therefore may want to see this business spread wide. In turn, killing off rivalry competitors toward Chelsea. Making Chelsea grow. Livenal also gave Chelsea millions during the 2008 Crash."

"Clear the smoke, son." Kordey urged him on.

"Yes, follow the money," Joe whispered in response. "Which makes perfect sense why the assassin Using is from Nigeria."

"I think you got it, genius."

"The million dollar question is, what can we do about this?"

Kordey took the file off his desk, turned on the shredder near his waste basket, and started feeding the paper into the machine.

"You still want your job?" Kordey asked, then shrugged. "You did your part. Let the CIA handle it. You have to admit, this case is one of your unique ones by far. If the CIA came down on you, there's not much I could do for ya, son."

"I'm closer than ever in solving the meaning to this case, and I can't even tell it. What about Allen? Was his life for nothing, sir?" Joe shook his head in disappointment, but gave a sly grin.

"You found his killer," Kordey said, "though I know that doesn't help bring him back . . . I don't know what to say, son. Life sometimes is funny that way." The last page of the file disappeared into the machine.

"Thank you, sir, for the file, for a little gratification," Joe said, and the two men shook hands.

Joe had to admit that something was accomplished. Allen would have made a great lead agent. A hard case like this he would have solved early on. Allen knew in the beginning Livenal had something to do with that assassin. "Follow the money." Allen would say.

Joe still wasn't fully satisfied. He didn't like Nzingha's arrogance. He knew in his heart she had something to do with all this or at the least knew what was going on.

Before he left the office Kordey scolded him on conversing with the

CEO of Chelsea. In the end, though, Kordey just shook his head. "You don't give a dried apple damn what I tell ya, do ya, son?"

Joe counted the steps to walk from Kordey's office back to his, two hundred and sixty-three. Counting calmed him. Some things never change.

CHAPTER 22

SHE RAN AS FAST AS SHE COULD. They had been chasing her and her four companions for what seemed like three minutes now.

The arctic tundra air was dry, making it hard to breathe as they ran. They wore blue and black pilot jumpsuits. The cold wind bit through their uniforms. They ran, but had no specific destination. They had no cover; only a white desert of snow and ice surrounded them.

The thought of heading for some grayish mountains in the distance came over her, but she knew that was unrealistic. The mountains were too far away—miles away, to be exact.

The men in the machines had been chasing them away from their craft that crashed in this forsaken world of snow. Black smoke about a half mile behind them rose hundreds of meters into the crystal clear blue sky.

It was hard to run in the knee-high snow. She had to pick her feet up so high to get a good stride.

The men in the machines had an immense advantage. The humans inside, wrapped in metal to the shape of their own body, had mechanical gears and hydraulics to make them move faster. They were in the warmth of body armor. Their pace was much greater as the suit made all three of them nine and a half feet taller than they actually were. They almost looked invisible. Their metal outfits were white, blending with the snow. Last, they had guns and lasers.

She knew the metal men with the benefits were going to achieve their goal in the end. If only she could make it to those mountains for cover.

Her friend to the left never had the chance to scream as his head was blown clean off, decapitated so fast the body was still giving itself commands to run for three more steps before it dropped.

She wanted to scream, but couldn't. She was far too out of breath, far too scared, and far too cold. The eerie whine of fire power filled the air. Bullets and laser-fire ripped into the snow as if a thousand rocks were thrown at them. Her friend to the right screeched as bullets ripped into his back and continued out his chest. Guts splattered everywhere, and he fell.

She dare not look back as she picked up the velocity in her run, like it mattered. Her companion, who was a step behind her, dropped and shouted her name until laser fire cut that off. She heard more blood curdling shouts. That was probably her last comrade, killed from somewhere behind. She could feel the entrails splatter on her back. If only she could reach those damn mountains!

Then, by some miracle, the men in the machines stopped. She smiled; she was going to make it. As she ran in great strides, she realized she wasn't in knee-deep snow anymore. She was gliding, and it felt wonderful for a moment. What she was skimming on crackled, like a tire on loose gravel. Then she frowned. She, too, stopped, but it was too late.

Looking around, she was now aware she ran about thirty feet out onto a thin ice-sheet. Slowly turning around, she saw where her footing made cracks all the way to where she stood now. There were about twenty-five of her shattered footsteps. More to her surprise, when she really looked around, she saw the ice was thin. She could almost see the deep-aqua ocean below in every direction for at least thirty to fifty feet. It was like standing on a mammoth scratchy white window.

The armored men put their hands on their hips. She felt if she could see their faces, they would probably be laughing at her. At a safe distance across the ice, she could see the armor clearly as they turned off their camouflage. The natural metal was a shiny gray and blue. One of the armored men, and it seemed as if he was amused while he did it, fired a single shot into her leg.

She yipped as the bullet passed through her thigh. She buckled and fell onto the ice with the splat of her full weight. The ice broke, making an ideal hole. Her body fit into the burrow with only her head and shoulders above. The only thing stopping her descent into the ocean below was her arms and elbows. She practically froze in that position.

The men in the machines walked away, back from where they came. She could almost hear them laughing as they slowly retreated.

The water that enveloped her from the shoulders down was so cold she couldn't feel the garments she was wearing anymore. It felt as if she was having a nude ice bath.

With all her strength, what was left, grunting, she tried to claw her way from the hole. She was too frozen and too fatigued to climb out.

After two minutes, her hair mimicked icicles on a bush. After a few more minutes her lips turned blue, and she shivered and trembled terribly. As her teeth chattered, she could see the exhalation from her breath getting weaker.

There was another problem altogether. Fish, about the size of her pinkie, bit into her thigh where she was shot. Her blood looked black in the water, like someone dropped an inkbottle onto a white sheet of paper. The tiny fish came by the hundreds, now thousands, attracted to the warmth of blood. The rusty-colored Piranha-looking fish bit into the womb in a frenzy, making the laceration wider.

She wanted to scream, but was too cold. She wanted to climb out, but her arms were too stiff. She wanted to cry, but her tears froze. The fish were eating her alive. She wanted to die now. Please, body, shut down and let me freeze to death. Please, fish, eat faster. Kill me!

She could feel the fish inside her leg eating away the flesh digging to the bone. She could hear the chomping of their teeth. All she could do was beg for death to come swiftly.

Freezing—eating was all Nzingha could think of this morning as she awoke sweating again. She had risen in her home in the confines of her room from another dream.

Today was a big day for her. She had to mentally prepare herself to show the Chief Executive of Designing and so-called friend, her M.E.G. program. He was practically begging to see it and in disbelief the technology of anti-matter could be harnessed. It kind of reminded her of her dream. The begging part anyway. She agreed to show him on one condition. She said before going to the facility where it was all done she had to first make a stop at a different type of facility; a prison, to be exact.

At the Youngstown Ohio State Penitentiary, Nzingha stood behind a tan podium in front of eight black male inmates in white jumpsuits. They were no more than about twenty years old.

The room was big enough to seat about fifty people. The bolted down pews were set up in rows like a chapel, with all the inmates seated in the front. They were unshackled, but watched by six security guards in navy-blue uniforms spread-out around the room. Maddox and two of her own security personnel stood on her right, and Warden, Bobby Ernst, stood on her left in his brown three-piece suit.

"Fellas, our image is going to have to change," Nzingha said, without a microphone. Her voice was loud enough for someone to hear in the back. She'd been speaking to them for forty-five minutes. Finishing her lecture, she stepped from behind the stand and paced back and forth in front of the eight-man crowd.

Nzingha wore a white shirt and dark-blue business suit. The group got to see her full figure of serious gestures. "How long is our culture going to be shamed with our pants sagging off our asses? This is a sign to other cultures of our disgrace. What other culture calls themselves a despicable name intended to hurt them for centuries, then still uses the name today? You can't stop calling each other the name, so you start making up excuses on how to continue degrading yourselves. So you make believe in your own mind that the word means a term of endearment. Ha, other cultures laugh at you.

"I'm not saying all of us will be rich. I'm not saying all of us aren't going through struggles and temptations. But in our poverty, struggles, and temptations, you could have some dignity. Dignity for rich or poor is more powerful than anything on this earth. Through dignity, you'll demand true respect. Through respect, you gain access to a new world of science, self, and the ability to grow intellectually on a global scale. It's time to think big, people, as we once did in our ancient past."

Nzingha went back to the podium, and the eight men clapped. "Today, six of you are here because of good behavior, and two of you will be released back into society. I hope you keep it up because soon all of you will be able to join my program of rehabilitation. Tomorrow, Paul and Kevin will be released into the program. According to their skills, they'll be helped into a good paying job with health benefits. A job that'll support their family. And I applaud them."

After Nzingha shook the eight young inmates' hands, they thanked her, then left the room in a single file. She also shook the Warden's hand, and he thanked her. They discussed how to set up the inmates Paul and Kevin in her program and who their Probation Officer was going to be.

It was the start of a good morning, Nzingha thought. She had done this like a routine three times every year. She'd either go to the Ohio State prison or Chicago. The many times she'd done this throughout the course of ten years, she helped release eighty-five male and female prisoners alike, with only six who went back. The seventy-nine who made it had special probation officers keeping a close track of them, watching them adapt comfortably into society. Twenty stayed in her program, went on to college and graduated.

Today she wanted to show Maddox she had always been more than just commerce and technology. She had a passionate heart for people.

They drove about twenty minutes before anybody spoke.

"Where're we off to now?" Maddox asked derisively. "To save more of society?" Thomas drove on the highway as she and Maddox sat in the back of her Rolls-Royce SUV. It was a smooth ride, no thanks to the road, more thanks to the cars suspension. As usual, her security entourage followed in the Hummer.

"I detect you didn't like our first visit?" Nzingha asked with sincerity.

"It's noble of you, but I just don't think people change. We're beings of habit. Once a criminal, always a criminal. Think of it like business. You're a business woman, you buy and sell. They're criminals, they thieve and kill."

"So you don't believe in second chances?"

"No. I mean, yes. It depends."

"Depends on what?" Nzingha asked, with wonder.

"I believe in the three strike rule. After the third time, hey, the guy's not going to stop. Lock him up and throw away the key. I also believe out of maybe fifty people who live a life of crime, maybe one over the years is sincere enough to stop completely. And that's a big maybe in my book."

"Interesting," Nzingha said, rubbing her chin.

"Just like maybe this anti-matter stuff isn't real."

"Patients, your skepticism will be feed. I'm about to get you some proof," Nzingha said, as she sat more comfortably in her seat. "We're going to Euclid, OH, the home of many inventions, like the cordless telephone we all own. Also home to a NPO Company called Stars Institute. To make a long story short, I give a bunch of scientists there a whole lot of money and they create things."

"Oh, so you're going to get a bunch of scientists to convince me?" Maddox queried and gave a devilish grin.

Nzingha responded with just a slight smirk.

They were quiet for five minutes until Maddox broke the silence. "You asked me once was I a God fearing man. I take it you don't believe in God. I think that's why it's so easy for you to play with Him."

Nzingha smiled, staring at Maddox.

"I'm willing to bet you fear death because you think you only live once," Maddox said. "You seem to have agnostic points of views. Maybe that's why you're so health conscious."

Nzingha almost laughed out loud, but Maddox held a serious face.

"Funny, Maddox," Nzingha explained. "I don't believe in the God theory of the western world. I, like you, believe in modesty, respectfulness, bravery, to be kind to others as you would want them to be gentle to you, and frugality. You're wrong. I'm not afraid of death. Health is longevity, yes, but death is the natural harmony of the universe. You and I are nothing but microcosms compared to the universe. Yet, to gain knowledge of the universe, we must understand ourselves first."

"Why does my belief have to be a theory?"

"Until the concept of any religion is a proven fact, it's a conjecture usually brought on by years and years of tradition."

"You almost sound like my father," Maddox said, leaning forward, looking at Nzingha. "He didn't believe in God much either, right up to the time he died. Where did you get these beliefs from, your foster parents?"

"Sit back, Maddox, we're almost there," Nzingha said, still beaming as if she was holding in a laugh.

Stars Institute was a white long three-story rectangular building. The front of the building from top to bottom was made of all blue glass. Green Ash trees evenly surrounded the building, their buds reddish-brown. One black tar road led to the front of this building with a parking lot. A huge long white rectangular sign sat on the side of the entrance. It read in black letters *Stars Institute Science Research*.

The place always reminded Nzingha of a shopping mall full of cars with no customers walking in and out. The place was almost completely surrounded by the Erie Lake beach, secluded from most villages in the area. Nzingha knew in the summer the place was like vacation time in Florida. Now there was no green, only light snow on the beach and ice on the mammoth lake.

Nzingha motioned with her head that this was the place, but Maddox insisted that she get out first.

"I'm following your lead here," he said, smiling.

Trying to be a gentleman, Nzingha thought. Strange guy. He was always interested in her technology, always doubting its authenticity. She wondered why, because today he was going to be enlightened. It was about twenty degrees outside as Nzingha, then Maddox, made it into the building rather quickly.

They went through the normal procedures of security. Nzingha glanced at Maddox's expression about her safety measures. She could tell by his astonished look that he seemed pleased.

The guards in dark-blue who carried handguns had them both go through metal-detectors to enter the building. They all spoke to Nzingha, "Good afternoon, Ms. Chelsea. How are you today? It's good of you to stop in again."

The place inside always gave Nzingha a feel of going back to college except here, everyone walked around in white lab coats. Entering an elevator, Nzingha took a keycard from her pocket and swiped it on a panel sticking out on the bottom of the floor numbers. A green light glowed on the side, and she typed in a six-digit code.

The elevator's numbers were from one to three, but they didn't light up, for they descended. It took about a minute before the elevator opened.

"We're about fifty feet below the surface under reinforced steel and concrete," Nzingha said. They walked down a gray bricked hallway about forty feet long before they came to a guard sitting behind a large black desk.

Nzingha watched Maddox look around and notice the dome cameras in the ceiling. The guard immediately stood, reached over the desk, shook Nzingha's hand, and glanced at Maddox suspiciously.

"Ms. Chelsea. How are you today?" The guard asked.

"Fine, Dex, and you?"

"Nothing going on here. Same as usual," the guard said, jadedly.

"Got a little company today." She smiled, nudging at Maddox.

"Great," the officer said sarcastically, amused. As he sat again, Nzingha stepped to a steel door with no handle. She typed in another six-digit number on a panel on the right side of the door. She placed her palm on part of the plate. It glowed bright blue as a laser scanned her hand like a copy machine, and the door automatically slid to the right.

The door slid back shut, immersing them into a maze of well-lit white corridors. Nzingha moved through the office-like passageways knowingly, with Maddox trailing.

Nzingha stopped a few times to say quick hellos to the staff who walked in and out of the offices. A Oriental lady who wore casual wear under her lab coat held a chart and looked twenty-five years old, briefly said hi. A young white male of about the same age dressed in a white shirt and gray dungarees also greeted Nzingha.

"Everyone around here is kind of young to be scientists don't you think?" Maddox asked.

"Yup, it's better that way," Nzingha responded, rounding a few corners. "The staff here is mostly recruited straight after graduating college. Their minds are fresher, more open to ideas, and aren't entangled in set ways. They admit when they're wrong and move on."

At the end of one hall they stopped at two knob-less doors with another panel. Nzingha swiped her card on the panel, and the doors slid aside like an elevator.

They strolled into a massive gray auditorium with black floor. Yellow lines on the dark floor showed a circular path like a track and field layout around the perimeter.

Three saucer-shaped vehicles the size of two-door automobiles sat in front of a console. Nzingha observed Maddox with a dumbfound look on his face. She knew why he looked that way. It was because the automobiles were suspended three feet off the ground in mid air. The vehicles had no built-in wheels, only lights, windows, and mirrors like a car.

Two individuals in lab jackets looked up from the console a few feet away from the entrance near the left wall of the hall. Nzingha walked up to them as Maddox trailed her with his mouth open. As she stopped in front of the two-male staff, Maddox almost bumped into her, not taking his eyes off the vehicles.

"Guys, the gentleman drooling here is Maddox Mathews. He's come for a test drive." Nzingha shook both of the guys' hands.

"Hi, I'm Roy," one of the men said, extending his hand, and Maddox shook it. He was also a young looking guy no more than twenty years old with a name tag that read *Roy Higgins*. The older, taller-looking fellow with name tag that read *Bruce Patterson* also introduced himself and shook Maddox's hand.

"Enjoy," Bruce said with a big grin.

Nzingha walked to a purple saucer automobile. Maddox bent down and put his hand under the wheel-less car between the space of the floor and smooth underbelly. Nzingha climbed into the driver's side of the shiny pansy-purple car. Maddox happily climbed into the passenger's side. They both shut the doors that opened and closed vertically, and she started the car, saying, "Ignition."

The car vibrated a bit, then smoothed out to the sound of a quiet hum. Nzingha steered the car onto the yellow track, and they drove around the auditorium following the path.

"Amazing," Maddox said, looking around at the interior of the lit colorful console dashboard. "I can't feel the acceleration when you step on the pedal. It feels weird."

"The single battery in my computers are the size of the nail on your pinky," Nzingha spoke, "with a life expectancy of twenty years. The battery in this car is the size of a D battery, life expectancy ninety years. What I'm about to power Ohio with is a power-cell the size of a normal car battery. Life expectancy, we calculate well over five hundred years."

"How did you achieve all this?" Maddox asked, showing interest in his brow. "Just like that rock in your house. I thought some kind of wire was holding it up. But this—I mean, how are we floating and moving through pure air? Can you explain this in layman's terms?"

"Well, for one, never count on your government for better solutions in energy and clean air.

"M.E.G. runs much like particle physics. The energy is harnessed in a thing called the Infinitenator, then that's controlled by mechanisms that give power to defy gravity and speed. We discovered Einstein's infinite power theory. It's not a theory anymore. It's a solid fact. Things are then compressed into nanoid-components." Nzingha smiled. "To understand all this, you first have to study quantum physics and mechanics."

"Gee, so who's the bright scientist who discovered this Infinitenator?" Maddox asked, raising one eyebrow. "I'm not a complete idiot. That part seems like the middle component that holds the matter and gravity control together."

"The scientist is undisclosed until this power is well known. I've already had spies in my company lurking around. This could leak into enemy hands and start a world-wide dilemma. You know, security measures."

"This stuff you're playing with is serious. Which brings me to my next question. When you say enemy, who's the enemy? Other countries?"

"Not necessarily. You know me; I'm all about the business, the highest bidder. Don't worry, I won't be selling it to any terrorist or anything. Other companies could be enemies, too."

"Have you ever thought about giving this technology to another country?"

"I don't know, Maddox. Why? Are you concerned?" Nzingha asked as she brought the vehicle to a halt near the door.

Maddox shrugged. "So what else can this car do besides drive off the ground in circles?"

"Everything a car does and doesn't. It has voice command, built-in

GPS system, and you can type in where you want to go and it'll drive you there automatically."

"Get the hell outa here."

"I figure that'll grab your attention," Nzingha said and got out the car.

Maddox followed, talking over the top of the car. "So you're saying I could go to sleep behind the wheel and wake up at my destination?"

"That's right. It avoids other cars in traffic, stops at red lights, and obeys the speed limit all by itself. Virtually impenetrable to accidents, depleted of polluting emissions. If everyone was driving these cars, it would greatly increase world life expectancy."

"All this. Yeah, you're right. The government's not going to like that. I see why the FBI is watching you." Maddox and Nzingha both chuckled. "So how fast can this car go?"

Nzingha cut her laugh short and stared at him solemnly. "You don't want to know. You'd never believe it."

"Hey, you got my attention. You convinced me so far. You don't seem to be a liar."

"Come on, Maddox, let's go." She felt she showed him enough.

MADDOX HAD TO ADMIT, he had a great morning and afternoon. He got to see Nzingha in action. He witnessed ambient intelligence at work and now was sure anti-matter was real and not just a concept. Nzingha had structured young chemists and physicists in a way to make all this possible. How she did it, he'd never know, but to him she was a genius, or a brilliant architect of technology in the least.

It was 5:00 in the afternoon when they made it to Bratenahl, Nzingha's residence. A nightcap with her would complete his day, Maddox thought. It would complete his whole week. She dismissed her security for the night, then invited him in, and they had dinner together again.

Maddox ordered his seafood platter, and Nzingha ordered her vegetarian dish. It was all requested through her wonderful ambient technology, of course. Once more they ate in her living room, sitting on the white leather couch with the huge mirror behind it. She again excused her butler after he served them for the night. Soft jazz played, déjà vu, Maddox thought, smiling to himself. "Don't mess this up," he whispered in his mind.

While eating, he tried talking to her about the scientist who unlocked the key to discovering how anti-matter worked. Like, how did that car, or rock in her yard float off the ground, continually? To no prevail, she side-tracked onto the idea of how the science worked more than who the person was.

She explained, and he got a good lesson in quantum mechanics, anti-particles, photon emissions, and kinetic energy. She also talked about a man named Rene Descartes in 1644 discovering the idea of a vortex gravity. Rene believed that no empty space can exist and that space must be filled with matter. Then Nzingha rambled on about the usage of dark matter and using the earth's magnetic field to help levitate the vehicles.

It dawned on Maddox for a second, and a second only, that possibly, Nzingha herself was that undisclosed genius scientist who discovered the Infinitenator. She knew too much, she was too detailed. Most entrepreneurs and philanthropists may start or steal an idea, but surely not know how the mechanics of their product actually worked.

After they finished eating, Nzingha collected their plates and glasses, leaving momentarily to the kitchen. When she came back to sit on the couch next to him, she sighed. Maddox had a sensation, that she sensed she was talking too much and stared at him in a *sorry I did that* kind of way straight face.

"The car you showed me today felt pretty powerful," Maddox said, breaking the silence. "What you're telling me on how it works is overwhelming. I mean, you're going in a path of global ground breaking technology at a pace never before seen. If the battery in this car or the battery that's going to charge Ohio was tampered with, could it set off an explosion? If so, what's the damage?"

"Good question, Maddox," Nzingha said, staring at his blue pinstripe shirt. She then eyed him genuinely. "I always liked an inquisitive mind. Like myself, about people.

"To answer your question, yes, if the battery for the car is fiddled with, it could explode. The explosion could reach proportions of a dirty bomb. Though this explosion could reach a Chernobyl disaster-type magnitude, there will be no fallout. There's no radiation.

"The person tampering with it would have to buy a detonator from the U.S. Army, or any army, for that matter, to set it off. I couldn't detonate it without a warhead detonator. While we're testing these things we, of course, use precautions. That's why we're so far below the surface under reinforced steel and concrete.

"Like solar and wind power this battery is clean energy. Unlike solar and wind power it doesn't need those natural things. This battery is self efficient and can self sustain itself for decades, centuries. We could build on the dark side of the moon for years without returning to Earth."

"Weighing your pros and cons, wouldn't this be a danger to the public by having free reign access to such a powerful battery?"

"We've designed a battery for the public to only work for the car. We've already tested hammering and torching it, no explosion."

"Would you classify this battery's disaster as a caesium-137?"

"Oh, you did some homework?" Nzingha asked with surprise, and she gave a bright smile. "Are you trying to impress me?"

"Maybe," Maddox said with a smirk. "Like I said, I'm not a complete idiot. I follow you a little."

"Yes, it may have the kick of a caesium-137, but not its radioactive fallout. It's no salted bomb."

Maddox moved closer to Nzingha on the couch, now resting his arm on the back near her head.

"Excuse me. You got me on that one. Salted what?"

As Nzingha answered, Maddox stared at the freckles on her face. "It's a bomb that could render an area uninhabitable for generations."

Maddox counted eight brown freckles the size of pin heads around her nose.

"But I'd rather not talk about tragedies," Nzingha went on.

He now gazed into her eyes. They seemed to luster, swimming in the color midnight-green, twinkling as he stared. "Me neither," Maddox whispered. "I'd rather talk about more positive things." He moved his head closer to Nzingha. For a split second she seemed like she was going to close her eyes and crinkle her lips. He could feel the warmth emanating from her body. He wondered was she overheating again. He never got the chance to feel her lips on his because he halted his budge toward her.

Almost like shaking out of a trance, Maddox blinked a couple of times, realizing he'd forgotten something.

"Oh, I just remembered, I have an important meeting with the boss tomorrow morning," he said disappointingly.

Maddox perceived, Nzingha looking down again at his shirt also disappointed.

"I understand." She gave a half smile. "I won't keep you."

"I truly had a wonderful day," Maddox said. "Very educational. I'm fascinated about your cutting-edge technology."

"I'll have Thomas see you home."

"That's alright, a friend of mine from the company is coming to pick me up. We have to go over some things before I go into work tomorrow. I just have to give him a call."

Maddox pulled his cell phone from his black trousers pocket and dialed a number, a phone he bought a year ago from her very company.

Nzingha got up and leisurely walked to the brown drapes covering the enormous windows.

"Yes, at the address I gave you the other day," Maddox said into his phone. "Okay, see you in about thirty minutes." He hung up and put the phone back in his pocket.

Standing, he slowly moved behind Nzingha. Through the slit in the curtain he caught a glance of a massive covered pool and colossal tan decked patio. It was dark outside as dull lights from the ground illuminated the courtyard.

"I'm sorry I have to go," Maddox said. "I truly had a wonderful day."

She was quiet for a few seconds. As he was about to put his hand on her shoulder, she spun around, facing him.

"I want to show you one more thing while you wait for your friend," Nzingha said sincerely. "Don't know when I'm going to see you again."

"Sure."

Nzingha led him through a white hallway to an elevator in her library. She pressed the elevator button, and the doors opened. They both entered the elevator, and the doors shut. She typed in a ten-digit code on a panel on the left and put a glass key in a slot next to it.

"This will only take a minute. I want to show you why I don't believe in your God. I want to show you a collection of mine." They descended for a few seconds before the doors opened again. "About eight feet under my house I have a private collection of books you should see."

When the doors opened, Nzingha took the key from the slot and put it back in her pocket. A rectangular hall stood in front of them about sixty feet long. In the center of the place sat a pool equal to the length of the room. Tan Egyptian palm-style pillars held up a lime-green arching ceiling. The columns, ten on each side, showed detailed hieroglyphics in an array of colors. Potted small palm trees also decorated the surrounding area of the pool.

Lights on the sides of the ceiling brightening the area made the pool water reflect green. Maddox followed Nzingha around the pool toward the opposite side. The jazz that played upstairs also played down here, now changed to Miles Davis.

"Nice, in a dreamy sort of way," Maddox said, passing huge paintings on the walls from artists like Aaron Douglas, William Johnson, and Gordon Parks. "I don't believe I know the artists who made these," Maddox added in an asking kind of way.

"They're extraordinary," Nzingha answered as they approached the end. A glass wall stood in front of them with two palm trees on both sides. Peering inside the glass wall, Maddox saw a library, dimly lit. Nzingha punched another code into a wall panel. This time it seemed like she didn't care that he saw the code. It was 12, 40, 3, and 7. Strange she picked those numbers, Maddox thought, for someone who didn't believe in God or the Bible. Maybe she was being sarcastic.

The number twelve was for the disciples of Jesus or the tribes of Israel. The cipher forty, was for Noah and the flood or when Jesus went into the wilderness. Three, was for the holy trinity and seven, for when God rested on the last day of creation. Those numbers had to mean that, or was it just a twist of fate?

Glass doors slid to the side, and Maddox and Nzingha entered. The lights above automatically glowed bright orange revealing a room about the size of an average living room. Four rows of floor-to-ceiling shelves housed thousands of old dusty books. Around the room incased in glass, the walls lodged artifacts.

"Pieces of the Dead Sea Scrolls," Maddox said out loud reading the plaque on the bottom of an item in glass on the right wall. The pieces resembled a five-year-old brown dirty badly torn t-shirt with Aramaic written on it. "Is this authentic?" Maddox asked unbelievingly.

"Of course, Maddox, what do you think?"

"I'm just saying, how, who gave these pieces up?"

"In 1947 when they found most of the scrolls, some pieces floated around among merchants finding their way into private owners' hands."

Maddox moved on, probing other ancient books with plaques that read, *The Codex Climaci Rescriptus*, medieval dated bibles, and a scroll called the *Gospel of Peter*. Interesting, Maddox thought. He always figured there were only four gospels.

"All this must be extremely valuable to a lot of people, especially Christians." Maddox then asked, "What's the security in here?" He gazed at some of the books in the aisle.

"Let's just say the code to get in here changes every day," Nzingha answered. "If you somehow break the code, unauthorized to enter this room, the doors will automatically lock, and the air will be sucked out.

Those glass doors are sound and reinforced bullet-proof. No one will hear you scream."

"So why own and show me all this and you don't believe in its God?"

"I believe the diseases of the world and man's propulsion into the future won't be funneled by biblical intuition. I'm fascinated, in the colorful history of how the ancient books passed from hand to hand, generation after generation, more than if the context of the stories are true.

"I'm fascinated that a lot of people believe in the miracles of these books. I always wandered why. I think people need to hold onto a belief system of fantasy because they don't understand the real world. I guess holding and reading these things pushes me more to realize the real world more than a fantasy world. The Bible has an opposite effect on me than most people."

"What's real to you?"

"The technology I always keep presenting to you." Nzingha smiled. "What you witness today was real, no castle in the sky."

"I suppose eventually you'll want to share your technology with the world."

"I suppose eventually in due time. Everything has its seasons."

Maddox stood behind Nzingha as she stared at a papyrus looking book in a glass case with a plaque that read *The Book Wars of the Lord*. He put his hands on her back and caressed her shoulders.

"I suppose I'm more like my stepfather," she said. "He doesn't believe in God much. Like your father Maddox."

Maddox slowly and passionately massaged the back of her neck. She was incredibly warm, as he figured, clammy even. She was sweating. He watched her rest her head slightly back on his shoulder and close her eyes.

"It's been a long day," Maddox whispered in her ear.

"It has," she responded as he kissed the left side of her head.

Maddox gradually wrapped his right arm around her neck. With his left hand he went into his back pocket, took out his black .45 pistol, and pressed it against the small of her lower back.

"I knew a day like this would come," Nzingha said, opening her eyes wide. "That's also why I brought you down here. I always wondered if I could really trust you or anybody."

Matt tightened his arm around her neck. She had to grab his arm with both her hands to breathe normally.

"How did you get that gun past security at the penitentiary and Stars Institute?" She asked.

"I left it in the car of course. Remember when we arrived at your facility, I insisted you get out first?"

"Yeah, of course, right. Now that I recall, you always wanted me to get out first."

"Why do I feel *you're* the undisclosed scientist behind this technology?" Matt asked in a way like he already knew.

"So you're the mole committing espionage? Who are you working for? Another company? The government? FBI, I suppose?"

"This technology you developed must never leave this country," Matt spoke sternly in her ear. Tightening his grip more, he felt it was getting hard for her to swallow. She was sweating more as he could see her hair sticking to the sides of her head. She didn't struggle: she stood still and loose. He could feel her trying to breathe, inhaling and exhaling rapidly.

"With a word I could command for those doors to shut, trapping us in here with no air. We'll both die."

"Nah, it won't be that easy. I'd torture you and make you open the doors before the air ran out, or I could just torture you before we die. Trust me; it could get real nasty in here."

Nzingha's eyes started to water as tears slowly one by one dropped onto his shirt sleeve.

"This technology can't be given to the public," Matt spat, "it must come through the government."

"I already put it out there, Maddox, or whoever you are. There are no guarantees."

"You have to give this technology to the DOE or . . ."

"You were sent to kill me anyway; what does it matter?" Nzingha said as if she already knew more than asked. She closed her eyes and cried more.

"Yes, I was sent to kill you," Matt said, clicking the safety off his gun. He felt her body tense up. "I thought you weren't afraid of death?"

"I'm not afraid of death, sir." She gulped hard now, trying to breathe. She struggled to take in the next breath to make her next statement clear. "I cry because you don't care that I forgive you."

Matt's phone rang, but he ignored it. "My friend is here. He'll ask if I completed the mission." Matt holstered his gun in his waist, went in Nzingha's pocket, and took out her glass key for the elevator. "You may not believe me, but I really like you, even though you don't believe in miracles and God. I've accomplished all of my missions flawlessly. I never failed one. This will be my first and your first miracle. So heed this as a warning. More people will come for you."

Matt released Nzingha as she coughed a little, regaining her breath. She glanced at him, sniffing, feeling her throat as he left quickly through the glass doors.

Matt felt Nzingha had to be the inventive scientist. She was too smart for her own good. Someone at The Company was going to be pissed about him aborting the mission. Hell, what were they going to say anyway? He was the best in the world at what he did. How can his government keep killing American scientists anyway? How will man advance, grow? What of the future, if I kept killing scientists? What about his peace? He had the mind of an executioner but just didn't feel like slaughtering today.

There was going to be a discussion on what to do with the Chelsea Company, so it wasn't over for Nzingha. She had a decision to make on who she was going to give her technology. He prayed it was going to be the American way. She was smart; he was sure she'd decide wisely, particularly after witnessing this so-called miracle.

He liked Nzingha; she had a lot of spunk. He didn't know why he let himself get that close to her as he did. He could have killed her by just being a good business partner. He supposed he got that close because he could. He was that good. All his life he followed rules by the numbers.

Taffy said to give this mission his all, then just walk away. He wanted to walk away once in his life with a clear conscience, his own real decision. He wanted to walk away this time on his terms, the way he wanted to do it. That was his best. If circumstances were different, he would have liked to really get to know her, date her.

In Matt's heart, his mission was complete. Retirement, he felt, was his only option.

CHAPTER 23

LAGOS ISLAND, NIGERIA, in the Central Business District, the office of The Agricultural Science Research Center sat on a block full with white two-story townhouses. The science office looked identical to the other houses except it was surrounded by a white twelve-foot fence.

Xavier Kcired walked behind his large brown desk in this office building talking into his speaker-phone. His wild gray and black beard fit his full face of untamed hair matching his head. If one could picture Frederick Douglass at sixty years old, he'd be a splitting image. Some would say he might have made himself to look like the American abolitionist purposely. He wore a brown three-piece suit and tan checkered tie in a preppie fashion.

His office had a British architectural feel. There was a bookcase to the left of the room full with blue and brown encyclopedias. Another bookcase sat behind him with all kinds of different books. An expensive maroon and brown wall to wall rug covered the floor, brown paneling on the walls, and posh thick tan drapes covered the single window on the right of his main desk. Under the window was a smaller desk with computer, printer, and fax machine.

Two items stood out in this spacious office, a model and a portrait. The six foot long detailed model of a year 1860 ship called the American Clipper sat on a pedestal near the wall at the door. The portrait on the wall above the boat showed a globe of an ancient map of the world. Standing on the globe was an Egyptian style Lady of Justice. It was set up this way so, when Xavier sat behind his desk, they stared back at him.

"He said he didn't need anymore persuading, and that he won't intervene with the Chelsea Company energy push in Ohio," said the voice on the speaker-phone.

"Great," Xavier responded in the direction of the phone as he paced behind his desk. "I'm sorry to say that it takes such drastic measures for some companies to understand."

"Mr. Walsh, I hear, is even talking about resigning."

"Really?" Xavier replied as there was a knock on the door. "Let me chat with you later. My company has just arrived this evening."

"Okay, we'll talk later."

Xavier pressed a button on his black desk phone, ending the call.

"Come in," Xavier shouted at the door.

A lady in her late fifties in a white dress with colorful checkered designs opened the door, smiling. She took her reading glasses off and let them hang on her bosom by a string they were connected to. "Morris is here to see you, sir."

"Great, bring him in," Xavier said, smiling back at her. "Oh, and Sandy, I'll see you tomorrow morning."

"Oh, thank you, sir," Sandy said, her smile brightening evermore. She hadn't closed the door fully as Morris Energ walked in nodding at Sandy. Sandy nodded back, hurrying past him.

"Someone's going home in a hurry," Morris said as he closed the door behind him.

"Yeah, mostly everybody is gone for today. I had her wait a little until you arrived."

"Ah, you shouldn't have. I know my way around." The two shook hands. Morris was a tall sixty-year-old man of six feet, short gray black hair, and clean shaven face. He wore a new royal-blue three-piece suit that seemed to almost shine in the dull light of the office. As Morris sat in a seat in front of the main desk he looked to the left, noticing Xavier wasn't alone.

The other office chair that usually was in front of the desk was occupied now by someone sitting in the left corner shadows of the room. Morris nodded at the figure, and the human shape bobbed back.

As Morris crossed his legs and folded his hands on his lap, Xavier sat behind his desk.

"I see another mission went well," Morris spoke pleasingly.

"Yeah, Mr. Walsh is talking about quitting."

"Really?"

"Yeah, but now we have other concerns."

"Nzingha?" Morris asked, unsure.

Xavier nodded that he was correct. "Morris, the world is an extremely violent place," Xavier began as Morris rolled his eyes. "I know you don't want to hear it, but it's true. As soon as you build something, there seems to be always someone there to tear it down.

"Man invented how to shape stone and fire. That brings the human race to the pinnacle of intelligence. Man then discovers oil, a new way to burn fire, the second apex of intellect. Now man has invented how to burn energy to move at the speed of light. That would bring us to the third zenith of intelligence."

"Don't you mean woman?" Morris quickly corrected him.

"Who created she?" Xavier retorted.

"So what's going on across seas now?"

"Apparently the Central Intelligence Agency has a hit out on her and has already made an assassination attempt."

"Is she alright?" Morris asked with concern, unfolding his legs.

"She's fine. She's a strong girl."

"How did it happen? What happen?"

"A gun was put to her head, and she got a warning. That was all."

"Is that all! She seemed so careful over all these years. So slow to move the technology. You'd think man would be ready for this. Don't give everybody a culture shock, we said. Give it to them inch by inch. Yet we knew something like this was still bound to happen. What are we playing with now?"

"It's simple. The United States wants the technology first."

"This could launch another worldwide investigation on us."

"If they haven't already. If you remember, not long ago they were snooping around here."

Morris glanced at the seated figure in the corner before responding. "What are you planning?"

Xavier saw his glimpse and smiled. "No, my friend, we won't be using our usual countermeasures this time. I was thinking something more subtle."

"Like?"

"Like just giving her another personal bodyguard."

Morris rubbed his chin quietly.

Xavier knew Morris was trying to insinuate, *was that it*? "She's a grown woman, intelligent," Xavier spoke, "she'll decide wisely on this crisis, I'm sure. Besides, I'd like to see how she'd go about something like this."

"This isn't like a secret adoption as you did long ago," Morris said, making a face like *I hope you're sure*. "It's your call. Your daughter. Testing and experimenting on her again I hope doesn't cost you—or her."

"We'll discuss this again soon with Mr. Xur to see what the three of us can come up with." Xavier shrugged. "Until then, I think she should have ample protection."

"Sounds good," Morris agreed, then sighed. "I hope we'll be able to contact Xur. He just left again on another mountain climbing trip."

"You know the European is truly insane," Xavier said with fire in his voice, changing the subject.

"Here we go," Morris said, rolling his eyes. "Don't you mean American?"

"Look, who basically over all started and still controls America and the world?" Xavier then demanded more than asked, "Just hear me out for a second. Think about this for a moment and tell me if it makes sense."

Morris nodded for him to go on.

"The European has lain with every woman on the face of the earth," Xavier elucidated. "He's the master of science on the earth. The master of the military on the land, sea, and air. Invades countries at will, claiming whole continents as theirs.

"The European is only a small percentage compared to the rest of the world. Eleven percent, to be exact. Yet people of color, most of the world, in Africa, India, and South America are in turmoil, give or take some are worse than others. They're Third World Nations. The Europeans have beaten the Japanese in World War II and have pretty much committed genocide on the American Indian.

"It's funny how one non-white tries to get ahead and that's evil to most of them. To kill one or two whites to put a single non-white person ahead, they would consider evil. They cry for justice but never understand what they have done to the world. Who'll arbitrate this obnoxious judge?"

"The Bible says, if a man strikes you on the right cheek, turn to him the other," Morris said with seriousness.

"My friend, you were always the level-headed one, but even you must see logic and have sense of this, too. How many times do you keep getting struck in the face? Does the Bible have a limit of a death total before protecting yourself, because the meter on offense is pretty high on white?"

"Don't answer that right away," Xavier said sarcastically. "I'm sure an answer will present itself soon, for now just call what I'm doing in America, atonement. Like countless nations throughout history I'm trying to make my score in the world, with elegance of course."

"You're still elegantly militant as ever," Morris said in a matter of fact way. "I guess that's not going to change anytime soon. So what of our friend these days?" He nudged at the shadow in the corner.

"Oh," Xavier said, looking in that direction. He waved his hand politely for the person to sit next to Morris. "Please come closer so we can discuss this thing about Gamba. I hear he's the new narcotics cartel, trying to blend in the night life of Lagos, giving the local authorities there a problem."

SHE SLOWLY STOOD from out the gloom of the room, grabbed her chair, and set it beside Morris. Suraksha straightened her black shirt, sat, and folded her hands in front of her. She was all ears.

THE NETHERLANDS, AMSTERDAM, behind the huge Church of Saint Nicholas known as Sint Nicolaaskerk on Oudezijdskolk Street, across a man-made canal, Lord Astor Cyril booked some rooms.

In a four-floor office building he rented the entire top floor. The hundred year old square building looked identical to the other houses that surrounded it, going a half mile in both directions. He liked this room because it sat directly in the middle of the block. Out a dark-blue draped window he was in straight sight of Sint Nicolaaskerk. The canal below separated the block from the church. Beautiful sets of trees and bushes lined the entire avenue that went for a mile, as did the channel.

Astor also liked the room because it was dull. Only small beams of light came from the window that was mostly obscured. The room had a gray look to it, a silent look; a secret look. The only thing that came to life on its walls were two huge oil portraits. One was of William the Silent and the other a battle at sea titled "Anglo-Dutch War, June 1666."

He had rented the office for a few weeks while he did business here in Amsterdam. Today, was different. It was three o'clock, and he sent his staff and personal secretary home an hour early. His usual business of banking wasn't going to be discussed today. There were more important things. Being an abiding member of the Bilderberger Group, he had to report back to the council of things about to be said.

"Chelsea announced yesterday that they were giving their anti-matter technology to the DOE," Isaac Von Thurn said.

Isaac was the only other American in the room besides Astor. He was also a banker and the Mayor of Georgia. He was the youngest in the room, only sixty-one. He was clean-cut, had short neat gray-brown hair—mostly brown, and wore a Persian-orange Brooks Brothers three-piece suit. He sat comfortably in a cushioned chair with his legs crossed, sipping tea.

"Yeah, well, it was in their best interest," Sir William Turner said, standing by the window. "But that only accomplishes half of our worries. What of this denoted vacuum c technology? Are we still in the red? Can it be vended on the free market?" William asked with his British accent and was Chief Executive of a petroleum company.

His hair was all gray, and he held an expensive ivory cane. Sometimes he'd lean on the wall by the window and sometimes his cane. His blue suit and tie looks like mine Astor thought, Ralph Lauren.

"I'm sorry to inform you, sir," Astor spoke. "Chelsea denies ever accomplishing this physical constant vacuum c technology. They say they want to charge the FBI and CIA for espionage."

"Look," Sir Elliott Nicholas said in a British accent. He sat next to Isaac in a blue three-piece suit. "Is this technology real? I thought you said your people duplicated it?"

Nicholas, who was the head of the Tavistock Institute, stared at Astor hard for an answer.

"We lied. We couldn't duplicate it," Astor said from leaning on the front of an office desk full with papers, pens, computer, and small three-striped red, white, and blue flag.

"Shit!" Nicholas tried to utter under his breath, but it just came out.

"The good news is that it's still assumption-able," Astor said calmly.

"Explain, what do you mean?" Nicholas asked, rubbing his head, frustrated.

"The technology is real. We already tested it. Attained by emissaries we're in possession of a prototype, obeisance to Chelsea. Scientists around the world couldn't back-engineer it. They examined it, dismantled it, but just couldn't find the key to exactly how it works."

"You mean to tell me we have the power of God at our fingertips and we don't know how it works?" Nicholas asked himself more than Astor.

Astor nodded.

"Who's the scientist?" Isaac asked calmly.

"Unknown," Astor answered. "We have our suspicion that it could be the CEO of Chelsea herself."

"We have ways of getting people to talk," Isaac said, looking over at one more individual in the room. Zamir was seated quietly with his arms folded at the left side of the desk.

"What's the latest report on that company now?" William asked Zamir.

Lawerence Zamir was a retired Director of the Mossad. Astor knew William was talking to Zamir as he watched the man gather his thoughts. Zamir had a well built muscular physique for a sixty-five-year-old man. The only one with dirty blond graying hair and sky-blue eyes, he wore a white shirt and black slacks; he wasn't as preppie as the rest.

"I have nothing that'll stick on Chelsea and nothing from recent CIA information on Livenal *yet*, but that'll change in time," Zamir spoke, in a deep Israeli accent. "Everyone has dirt. It just depends how you wash them. We've recovered some pictures of the inside of a Livenal aluminum mine showing residual of a cloning factory. We could heighten the FBI file already on Chelsea. We could look into that?"

"You might be right about looking into Livenal," Astor spoke. "I got the coroner's report about that mishap in the States in LA. Those dental records we acquired don't belong to the assassin they found. The body of the female at the site was already dead hours before the explosion. I concealed it from the FBI so they could drop the case. For now, the less they know, the better."

"What kind of people or organization are we dealing with here?" William posed to anybody as he moved from the window. Leaning on his cane, he moved closer to the group to stand by the desk. "Covert war, terrorist, revolutionary evil scientist—have we found out their goal?"

Everyone was quiet for a whole minute as only the sound of Isaac slurping his tea could be heard.

"This could be a case of a capitalistic battle for who could make the most currency," Astor voiced, breaking through the moment of silence. "Maybe a simple move to seek power and dominance among the world? Are we no different? Or maybe, as the Chelsea Company says, they just want to make a better world through technology. You know, create their own future for the world. Are we not doing that?"

"Then we better double our efforts on watching these people," Zamir said with much seriousness. "And if this vacuum c technology can't be duplicated, then we'll hunt these scientists down and break them."

Everyone nodded in agreement.

EPILOGUE

THE NIGHT WAS INK BLACK. Like a black oil canvas, the sky met the ocean in this clear darkness. No moon shone this evening as a million stars lit up the sky like white fireflies. The luxury yacht Firestone drifted now two hundred miles moving away from St. Helena Island.

Her stepfather Xavier, Morris, and the helmsman Ralph stood in awe. Did they encounter an unidentified flying object? She wondered. Was it some kind of man-made craft that could defy gravity?

Though the vessel's engines and lights were normal, the computer among the console of navigational indicators was still on the fritz. Letters, numbers, and symbols still flashed across the screen in sessions of glitches.

At first she witnessed gibberish as she stared at it in confusion, watching Ralph lightly hit the side of the computer.

"Stop! Wait a minute!" Xavier practically shouted. She realized as she began to see her stepfather notice the green jumbled symbols were some kind of cryptogram. She'd seen it before. The numbers and letters read, A, G, C, C, G, GAT, HAR1, NH2, NH, O, 5-GAT.

"Oh, my God!" Xavier said to himself more than his company.

The flashing ciphers were enzymes, binding proteins, and genes of a cell nucleus. A Hydrogen band and double helix flashed. She knew this was the nucleic acid that contained the genetic instructions to develop all known living organisms. Could be human or something xenomorphic. She was sure of one thing, though. It was the language of DNA.

"Do you have a blank computer disc?" Xavier asked anxiously.

"Yeah, in the cabinet, but I don't . . ." Ralph said, pointing to the back

229

of the helm. She detected Xavier didn't hear the rest of Ralph's statement as he made a mad dash for the cabinet.

What they encountered on this trip out to sea was differently supernatural, she thought. Though she wasn't a big believer in the Bible, ghouls, and U.F.O.'s, something was certainly trying to give them information.

HER ENTIRE BODY WAS FREEZING. She was nude, frozen solid in the middle of a huge ice cube. What surrounded her appeared to look like crystals. She was imprisoned in a sub-zero quartz tomb.

Was she alive? Why couldn't she move? Why couldn't she talk? Who suspended her like this? She wanted to scream, but all she could do was cry. No tear came out. She tried to shout; no sound came out. How was this possible? She thought. She was literally frozen in time.

Focusing, she could just see past the scratchy glass-like window that incased her. She spotted a long yellow label on what seemed like a white door that said *Keep Out Biochemical.* She read other blue labels on pure white walls that read *Danger Liquid Nitrogen, Cryopreservation, Vitro Fertilisation, and Frozen Embryo.*

What did all this mean? Nzingha thought as she awoke, sweating. Again she laid under satin brown sheets aboard her yacht on the Atlantic Ocean.

NEW PROVIDENCE, BAHAMAS, on Paradise Island, Nzingha slowly strolled on the white sands of Paradise Beach with Anna. They were nearly alone on the beach as only a boy with his black dog ran together in the distance.

Palm trees waved uncontrollably in the strong breeze, and waves crashed the shoreline relentlessly every few seconds. Nzingha breathed in heavily. She loved the fresh smell of the salty sea air. She adored the clear sky-blue sky that harmonized the color of the ocean. The sun beat down on them this February, the temperature, sixty-five degrees—that's what read on her watch.

Nzingha remembered Anna Barron as she was in New Orleans in 2005. Anna was retired now from the Louisiana PD and only fifty-five years old. Her radiant tan skin still looked as fresh as it did seven years ago. She wore a yellow dress and short tan sweater with yellow elder flower in her black, silky shoulder-length hair.

Nzingha wore a white shirt and black slacks. Her shirt was open three buttons down, and she walked barefooted, making sure her toes dug into the powdery sand.

"You're not cold?" Anna asked. "It's a little cool today."

"I'm fine," Nzingha responded with hands in her pocket. "I have to thank you again for that bit of information. You've been a great help."

"You didn't have to come all the way out here to tell me that," Anna spoke sincerely. "What you did for me and my community back in—"

"Please, you remind me enough," Nzingha said and smiled. "Besides, I didn't want to use the phone. I'm here today to personally give my gratitude."

Anna's friend had provided her with the file, Fortunes and Misfortunes. She was also told that Special Agent Joseph John Clay's partner died by the assassin's hands. Anna then transferred that knowledge to Nzingha.

The interview with the agent was over before it began. Besides thanking her source, other things clouded her mind.

Who really was this Suraksha Using? Was Livenal involved? If it was, then all this was connected in deaths dating back to the nineties, far before she started in business. Was her stepfather trying to shape her future? If he was, he was virtually destroying her reputation in the process. It enraged her that he might have done this. She had to talk to him about it, and soon, among many other things.

She liked Maddox, or whatever his name was. He was slick, for one thing, and managed to slip under her detectors. He decided not to pull the trigger. She wondered why? Was he really trying to prove miracles are real? Or did he have some kind of feelings for her deep in his heart?

She was growing suspicious of him and could have at any time fled from her underground library glass chamber, trapping him inside. But she didn't, she just stood there and let him grab her. She wondered why?

She wondered did he ever once truly like her, or was it all just business? Nzingha felt she was foolhardy for letting him get close. She did for a moment, feel that she had some sort of connection to him. She felt they were both lonely, and at the time as far as she knew, they didn't have kids—well the Maddox character anyway. If circumstances were different, she would have liked to get to know more of the Maddox character. But Maddox wasn't real.

There was one sure thing about him. He always believed in her technology. He only pretended he didn't—pretty impressive. It served her right, this outcome. Never mix business with pleasure.

Derrick John Wiggins who did two years in Lehman College has worked as a reprographics associate in Goldman Sachs, an investment banking firm, for four years and Paul Hastings a law firm, for two years.